He didn't know how the cartel found out he was leading the investigation…but it was obvious they had.

Joe noticed that the two older Toyotas had pulled out into the middle lane. They were coming up fast behind him. He wasn't sure what to expect, but he didn't think it would be anything good. The first car blew by him and pulled in front of him, only about two car lengths ahead. The second car moved in behind him at the same time. As soon as that happened, Joe hit the gas and moved across to an outside lane. Traffic was sparse in this area so he didn't have to worry about other vehicles. In his mind, he knew that this spot was perfect to take him out, whatever the reason was. He didn't wait to figure it out.

The car in the front rolled down its windows, and Joe could see a gun pointed at his car as soon as he pulled even with it, two lanes away. Seeing the gun aimed at him, Joe took his own gun off his lap. He had already opened his own passenger side window when the first car passed him. He turned and shot out both the two side windows on the first Toyota. He pulled over to the far outside lane, where there was room, slammed on his brakes, and, as the second car passed him, he shot out both windows of the second car. Both Toyotas slowed up and pulled off to the side. Joe wasn't sure if he hit anyone but he was sure that he surprised the shit out of all of them.

He took his phone out, hit 9-1-1, and yelled at the operator that shots were fired on I-95 N, just south of the first Fort Lauderdale exit. He then watched traffic, pulled out, and made the exit in just under three minutes, then ducked into a Mobil station to call Mark.

He dialed Mark's cell number but there was no answer. *Maybe he's in a meeting.* He then dialed the station's main number and someone picked up.

"Mark Silva, please. Joe Traynor calling."

"Sorry, sir, but all hell just broke loose. Someone shot up the station just minutes ago."

It's just another day in paradise for US Coast Guard Lieutenant Joe Traynor, stationed in the Florida Keys…until he gets a call from his boss, Rear Admiral Jake Barnes. Barnes suspects that some Coast Guard members in Miami have been selling seized cocaine back to the Colombians, and Joe and his team are called in to investigate. But as Joe leaves the rear admiral's office, he runs into an ambush, at the same time that his second-in-command is shot and nearly killed. It seems that members of the US Coast Guard Seventh District are selling more than cocaine to the drug cartels. They're also selling information obtained from bugging the Coast Guard offices. How deep does it go, who is involved, and how are they getting away with it when audits of the warehouse where the drugs are stored show nothing is missing? Joe needs to find out—and fast—before any more top personnel and their families are threatened, including his own fiancée, Julie. However, keeping Julie safe while she negotiates a movie deal for her new book with Walt Disney Studios, outsmarting drug lords and their minions, and tracking down missing fifteen-year-old girls who have been sold into the human trafficking network are all in a day's work for Joe and his team of special investigators…if they can just survive long enough.

KUDOS for *Taking Care of Your Own*

In *Taking Care of Your Own* by Daniel J. Barrett, we are once again reunited with Joe Traynor and Julie Chapman, now engaged to be married. Joe is called in on a special investigation for the US Coast Guard and is nearly killed in an ambush as he leaves his boss's office. Angry that someone is out to kill him, as well as stealing cocaine from the Coast Guard warehouse where the drugs seized for evidence are kept, Joe is devastated to discover that some of his coworkers could be working for the drug lords. But he and his boss are determined to root out the bad apples in the Coast Guard and police their own, especially since both of their careers are on the line. In the background, Julie is dealing with issues of her own. Walt Disney Studios wants to make a movie of her book trilogy *A Girl's Life*, and Julie isn't at all sure that she wants to do that. Meanwhile, her life could be in danger as much as Joe's, since drug cartels don't care who they hurt as long as they get what they want. Like the first two books in the series, this one is fast-paced, with a strong plot, lots of twists and turns, and quite a few unexpected surprises. ~ *Taylor Jones, Reviewer*

Taking Care of Your Own by Daniel J. Barrett is the story of corruption and greed in the US Coast Guard. Our hero, Joe Traynor, is a lieutenant in the Coast Guard in charge of investigations in Miami and the Florida Keys. But this time, it looks like the bad guys are some of Joe's own Coast Guard members who are selling back to the Colombians the drugs seized in the investigations that Joe works so hard to solve. Joe knows why they are doing it—money, the Colombians pay well—but he can't figure out how, especially since the secured warehouse where the drugs are stored until they can be destroyed claims that no drugs are missing. And according to the audits of the bales of cocaine, all the bales that are supposed to be there are. Vying for Joe's attention are his fiancée Julie and the movie deal for her book. Of course,

Joe has to keep himself alive long enough to catch the bad guys who are trying to kill him and would certainly harm Julie as well, if they could get to her. Throw in a an ambush, a wounded partner, a bugged office, and couple of missing teenage girls, and Joe is having a very bad time. *Taking Care of Your Own* is another Barrett page-turner. With fast action, a complicated plot, and intriguing characters, it's a worthy addition to the series. ~ *Regan Murphy, Reviewer*

ACKNOWLEDGEMENTS

Once again, thank you to Black Opal Books for making this third book in the *Conch Town Girl* series possible. A special thank you to Lauri Wellington, Acquisitions Editor, and to Faith for making *Taking Care of Your Own* the best that it can be. Your dedication and hard work is very much appreciated.

Taking Care

of

Your Own

Daniel J. Barrett

A Black Opal Books Publication

GENRE: MYSTERY/THRILLER/NEW ADULT/ROMANTIC ELE-
MENTS

TAKING CARE OF YOUR OWN
Copyright © 2016 by Daniel J. Barrett
Cover Design by Jackson Cover Designs
All cover art copyright © 2016
All Rights Reserved
Print ISBN: 978-1-626944-11-4

First Publication: FEBRUARY 2016

Published by Black Opal Books **http://www.blackopalbooks.com**

DEDICATION

To my wife, Sandy,

And to our grandchildren: Shannon, Caden,
Megan, and Declan.

And to

All those many friends who served
as readers and advisors.

Thank you to all. You are all greatly appreciated.

Chapter 1

"Please hold for Rear Admiral Barnes," the voice announced.

Joe Traynor was in the middle of a meeting in Islamorada with his investigation team that included Joan Talbot and the facility's Chief Warrant Officer, Jacob Cramer. Ever since Joe had been promoted to lieutenant, Cramer had been on edge, and it was apparent. Joe tried to make life simple for Cramer by telling him that, even though he outranked him, Joe had no desire to take over Cramer's duties. He told him that he'd report to both the Rear Admiral in Miami and to Cramer in Islamorada, when he was at either place. Joan had no problem with the reporting mechanism but evidently Cramer did. Joe figured his attempts to appease Cramer fell on deaf ears. So he stopped trying and simply did his job, which was to take down drug smugglers in the Keys, utilizing his vast experience in investigations and his linguistic skills in both Spanish and Russian. At that very moment, when the rear admiral called, they were reviewing a pending case that needed Joe's attention in both Spanish and Russian.

The call came in from Warrant Officer Al Cummings, the chief aid to the district commander, Rear Admiral Jake Barnes, who had his office at the seventh district headquarters, in the Brickell Plaza Building, located at 909 South East First Avenue in Miami. This was the address for Joe's new assignment, with an office only three doors down from the rear admiral's. It was fifty-eight miles, door to door, from Joe's office in Key Largo to the one in the federal building in downtown Miami. Joe made the trip three times a week to meet with the rear admiral and then worked on Islamorada cases around that schedule.

"Joe, it's Rear Admiral Barnes. How are you? Sorry to interrupt your meeting but it's important. I know this is one of your two days in the Keys but something has come up. Can you get up here quickly? I need to speak to you face to face, in private."

"Will I be staying over, sir?"

"Probably for a few days, for now," Barnes said.

"I'll leave as soon as I pack a few things, sir. Will I need my dress uniforms or just my regular everyday Coast Guard work clothes?"

"Bring one dress uniform and some of your civilian clothes for now. You may be in circumstances where I don't want you standing out," Barnes ordered cryptically.

It was now 11:00 a.m. and they were about to finish the meeting, anyway. The meeting's give and take was hanging there by a thread and Joe knew that he'd have to speak to Cramer privately and let him know that he wasn't happy with his attitude. He thought Joan had probably realized that and may have already tried to smooth this over with Cramer. As good as Joan was at this, she might have to step aside and let Joe handle it himself. Joan was nearing the end of her career in the Coast Guard and he didn't want her to be in the middle of anything. She'd been too good to him for too long and he knew that, upon her retirement, both she and her husband wanted to continue to work as contractors in Jeff Talbot's side business, which included all the maintenance on the Coast Guard vessels docked in Islamorada. Jeff ran his own small marina and repair shop, side by side, next to the Coast Guard facility. They lived in Coast Guard housing at the station, only steps from Jeff's business.

After the call, Joe told Joan that he had to leave for a few days. She never questioned him, especially since he now worked directly for the brass in Miami. She knew that he wasn't just handed his promotion to lieutenant. Both he and Mark Silva had earned it through smarts and hard work. Solving critical investigations, one after the other, didn't hurt either. As he was leaving to pack at his officer's living quarters, Joe stopped in Cramer's office to tell him why he had to leave.

"Jacob, I need to speak to you for a minute before I leave."

"Where are you going now?" Cramer asked. "I wish you wouldn't leave us stuck with these investigations. When are you coming back?"

Joe had just about had it with Cramer. He picked up his cell phone and dialed the rear admiral's private cell number. Only Joe and two others had the number. One of them was Jake Barnes's wife. The other was the rear admiral's boss in Washington. As the phone rang and the rear admiral picked up, Joe asked him if he'd please speak to Chief Warrant Officer Cramer to tell him that he was going to Miami at the rear admiral's request and that Mr. Cramer probably should stop questioning him about his comings and goings and his future duties.

Joe handed the cell phone to a very startled Cramer. At the end of the call, the chief warrant officer nodded to Joe. "I'll never question you again."

Evidently, he was given a direct order to that effect.

"I have a call to duty just as you do, and I wouldn't question my commanding officer's orders," Joe told him, looking him right in the eyes. "I have no problem with you, but it's clear that you've had a problem with me. I've never pulled rank on anyone since I've been in the Coast Guard and I have no intentions of doing so, ever." He paused a moment for effect. "Of course, my personal preferences could change if your attitude doesn't."

Joe reached out to shake his hand and Cramer reached

back to shake Joe's as well. Joe hoped that this was the end of this little pissing contest. He wanted to be in Islamorada for as long as Julie wanted to remain in the Keys.

This was a perfect setup for him, but he wouldn't allow himself to be stepped on by anyone. Joe knew himself very well. He could be a very belligerent Irishman. When provoked, he got even more obstinate. His own mother had told him that while he was growing up. He worked on it constantly, but once in a while, it reared its ugly head. This temper of his was both a hindrance and a help. Joe needed that attitude when he was in very trying and deadly circumstances. It gave him strength and fortitude not to fail under pressure. He'd get angry and turn that anger into aggression toward the lawbreakers he was hunting. Only a few times had it come out when his friends noticed. Julie's grandmother, Tillie, even commented on it one day after Joe shot Julie's father, Tom Chapman, who at the time, was holding a gun on both Julie and Tillie. Tillie was shocked that a man like Joe, who appeared so in control, actually had this other side to him.

At the time, Mark had told her about what happened in Albany when he had to shoot Luis Hernandez and his three gangbanger goons in the president's office of the Albany Coalition for Families several years and many cases ago.

All of these thoughts were slowly going through Joe's mind. It was difficult having a photographic memory. It brought up the good and the bad. He had to put everything out of his head and concentrate on heading up to Miami to meet with the rear admiral. Joe had no idea what Barnes wanted. He never questioned the rear admiral's orders. Barnes had been very good to Joe and had bent over backward to accommodate his request to remove Dmitry Assinoff and his associates from Miami. Joe would never forget his support, and he wouldn't let him down.

He hoped that traffic would be light getting out of the Keys at noon, when he finally got into his car for the drive to Miami. He had to call Julie and leave a message that he'd be gone for a few days and that he'd call her this evening when he got settled. The Coast Guard had a condo, right around the corner from headquarters, for visiting officers, who could then walk to the building and not waste time parking and getting back and forth from expensive downtown hotels. Joe knew how expensive it could be since he and Julie had stayed at the Ritz-Carlton Key Biscayne the time Joe had picked Julie up at the airport when she finally got back from New York City. At $369.00 per night, he'd hoped she'd enjoy the room. She did. It was rated 4.7 out of 5 stars. Joe couldn't figure out, at those prices, what would be missing, but it couldn't be much.

Their guestroom had featured an ocean view. It had a beautiful balcony, marble bathroom, flat screen TV, and, of course, a fully stocked minibar. Joe could take or leave the WiFi hookup. Julie had to get some emails but, at the time, he certainly hoped that her online time would be short. It was. Now, staying alone, in the free condo, one block away from headquarters suited Joe just fine. It suited his pocketbook as well.

Joe headed right up Overseas Highway, which was US Route 1 North, to Florida Route 5. He merged onto 821 N, the Florida Turnpike, for seventeen miles toward the Miami International Airport. From there, he headed to the Don Shula Expressway toward FL 826 Miami. He took FL 878 E toward South Miami back to US 1. The Dixie Highway, which was also US 1, took him right to I-95 N. Taking Exit 1B brought him straight to Brickell Avenue. He drove the one-mile distance to the Brickell Plaza Federal Building and parked in the Coast Guard lot. He was here and had no idea why. In a few minutes, Joe knew, he'd find out there was a very good reason but, right now, he didn't have a clue.

He walked in the front door, presented his credentials, and proceeded through the security checkpoints. Once through, he got back his cell phone, his bag, and his service weapon. He headed up to the rear admiral's office and walked in.

Chapter 2

As Joe walked into the office, Al Cummings, the rear admiral's administrative assistant and warrant officer met him and told him to go right in. The rear admiral was waiting for him. This time at least, Cummings was pleasant to Joe. On previous occasions, he hadn't been very pleasant at all. Joe thought that, maybe, things were looking up. After confronting Cramer before he left Islamorada, he didn't want any more personnel issues, especially at headquarters.

The rear admiral waved him in. "Hi, Joe. I'm just finishing up. Please close the door. Thanks."

Joe closed the door and sat in front of his desk. He didn't have a clue why he was there. He thought everything was going well and hoped that he hadn't stepped on any toes recently. God knew he'd stepped on enough of them after the last case. He remained quiet and waited for the rear admiral to speak.

"Joe, I've a big problem on my hands and I really don't know how to proceed at this point because, quite frankly, I don't have enough information to go on."

"Is this anything concerning me, sir?"

"No, of course not, Joe. I hope I didn't give you that impression. You may be my only ray of light this week." He then went on to explain exactly what his problem was. "The local FBI office in Miami just called me this morning about a situation that they heard about second hand through Homeland Security. It seems that one or more Coast Guard officers and crewmembers, assigned to the southeast region, might be on the take," he told him. "This was the first time in my thirty-plus-year career that I've had to confront such an issue. But with drugs becoming so prevalent in America, it has seeped into the armed services, including the Coast Guard as well. There have always been drug issues with soldiers oversees, but now that they've come back, hooked on drugs, it's the worst I've ever seen, including Vietnam.

"We just caught two Coast Guard lieutenants in California hooked on cocaine and heroin. We've seen it before in the ranks but never so blatantly as now, which includes first-line-defense officers. One officer in California was in charge of the entire Pacific fleet, out of San Diego. It got so bad that the officer was caught stealing cocaine from seized shipments, just to support his habit, which was now out of control.

"From what I've been told, Joe, we had a major seizure in mid-April of this year. The seized drugs came into the Miami Beach Coast Guard Station. The wholesale value was almost one hundred ten million dollars. They seized 3,300 kilograms, which was 7,275 pounds, to be exact. The wholesale value was $33,000.00 a kilo or over $15,000.00 a pound. A kilo is a little over two pounds, as you know."

Barnes sighed and shook his head. "This offload was a result of two separate drug interdictions. In mid-March, a US Coast Guard Law Enforcement Detachment aboard Her Majesty's Canadian Ship, *Glace Bay*, assigned to Joint Interagency Task Force South, patrolling the Caribbean Sea, identified a vessel suspected of smuggling drugs. The vessel was boarded by the LEDET, but no drugs were found. During the boarding, the fishing vessel caught fire and sank. All passengers aboard the vessel were safely disembarked. A subsequent search of the general area located approximately 130 bales containing approximately 3,300 kilograms of cocaine floating in the water, worth an estimated wholesale value of one hundred ten million dollars. That seizure wound up in Miami and, when the final tally was taken, no bales were missing. There was nothing suspicious. They recorded all 130 bales at full value. Even though all the bales were accounted for, the FBI, through Homeland Security, believes that thirty bales still wound up back in the hands of the Colombians. No one had a clue.

"Joe, I'm not accusing the Miami Beach Station of stealing the cocaine. I've no idea what happened and nothing appears to be missing from the warehouse that's fully secured twenty-four/seven. However, after talking to the local FBI, I found out it's been rumored that over thirty bales wound up back where they started, with the Colombians. It could be over a matter of days or months. No one has any idea. Evidently, they've got warehouses all over Miami and shipping containers at their disposal. It could be anywhere. What would you suggest we do from an investigative standpoint? All I'm saying, right now, Joe, is that we need to be taking care of our own problems. If not, how can we protect and defend this country? If my own men are stealing and contributing to the drug problem of this country, I'll be not only embarrassed but also fucking mad as hell, and I want them caught. What I need from you, knowing now how your brain works, is a strategic plan, not only to catch our own internal crooks, but also to stop it from happening again."

Joe shifted in his seat. *Holy hell.* "First, let me say that I'm honored that you asked me to look into this. A strategic plan will only help if we get all the facts. From my experience, people seem to each have their own set of facts. They call them facts, when what they actually are is their guesses. Can I use your whiteboard?"

"Sure, Joe. Let's see what you came up with."

Joe rose, went to the whiteboard, and started a matrix. On the left side, going down vertically, he put the names of the organizations and personnel involved, starting with the Coast Guard ships in question, the Canadians, the Miami

Beach Station, the FBI, Homeland Security, the rear admiral, and, finally, the Colombians. On the top, across horizontally, he placed the key dates from March until now, well into the fall of this year. He placed the kilos/pounds and the value from seizure to delivery and then put a big question mark on what took place from April until now, when the FBI called. Joe was taught, at Rensselaer Polytechnic Institute, where he went for his MBA, that this wasn't just a matrix but a rather complex fishbone diagram.

Joe explained to the rear admiral, step by step, where his thinking was headed. "In order to get where you need to be, you start with the end date and work your way backward to determine gaps in time. Those gaps needed to be clarified. Who was in charge of the storage of 130 bales of cocaine? How big in physical space are 130 bales? The bales are each about three feet square in size, all in plastic wrap. How were the bales numbered, 1 through 130? Were they missing any? Did each bale have its own Coast Guard inventory code, in addition to the numbering system supplied by the drug smugglers? How often did they take inventory? How often did they get shipped and to where? Had any shipments gone out that totaled thirty bales? Where did thirty-plus bales go, if they ever got there? You said none are missing in the warehouse, correct?"

"Correct," said the rear admiral. "Those are all good questions, Joe. Please continue."

"In sheer size alone, the bales, each at three feet by three feet cubed, times 130 bales equals 1,170 cubic feet of space." Joe did a quick calculation in his head. "The storage area holding the 130 bales has to be a minimum of a room that is equivalent to twelve feet high, fifty-one feet long and twelve feet wide. The actual dimensions of the bales, when stacked on top of each other, would be nine feet tall, nine feet wide, and forty-five feet long. You need three feet all the way around the huge pile just to get to it. So, one thing I want to do is to go to the storage area and see if it is, first, physically possible to store 130 bales, and if the bales are all accounted for correctly, not just on paper. If not, the bales never got to the storage area, even if the paperwork said they did. That would cut the investigation by two-thirds, if true. If the room is big enough, you still wouldn't be sure that they got there but you'd be sure that it had the right amount of space, if they did."

"Joe, how the hell did you just do that? Did you do that in your head? I'm impressed."

"Thank you, sir, but it's no big deal. My father taught me how to measure space when he was putting in construction contract bids. He told me that you had to think geometrically in dealing with issues like this. It stopped a lot of wasted effort, trying to figure out if things were bigger than a breadbox, he used to say."

"Well, I'm still impressed and this is bigger than a breadbox. How do we keep this quiet for now and still have you look into it?"

"As you know, sir, I work with Mark Silva and Jack Forest up in Virginia when we do our investigations. They're brilliant at what they do. I supply the strategy and mode of attack, but I can't do anything without facts, and they get me those. As I said before, sir, not guesses, but real facts. Jack can download the blueprints from the storage facility and see if the dimensions fit. I'd like to go there anyway just to visually check things out. I have to visualize a problem before I understand it."

"Joe, do whatever you have to do, but quietly for now. I don't want to accuse anyone yet, but the FBI and Homeland Security have their collective eyes focused on us. I don't want to drop the ball."

"If I may ask, sir, who called you from the FBI in Miami?"

"I don't know these people personally. I know I should, and I will before this is over, but I was called by Paul Philips, the Miami Office FBI Director, and then I was placed in a conference call with Mr. Philips and his boss, Terry Owens, who's the Florida Regional FBI Director.

They've got as many people falling over themselves as we do, I suspect. At first, I didn't know if Terry was a man or a woman. She's a woman."

"Sir, I know Mr. Philips and Ms. Owens very well. In fact, they put me in touch with the Albany FBI Director, Tom Mathews, when the Mexican Mafia takedown took place last year. All three were very helpful and very professional. As you know, I carry identification not only for the Coast Guard but for Homeland Security and the FBI, as well. I used all three in Nashville just recently. If you want, I'll be glad to see them first before I do anything else or even contact Jack and Mark."

"That's a very good idea, in case I missed anything from the short conference call. I didn't tell them that I was bringing you in to investigate this situation but, hopefully, you'll have a better working relationship with them since you've already done so previously."

Joe was getting fidgety and wanted to leave as soon as possible. His mind was racing a mile a minute. "Do you need me for anything else, sir?" he asked. "I'd like to get started on this right away."

"No, you go ahead and do what you need to. Just keep me posted."

"Will do, sir."

Joe left the rear admiral's office at a fast walk. He had to go to his office down the hall and see if he could set up a quick meeting with Paul and Terry for this afternoon. He wanted to make sure that they were all on the same page before jumping in cold. He also wanted to call Julie and tell her he wouldn't be home for a few days. And he wanted to call Mark right away, but it was best if he spoke to the FBI first to get a better idea of what was involved.

Mark was more of an operations guy who really knew how to get things done once a plan was in place. Jack on the other hand, was a major resource who could get information quicker than anyone else in any of the armed services. He was a technology genius.

As Joe headed to his office, he thought that this new job would be a never-ending battle but it was what he was hoping for when he rejoined the Coast Guard. He still needed his own people, whom he could always trust. Hell, they'd been close friends for almost fifteen years now. You couldn't do better than that. Whenever Joe needed anything, they dropped what they were doing to help. And Joe did the same for them.

Chapter 3

Joe headed north to I-95 N, to Exit 9, to get to Second Avenue in North Miami Beach. It was only ten miles, door to door, from where Joe would meet with Paul and Terry. Hopefully, after the meeting, Joe could drive up to Fort Lauderdale to meet with Mark and start a plan of attack. Mark was only fifteen miles north of the FBI headquarters. They'd get on the phone with Jack Forest to see what kind of information they could get quickly to start the investigation.

Joe walked into FBI headquarters and at least the guard at the front desk recognized him. Joe told the guard that he didn't have an appointment but wanted to see if he could speak to Paul Philips and Terry Owens. The guard called upstairs and Terry was available. Paul just got called out of the office on another matter that he couldn't avoid. Terry told the guard to let him through and that he knew where her office was.

Joe thanked him but still went through the checkpoint, giving his gun and other metallic items to the inspector. After going through the machine, Joe retrieved his belongings and headed up the stairs to Terry's office. On the way, he stopped in the men's room. He realized he hadn't eaten since that morning and looked a little disheveled as well. He'd hoped Terry had something to nibble on and drink while he met with her.

When he arrived at her office, he knocked on the door-frame of her open door.

"Hi, Joe," she said. "Please come in. Paul just got called out on an emergency. He had to go but I'm here. No problem," she said. "I'll fill him in as soon as he gets back."

"Thanks for seeing me with such little notice. I'm heading up to see Mark next and I wanted to talk to you first before I did anything. Mark doesn't know I'm coming either."

"Is this about our discussion this morning with the rear admiral?"

"Yes."

"Did Rear Admiral Barnes give this investigation to you and Mark?"

"Just to me for now. I asked to bring in Mark and Jack Forest from up in Virginia. You know Jack. He worked on our other investigations."

"I'd spoken to Jack but never had the pleasure of meeting him," she said. "He seems like a very bright guy."

"He is and he's even brighter than you might suspect. He's a technological genius and we couldn't have cracked any of the cases without his facial recognition and new DNA testing, let alone his ability to get me almost anything I request. Don't ask me how he does it. I don't want to know," he said, smiling.

Terry smiled back. "I guess I don't need to know either. Joe, here is the situation. Paul got a call yesterday, late afternoon from Homeland Security. He came to me right away and we got on the phone together with the Miami Homeland Security mucky mucks. They said they heard chatter that a number of bales of cocaine had gotten back into the hands of the Colombians. No matter how hard they've looked in the Miami area, they don't know where their storage facilities are located. Hell, they may still be in shipping containers at the Miami port along with the twenty thousand other containers that come in every day.

"They also believe they have warehouses somewhere in the greater Miami area where they breakdown the bales into

kilos, shrink wrap the product, and send it out for processing, either locally or somewhere else here in Florida. As
you know, each bale is well over 50 pounds and a kilo is a
little over two pounds, almost two and a half. So breaking it
down to smaller packages means they've a multitude of
ways to ship product. If left in bale size, they'd need a fleet
of forty-eight foot trailers for deliveries. They probably still
have those but, if caught, they'd lose a great deal more than
shipping it out in vans and cars, which would only carry a
fraction of the total amount. Other than that, we haven't
heard any more. However, they believe that the Coast
Guard and some of its officers and noncoms are responsible
for this. They also don't believe that this was the first incident."

Joe sat back and thought about what she just said.
"Here's what I know about the process of destroying seized
cocaine. Once the bales are seized at sea, the Coast Guard
cutters come into the Miami Beach Coast Guard facility.
From there, the product is tagged, inventoried, and shipped
by Coast Guard trucks, set up for this process. The product
is taken to a specific Coast Guard facility, a location that I
am not able to discuss. The trucks are tagged as soon as
they're loaded, have proper bills of lading, and paperwork.
The trailer doors are locked and sealed with a special Coast
Guard lead stamp, crimped right onto the sealed doors. The
product comes off the trucks under the supervision of the
site officer and two other signatories. The bales are then
placed into a sealed room, secured and, again the locked
doors are secured with the Coast Guard seal. The Coast
Guard maintains the facility, even though it is under the supervision of Homeland Security. Even the maintenance staff
is Coast Guard. If there's a problem, I know that it would
most likely fall back into my lap and under the watch of the
rear admiral.

"The paperwork says nothing is missing, Terry. However, I'm going to personally audit the warehouse and make
sure that all the bales are there and match the paperwork. If

what you're saying is true, and I believe you, the bales probably came from somewhere else or someone is lying internally. I'll get to the bottom of it." Joe sighed. "There is a destruction policy and the product is held for six months and then destroyed, or destroyed sooner if the evidence is no longer needed for the criminal cases of those involved. Usually, there's so much plea-bargaining going on, that it is sooner rather than later that the product is destroyed. There's a schedule of destruction, following the same procedures as the delivery. The cocaine bales are taken by a Coast Guard truck to a designated ship that is set up for the destruction process. There are two ships that I know of that are designated for this process. The bales are loaded onto the ship and taken a minimum of ten nautical miles from the Miami Beach Coast Guard Station. Each bale is lowered individually into the ocean by a specialized machine that crushes the bales, shreds the plastic, and allows the cocaine to drop to the bottom of the ocean, rendering the product useless. The shredder is raised and the shredded plastic, taken from each bale, is put into a larger evidence bag and tagged as to the time and date of destruction, signed and sealed. They are stored at the same Coast Guard facility to match with the incoming and release paperwork."

"Joe, how the hell do you know all that?"

"A while ago, after a bust, I asked to see how the product was destroyed so I'd understand the process from the beginning of a takedown to the end, the final destination of the product. If I can't understand the whole picture, things become fuzzy to me and I can't grasp what I need to in order to complete the tasks. That's just the way my brain works, I guess."

"So where do you think the problem lies, if, in fact, there's a problem."

"Well, first, this is very premature but, like I said, I think I want to follow the trail from beginning to end. Does anyone have an idea how much cocaine we're talking about going back to the Colombians?"

"Homeland Security heard that perhaps around thirty to thirty-five bales or so were involved. That means about 1,500 pounds of cocaine at wholesale level. The wholesale price for cocaine right now was around $33,000.00 a kilo or over $15,000.00 a pound. That would put the wholesale value over $20.0 million, maybe up to $28.0 million dollars. The retail value, once cut, could be over $80.0 million," she said. "The last big haul that came in to the Miami Beach Station was in mid-April of this year. The Canadians and our guys brought the haul in, about 130 bales or 3,300 kilos with a wholesale value of $110 million."

"Did anyone check to see if it's still there or had it been destroyed?"

"Joe, all I know is what I heard from Homeland Security, and I passed it on to Rear Admiral Barnes, who gave it you. That's where we stand right now."

"Okay. At least that's a start," Joe said. "I'd caution you, Terry, along with Paul, not to discuss what I just told you, if you wouldn't mind. I have to put together a game plan that doesn't piss off the world but at least lets us get closer to the problem and, hopefully, the solution. It sounds like this has been ongoing and no one knew a thing until now. I find that hard to believe with everyone's hand in everyone else's pockets."

"I hear you, Joe. We won't say a thing. I know you represent all three organizations. God knows why," she said and smiled. "Why would you take on so much at one time? Didn't you just get back from Nashville? Didn't you just get engaged, for God's sake?"

"Yes, yes, and yes," Joe said with a frown. "When asked to serve, I have to serve. Does it screw up my personal life? You've no idea."

"When are you getting married," she asked.

"With everything going on, maybe next spring, which will be here sooner than we think. It's only been a few months since I asked Julie to marry me in New York City. Hell, I haven't even gotten her a ring yet. I think she wants to incorporate Tillie's ring into a new setting. Tillie is Julie's grandmother who raised her. Julie just got back to the Monroe County School District for the fall semester, with twice as many duties, and a new book due shortly. She's also been asked to meet with Disney about either a movie or television project."

"You didn't get her a ring yet?"

"That's all you heard, wasn't it, Terry? God, women are all alike. I asked her four times to go get a ring and she hasn't had time. So there." He smiled smugly.

With that admonishment, Joe said goodbye. "As soon as we formulate a plan, I'll meet with the rear admiral and then bring you into the investigation, along with Homeland Security personnel. I need to hurry up and get to Fort Lauderdale to catch Mark before he leaves the Dania Beach Station."

ৎৎৎ

Joe got back on I-95 N and headed toward Fort Lauderdale and then only a few miles east to Mark's office. After taking the entrance ramp coming out of North Miami Beach, he noticed two cars behind him, both older Toyotas, maybe late 1990s. Hispanic men drove both and each had another man in the passenger seat. Joe always looked behind him while driving. If someone came up behind him too quickly, he'd blow his horn to let the person know to back off and that he wasn't happy. Neither of these cars came close to him, but there was something he couldn't put his finger on. It looked to him like he was being watched. It never took Joe long to figure that out, especially after the last few operations. He always had to be careful. One wrong step could be his last one.

When he was sixteen, he'd gotten his driver's license in a dump truck that belonged to his father's business. In fact, Joe took his test for his chauffer's license on his sixteenth birthday. Most kids his age didn't even have driver's licenses for a car let alone a commercial license to drive a large dump truck. Joe had been taking lessons from his father for over two years. God knew why John Traynor allowed his son to drive around the neighborhood in a dump truck, but he did.

That was why Joe told people, who asked him why he did certain things, that he was raised by wolves. He worked for his father, who paid him a good salary under the table, until he left for college at eighteen. Joe had done a lot of things that only grown men were allowed to do, including working a full construction crew job while in high school. The only time he took off from work was for baseball season. Joe was taught to drive the truck as if everyone else was out to kill him. That was what his father taught him and that was the way Joe drove. He left plenty of space between cars, either in front of him or in back of him. He knew that some idiot in South Florida would take an exit ramp from the third outside lane and cut right in front of him before the exit. It was a daily occurrence in Miami, and Joe never drove with the radio on or when using a cell phone. He didn't need the distraction.

He was about five miles from the Fort Lauderdale exit when he noticed that the two older Toyotas, that had followed him all the way from North Miami Beach, pulled out into the middle lane. They were coming up fast behind him. Joe had his gun in his holster. He unsnapped it, pulled out his weapon, and took off the safety. He wasn't sure what to expect, but he didn't think it would be anything good.

The first car blew by him and pulled in front of him, only about two car lengths ahead. The second car moved in behind him at the same time. As soon as that happened, Joe hit the gas and moved across to an outside lane. Traffic was sparse in this area so he didn't have to worry about other vehicles. In his mind, he knew that this spot was perfect to take him out, whatever the reason was. He didn't wait to figure it out.

At that moment, he'd been going around seventy miles per hour, a little over the limit, and now he was moving fast, around eighty miles an hour.

The car in the front rolled down its windows, and Joe could see a gun pointed at his car as soon as he pulled even with it, two lanes away. Seeing the gun aimed at him, Joe took his own gun off his lap. He had already opened his own passenger side window when the first car passed him. He turned and shot out both the two side windows on the first Toyota. He pulled over to the far outside lane, where there was room, slammed on his brakes, and, as the second car passed him, he shot out both windows of the second car. Both Toyotas slowed down and pulled off to the side. Joe wasn't sure if he hit anyone but he was sure that he surprised the shit out of all of them.

Joe took his phone out, hit 9-1-1, and yelled at the operator that shots were fired on I-95 N, just south of the first Fort Lauderdale exit. He then watched traffic, pulled out, and made the exit in just under three minutes then ducked into a Mobil station to call Mark.

He dialed Mark's cell number but there was no answer. *Maybe he's in a meeting.* He then dialed the station's main number and someone picked up.

"Mark Silva, please. Joe Traynor calling."

"Sorry, sir, but all hell just broke loose. Someone shot up the station just minutes ago."

"Was anyone hurt?" Joe asked.

"Mark was walking out the door and he got shot in the right shoulder. He was smart enough, and it happened quick enough, that when he got hit, he rolled near the door and one of his men opened it and pulled him back into the building. He saved Mark's life. There were several shots in between Mark being shot and the door opening, but no one else got hit. We put a compress on his shoulder and called 9-1-1 for officer down."

The ambulance and Joe got there right at the same time. Joe left his car in the lot, threw the keys to one of the people he knew at the station, and hopped into the ambulance with Mark. They were headed to Broward General Medical Center on South Andrews Avenue in Fort Lauderdale. They'd be there in five minutes.

Joe looked at Mark who was being worked on by the EMTs. They looked at Joe and said nothing. Joe flashed them his credentials. "We're Coast Guard lieutenants and members of Homeland Security and the FBI." Joe said emphatically. "This was the shooting of an officer."

They drove up to the emergency room entrance and pulled Mark out on his gurney and into the hospital entrance. The EMTs called ahead and the crash emergency team was waiting at the door for them.

Right before Mark was taken from the ambulance, he squeezed Joe's arm. "Call my wife, please, Joe."

"I will. Don't worry."

They took Mark straight into surgery. He'd lost a lot of blood, but it looked like the bullet went through his shoulder and out, just missing a few critical areas. Joe knew that it was much worse than what had happened to him in Albany when he got shot by Luis Hernandez, during the Mexican Mafia crisis.

Before he called Mark's wife, Louise, though, Joe needed to make sure that Mark was secure. He immediately called the rear admiral on his private cell and told him about both incidents.

The rear admiral called the FBI, who immediately sent four special agents to the hospital to secure Mark's safety.

Once again, Joe's mind was racing. He was really upset that he could have lost his best friend. But he didn't want to show it. He needed to stay calm for Louise and the kids' sake. He had to get to them and also have agents sent to guard them. She'd want to leave for the hospital. He decided to pick her up then remembered he'd left his car back in the station lot.

Calling the station, he spoke to the Chief Petty Officer Michelle Bower, who reported to Mark, and told her to get to Mark's house immediately with two armed guards. Joe then made the call to Louise.

He got her right before she was heading out to work at the Hard Rock Café. She worked as a waitress at night from 5:30 p.m. until 11:00 p.m. Mark usually got home right before she left and watched the kids. She had days and he had nights. The arrangement worked but was getting tiresome, especially after Mark had been away from home for so much time over the last several months. Joe and he had worked almost nonstop to solve several major crimes and they'd barely had time to breathe.

"Louise, it's Joe," he said. "I need you to listen to me very closely. Mark has been shot in the shoulder and he's now at Broward General. He's been rushed into surgery but he'll be fine."

"Oh my God," she shrieked. "When did this happen?"

"Less than a half hour ago. I'll explain it to you as soon as I see you. Are your mother and father home?"

"Yes."

"Mark's second in command, Michelle Bower, will be at your house in five minutes. She'll drop off two armed guards. Have your mother and father watch the kids. She'll take you to the hospital, and I'll be waiting for you at the emergency room entrance. Louise, Mark will be fine, I promise you," he said before hanging up.

He went back up to the surgical suite and made a call to Julie and Joan. He told Julie what happened and that she didn't need to worry. It wasn't the Russians and had nothing to do with that. He believed that either the rear admiral or the FBI had a leak in their offices and someone decided to take out both Joe and Mark at the same time before they could start their investigation.

ᥱᦂᥱᦂ

Louise arrived less than a half hour later and ran to Joe

as soon as Michelle stopped the car. Michelle parked in the police parking spot and went up with Louise and Joe to see if there was any news. As soon as Louise saw Joe, she burst into tears. "What the hell is going on?

"I'll tell you in private," he whispered.

When they reached surgery, they walked into the waiting room. Joe went up to the nurses' station and told them who they were. The head nurse, knowing that this was an officer-shot situation, came right out to see Louise to reassure her that her husband was in the best possible hands. "This is a major trauma hospital and we see gunshot wounds and mayhem throughout the year. Our staff of surgeons know their stuff."

At this point, all Joe could think about was seeing Tillie in the Mariner Hospital in the Keys after her hit and run. She was unconscious and at death's door but pulled through, thanks to her being one tough lady and the bene-factor of a lot of prayer. Joe had just gotten back from his own father's triple bypass at the Albany Medical Center in upstate New York. He remembered how that song went—if it weren't for bad luck, they'd have no luck at all.

Country and Western music, he thought. He remembered Tillie telling him that, when you played a country song backward, you got back your pickup, your dog, and your wife. He laughed at the parody for the Beatles record.

After the nurse left, he pulled Louise off to the side. "Here's what I know. Mark knows nothing of this. I was on my way up to see him, and I couldn't say anything until it was cleared by the rear admiral and the FBI in North Miami Beach. As I was headed up I-95 to see Mark, I was nearly killed by four Hispanic men in two cars on the highway. I was able to take them out but when I got off at Fort Lauder-dale and called Mark, he'd already been shot. There's a se-rious issue that we were to investigate and I believe there was a leak that almost got us killed. We need to keep the guards around you and Mark, for now. I called Julie and she'll call Tillie. I called Joan Talbot as well to let her know. That's what I know at this point. Both the rear admiral and the FBI have been informed. The rear admiral is on his way to the hospital right now. Mark is well thought of and no one will let anything happen to him, or to you and the kids. That's my solemn promise."

With that, Joe remembered that he was starved. He needed to get something to eat before the rear admiral got there. He also needed to find out what happened to the four men on I-95. He was glad he hadn't stopped at the time because he wouldn't have been there for Mark. Now, he needed to know who they were.

There was a leak. There was no doubt about it. He laughed to himself about dinner at the hospital. He and Julie had spent so much time at the Mariner Hospital that he actually grew to like the food and the prices. He hoped Julie didn't break his chops when she found out where he'd be eating dinner for a while. He also wondered if Chief Warrant Officer Jacob Cramer would now like to change places with him, since his job was such a piece of cake and he could come and go as he pleased. *What an asshole*, Joe thought.

CHAPTER 4

Joe finished his dinner and went back to the surgical wing. Louise was still there and Joe brought her a sandwich and coffee. He would have normally felt bad that he'd eaten before Louise but, as he and Mark had discussed many times, you ate and slept when you could. You never knew when your next meal would come in the middle of an investigation. You hardly slept at all, either.

As soon as he sat down, the surgeon came out and asked for Mrs. Silva.

Louise responded immediately. "How's Mark doing?"

"He came through with flying colors," the surgeon said. "The wound wasn't life threatening but if we hadn't fixed the problem immediately, Mark would have difficulty raising his arm because his shoulder wouldn't move properly."

That alone could have jeopardized his Coast Guard career. He only had a few years left, but they needed the income now. The retirement would be nice but wouldn't come close to covering the costs of college for their two kids.

Joe was standing right next to Louise. "How long will his recovery be?"

The doctor shrugged. "It will take from a few weeks to three months, depending on physical therapy and the healing process."

Being a baseball fanatic, Joe thought it was like a pitcher tearing his rotor cuff. They just had to wait and see. He knew immediately that he'd be on his own for this investigation, but he was thankful that Mark was going to be okay. He turned to Louise and gave her a hug. She wiped her eyes, sat back down in the waiting room, and called her parents.

The immediate crisis of Mark being shot was over but the problem of protecting him and his family had just begun.

Joe turned to Michelle, Mark's second in command. "We need a fulltime plan to protect Mark and his family." He'd never gotten a chance to tell her what had happened to him on I-95 N before, so he asked her to step outside the waiting room for a minute. He told her about the investigation that he was just handed by the rear admiral "I never got a chance to tell Mark. I was quietly on my way up to see him to tell him what we'd be working on next, but I was too late."

Michelle had known that Mark had "borrowed" several of his subordinates a while ago when Joe needed them. Mark's men were invaluable in taking down Dmitry Assinoff in downtown Miami when the drone took out Assinoff's limousine. With Mark's help, Assinoff and his bodyguards were renditioned out of the country. "I'm going to need those men once again, but it has to be done very quietly due to the nature of the investigation. 'Taking Care of Your Own' will be the name of the operation, TCYO for short."

From the operation's name, Michelle knew the Coast Guard had a few bad apples. She was just starting to realize that she was now in command of the Dania Beach Station until further notice. Joe would make sure that the rear admiral understood the ramifications of bringing someone else in over her command.

Joe couldn't afford to start over with a new station commander, and he needed the combat-ready men that he'd already worked well with previously. It was selfish on his part, but critical if they were to get to the bottom of the missing cocaine.

"I'll back you one hundred percent," Joe assured her.

ᏬᎠᏬᎠ

Joe always carried a small pad and a pen. He made notes about everything he did. He had a page for every day of his life since he joined the Coast Guard at eighteen. Every night, he took out his notes and added his thoughts to one daily page. He'd then write out what he needed to do for the next day, in order, and for the rest of the week. He never went beyond a two-week period because he knew everything that he was working on could change in a heartbeat. The shootings that just happened changed his mind about what he needed to do now to move the investigation forward. As he sat there and thought about what happened, it became very clear that between the rear admiral's office and the FBI meeting, someone had put out a hit on both him and Mark.

Joe drew a timeline from the moment he got to Miami that day. Up until he met with the rear admiral, he had no idea what the meeting was about. The rear admiral said he'd told no one but Joe what he was told by the FBI that morning. The meeting took about an hour, maybe a little more, and then Joe had headed to the FBI office. He was only there for about forty-five minutes. As soon as he left the FBI office, he felt like he was being followed up the ramp on I-95 N headed to Mark's Dania Beach Station. So if there was a leak at either place, how were he and Mark identified as the investigators for this case? *No one could set up that fast after the FBI meeting. I was only there for forty-five minutes.*

Whoever tried to take him out and Mark at the same time had to have time to set up across the street from the Dania Beach Station and wait for Mark to walk out the door so they could shoot him. They also needed pictures sent of both Joe and Mark to make sure the right two guys were being hit. Joe didn't believe the leak was at the FBI office because there just wasn't enough time to follow him and to shoot Mark. The leak had to come from the rear admiral's office. That was the only explanation.

It gave them about three hours to get someone in place to shoot Mark. For the two cars to follow him up the ramp, they had to know that he was at the FBI office. Someone had to get the cars and men ready to follow him as soon as he left. They had to know that he was headed to Mark's. He'd only discussed it with the rear admiral, saying he'd go to see Mark after meeting with Paul and Terry.

Joe wrote down notes feverishly. He tore out one small sheet from the pad and wrote in large letters, *REAR ADMIRAL, YOU HAVE A LEAK IN YOUR OFFICE.* He'd hand it to Rear Admiral Barnes when he arrived.

❦

As soon as he finished his notes, Joe turned around and watched the rear admiral walk into the waiting room. Barnes was accompanied by three very large noncoms. He nodded to Joe and went over to meet Louise. If anything, Jake Barnes was a presence and a calming influence. People around him felt better for knowing him. He commanded loyalty and respect.

Coming up through the ranks, with a thirty-plus-year career, he understood how the enlisted man and officer felt in the face of tragedy or danger.

He shook Louise's hand and, as she stood up, he gave her a hug. "I'll do everything I can to ensure your safety and Mark's full recovery. I've suffered the same fate as Mark many years ago and I understand what's going through your minds. You'll have around-the-clock security. When Mark is on his way to recovery, I'll personally send your entire family to San Diego to stay with Mark's mother if you want."

Mark's sister and her family lived close to his mother and his other sister was only a half-day away in Los Angeles. She was in the movie business as a sought-after cinematographer.

The rear admiral turned to Joe and mouthed, "Meet me outside."

Joe waited for him to finish up with Louise and then met him down the hallway near the elevator. Joe pressed the button and he and the rear admiral stepped inside. Barnes had left his guards with Louise for the moment. He didn't think he needed anything more than Joe right then. They went into the cafeteria and each got a cup of coffee.

When they sat down in the corner, away from everyone else, Joe handed him the note. The rear admiral's eyes went wide. He looked at Joe and quietly asked how he knew that. Joe handed him his notes. Barnes read them carefully and started to shake his head. "Joe, I'm so sorry. I can't believe that this is true but you seem to think so. How do we prove this?"

At that point, the rear admiral knew nothing of Joe's problem on I-95 N. Joe then told him about his incident and how he figured it out that the leak had to come from the rear admiral's office and not the FBI.

"There just wasn't enough time to take out Mark. If it were just me, it could have come from either place. But to be set up so quickly to take out Mark, it had to take time. Either someone overheard you before I got to your office, or the office is bugged. Did you remove the information from the whiteboard?"

"Yes, I printed out a copy and then had the board cleared." The rear admiral sighed. "Go through the process of how you knew that you were being followed."

"I was taught by my father that, while driving trucks, you mostly watch the rear not the front. That's where problems occurred. Even the police come up from behind your vehicle, not in front of you. You keep your eyes on the road to know where you're going but you watch traffic from behind. They weren't following me closely going up the ramp to I-95 N. It was just that I had a premonition that something was about to happen. Ten miles later it happened exactly like I thought it would. I wasn't 100% sure, but I'd had an inkling that it would," Joe told the rear admiral. "That's all I needed."

"What made you shoot out the windows, not just of the first car but of both?"

"Sir, I act. I don't react. It's much easier to tell you exactly what happened after the fact, since I'm still alive. It wouldn't be so easy the other way around," Joe said. "I'm not being facetious. As soon as the first car moved in front of me, and then the second came right behind me, they declared war. I hit the gas and pulled out to the third lane. I already had the passenger window opened as I saw things unfold. I saw a gun moving toward the window and, instinctively, I pulled the trigger and didn't stop until both cars were taken out. That was the way I was trained. If you pull out your gun, use it."

"I must say that's remarkable, Joe. You've got great instincts. I don't know if I could have reacted that fast. What happened next?"

"I didn't wait around for the Florida Highway Patrol to get there. I-95 N has no toll roads so neither I, nor the two cars, would be picked up at any tollbooth, like on the Florida Turnpike. I didn't need to know the individuals who were doing the hit. It didn't matter. They were just soldiers. They'd have never given up their bosses, anyway. They'd probably plead guilty to reckless endangerment at the most and I couldn't prove anything else. They'd probably just be deported and backfilled with the next team. I didn't have time to go through the legal process with the Florida Highway Patrol, unless I was made to do so by you. I made a quick decision and it turned out to be the right one."

❧❧❧

They checked later about any accidents at that spot, and there were none. The gangbangers took off as well. Or some of them did. Perhaps, those who weren't shot by Joe. It was obvious that someone wanted both Joe and Mark dead. It wasn't as much a warning as it was an attempt to stop the investigation before it began. Although that was kind of a warning, in a way. Dead men didn't continue investigations.

"Rear Admiral, I need Mark's men, those men who helped me before, and I also need Michelle Bower to be in charge while Mark's laid up."

"Why?"

"I don't have time for explanations to a new guy. I also don't have time to explain things to the Islamorada commander, either."

The rear admiral smiled. "You're in charge and you can do anything you need to do to get to the bottom of this."

"I might need the drone team back again. I was thinking about using the drones for surveillance around the Coast Guard warehouse holding the bales of cocaine."

"Make the call to Texas to get the team back whenever you think you'll need them."

"Thanks." Since Joe was a marked man, at best, he needed to be in charge of the full investigation, just to make sure he didn't get killed. "I'm getting equipment from Jack Forest and I'll have it shipped offsite from any known Coast Guard facility. Within the next two days, I'll fully debug your office. From there, I'll have to find out where the leak came from and who's working with the Colombians. The Colombians didn't just walk into the most well-guarded facility in the country and walk out with thirty to thirty-five bales of cocaine. This was an inside job from beginning to end, especially since it appears from the paperwork that nothing's missing."

CHAPTER 5

Joe was going to use his SAT phone to call Jack Forest but thought better of it. After the last incident, Jack thought it would be wise if Mark, Joe, and he were all on the same secure system. Joe would get burner phones from the local corner store but in the meantime, he called Jack from Louise's cell phone that he'd use while he was there.

Joe had hoped that Jack was still in the office because he didn't want to leave a message. It was now after 8:00 p.m. and he knew that Jack never left the office before 9:00 p.m. That was until Jack got a girlfriend, the first significant other in his life since Joe had known him. Joe had never met her but he asked Jack to come down to Key Largo with her for a vacation when he could get free. Knowing Jack, he never got free, just like Mark and Joe.

Luckily, Jack was still in his office. "Hey, Joe, how are you? What's with the new number?" If Joe was calling from another number, Jack knew it had to be important. He'd already checked and it was Louise Silva's phone.

"I've been better, Jack. I don't know if my SAT phone is compromised or not, so I'm using Louise's cell phone."

"I already know, Joe."

"How?"

"How do you think?"

Joe laughed. "Yes, of course. You're all knowing and all

seeing." He went on to explain the situation and how Mark got shot and was in the hospital, just out of surgery. "I'm staying at Mark and Louise's house for the night, even though several armed Coast Guard men are sitting in the living room."

He went through everything that had happened, and at the end of the tale, Jack volunteered to come to Fort Lauderdale immediately to help out. Joe had a few other things in mind first but he knew he needed Jack down in Miami to help him out. "I need several state-of-the-art protective vests for myself and Mark while he's in the hospital, just in case. I need a few more for Mark's guys who'll be helping me and an extra small for Michelle, even though she'll be at the Dania Beach Station, running the operation for a while."

He also requested six pairs of night-vision goggles, optical devices for firearms, laser devices, long distance goggles, handheld UHF/VHF portable transceivers, additional Iridium satellite phones, video camera recorders, and comprehensive first aid kits. He also wanted the same thermal imaging equipment he used in Nashville, while taking down the meth distributor. He said he'd pick up burner phones if their phones were compromised.

He also told him he needed two Super Sweep 2000s, which were devices used by all the military services, including the Coast Guard, law enforcement, and private investigators. He needed the first one for the rear admiral's suite of offices and the second one for Dania Beach and the Islamorada Stations. This counter surveillance probe/monitor provided five of the most desired sweep functions in one package. An RF probe was a device, which allowed electronic test equipment to measure radio frequency oscillation (RF) in an electronic circuit. The RF probe sniffed the environment for hidden phone, room, or body bugs; remote signals; computer; fax or telex transmitters; video transmitters; pulsed tracking transmitters; and even wide band frequency hopping or burst bugs.

The very low frequency, VLF, probe tested AC outlets, phone lines, or suspicious wires for very low frequency carrier current signs. Auxiliary audio input allowed you to listen to telephones or lines for hot-mike hook switch by-pass and infinity bugs. Also, unknown wires and cables could be tested for wired microphones. A hot-mike was a form of signal reconnaissance. To hot-mike was to tap into a cell phone frequency and catch all of the data coming over that frequency. The person who did this could hear all of the calls and the things said near the cellular phone in question. The phone didn't have to be physically touched to do this. The perpetrator could tap into a phone without even putting their hands or equipment onto it. The only way to temporarily defeat hot-miking, without having the equipment to scan the connections coming from your cell phone, was to turn the phone off.

After a sweep, the alarm monitor guarded against new devices brought in, remote control activation, or someone tampering with the equipment. The twenty-four-hour evidence recording output stored suspicious sounds on a standard cassette recorder while you were away. This equipment detected and located, quickly and silently, all major categories of electronic surveillance, including room, phone, and body bugs that had transmitted conversations; video transmitters, watching every move; vehicle tracking beepers, giving away locations; infinity bugs; hook switch bypass or reversals turned-on to your conversations; wired microphones, listening inside a wall; computer, fax or telex transmitters reading your information, and any other electronic leakage.

In addition, the alarm monitor mode protected the facility after a sweep by continuously checking for new devices brought in, remote control activation, nearby two-way communications, and phone line tampering.

"Christ, Joe, do you need anything else? And when do you need this by?" Jack asked. "Only kidding. I'll get everything to you as soon as I know what I have. I've got most of it but I'm sure you need the Super Sweep 2000 first. Don't you?"

"I'm glad I wasn't paying attention to that rant, Jack. Yes I need the sweepers first, no later than tomorrow. Can I get both by then?"

"Where do you want the sweepers sent? It wouldn't be wise to send the equipment to the rear admiral's office labeled 'To be swept upon notification,'" Jack said, laughing.

"Ha, ha, Jack. No send the equipment, all the equipment, to Louise's parent's house. It's just a short distance away. Here's the address. I'll ask them to stay there until it comes. Can you call me and let me know exactly when it's getting there? Are we using Coast Guard Express?"

"Good one, Joe. Can I use that? Coast Guard Express, I like that," Jack said. "Will do." Then he hung up.

Joe shrugged. *A man of few words. Must have a hot date again tonight.*

✄✄✄✄

Mark was finally awake after the operation. He was groggy, lightheaded, and dying of thirst. Louise poured water from a nearby pitcher, took the plastic off a sippy straw, and brought the cup close to Mark's mouth. He drank so quickly that he started to choke. He stopped for a second and then, after he began to breath normally again, he asked for more.

As he continued to wake up, he looked around the room and saw Joe. "Hi, Joe. What the hell happened? When did you get here? What's going on?"

"Stay calm," Louise told him. "And Joe will sit with you while I go out for a cup of coffee and a snack." She turned to Joe. "He's all yours, Joe."

She gave Mark a kiss on the forehead and walked out of the room toward the elevator. One of the guards still there walked with her to the cafeteria. In the hallway were two

Broward County Sheriff's Office detectives waiting to speak to Mark. There hadn't been a shooting in Dania Beach in a long time, so they were quite anxious to speak to him as soon as they could. The detectives were actually stationed at the Dania Beach Sheriff's satellite office. They popped their heads into Mark's room and asked if they could speak to him briefly.

Joe turned around and said softly to Mark, "Let me handle this." He walked out into the hallway. "Can we step outside for a moment," he asked the detectives.

They weren't pleased to be speaking to Joe instead of Mark. "Who are you, why are you here, and what do you have to do with it?" one of them demanded.

Joe pulled out his ID and showed them his Coast Guard credentials. Then he flipped open his FBI and Homeland Security badges as well. "This is an FBI and Homeland Security issue at this point," he said, telling them as little as he could get away with.

They seemed to be very surprised at this. They, like most people, had no idea that the Coast Guard and FBI reported to Homeland Security and that Joe could represent all three organizations.

"Mark has no idea why he was shot, but I do," Joe told them. "I've just been put in charge of highly sensitive investigation and was on my way up to the Dania Beach Station to tell Mark all about it. By the time I got there, Mark had been shot." And that was all the information he was going to give them.

"Is this related to a shooting on I-95 North?"

Joe looked them straight in the eye. "I don't believe so but I don't know anything about that."

"A passing motorist called in the shooting but, by the time the Florida Highway Patrol got there, there was no one to investigate," the other detective said.

Joe shrugged. "That's interesting but I still don't know anything about it."

They each gave him their cards and left.

Joe was a little nervous, but he figured that no one had a clue. No one had seen him or anything else that had gone down on I-95. He walked back into Mark's room.

"The detectives left after my brief meeting with them," he said and told Mark everything that had happened since the rear admiral called him that morning. He knew Mark would like to participate in the investigation, so Joe told him he could if he was doing okay but he couldn't participate physically. Joe needed Mark's operational smarts, only, at this point. He smiled at Mark. "Well, I guess we've got matching bullet holes in our right shoulders, huh?"

Mark chuckled. "You call that scrape you got in Albany a bullet hole? Are you kidding me? This is ten times worse than yours."

"You always exaggerate," Joe said with a grin.

"Exaggerate? I'll be out for quite some time. They put a band aid on your booboo and you went back to the office."

Joe looked at Mark. "Seriously, I'm glad you're alive, Mark. I really don't know what I'd do without you. I'll make sure that you, Louise, and the kids are safe before we do anything else, so help me God."

"I know you will, Joe but I want to help. I can do things without being in the front lines. If Louise doesn't kill me first."

"Get some sleep, Mark. You'll need it. I'm taking Louise home and staying with her and the kids. There's all-day-and-night protection until this is done. So try not to worry. You'll have guards at this door, FBI men, who'll keep you safe."

With that, Joe turned and watched as Louise came back into the room and said goodbye to Mark. Joe had to call Julie and let her know what was going on now that Mark was okay. He'd call Joan as well.

They headed out and both forgot that neither had a car. Michelle brought Louise and Joe came by ambulance. He went back in and asked the FBI for their keys, since they weren't going anywhere.

He'd trade cars at Dania Beach in the morning. He needed to meet with Michelle and then head down to Miami as
soon as he got the spyware.

CHAPTER 6

By 7:00 a.m., Joe had already put his "To Do List" together for the day. He had to wait for the delivery from Jack. He needed to meet with Michele and get his car back. He wanted to see Mark before he left for the rear admiral's office. He'd meet with him after everyone had left for the day. He needed to meet with Mark's men. He needed, at least, the three that helped him the last time and maybe even more, depending on what he found out. He also needed to see Julie to discuss her meeting in Orlando with the Disney people and her attorney. He also needed to be fully involved in the wedding plans, which really wasn't his style, but he'd push himself to participate in every aspect—if it didn't kill him. He laughed. She'd kill him if he didn't.

He didn't think he'd be back to Mark and Louise's house for a while. He kissed the kids goodbye and gave Louise a hug. He told her what his plans were for the day. He'd try to involve her as much as he could but he also wanted her to remain safe. She didn't complain about the armed guards at her house, but he knew it would wear thin if they didn't solve this soon. He hoped that Mark got well enough, soon enough, to be shipped off to San Diego with his family. Then Joe could relax and throw himself into this investigation.

Now it was hard to think about keeping himself safe

when he had Mark and his family to worry about. Getting them out of town was paramount in his mind.

Joe made it to the Dania Beach Station in ten minutes. As he walked through the front door, it was hard not to notice the plywood over the shattered glass by the front door. Training, instinct, and just plain good luck had saved Mark's life yesterday. For that, Joe would be forever grateful. He walked right in and stepped to the front desk. Michelle saw him and waved him into to her office. Everyone came over and wanted to know how Mark was doing. They'd also heard about a shooting on I-95 N and wanted to know if Joe was all right as well. No one had to say a thing. They knew Joe had been involved in a life-and-death shootout on the highway.

"How are you, Joe?" she asked.

"Good," he said. "I slept and I'm rested but we've got a lot to do over the next few days. You'll be leading the Dania Beach Station."

For that, she was grateful. "I won't let you down."

"I'm waiting for equipment to arrive." But he didn't tell her where.

He had a note written out for her that she read quietly, shaking her head in disbelief. She couldn't believe that a fellow Coast Guard officer or enlisted man or woman would turn on his or her own. His note read, *Before I leave, if I have time, I'll use the spyware here in the Dania Beach Station. Make sure that everyone is out of the office when I come back. No one is to know what I'm going to do. I also want to meet the men, who will be working with me, around 4:00 p.m., before I leave for Miami.*

It took less than an hour to get there and he wouldn't be meeting the rear admiral until everyone had left his office. Joe got his car and handed back the keys to the vehicle he took from Mark's FBI agents last night. He went to the hospital to see Mark and discuss with him what he needed from him. Before Mark did anything, Joe wanted to make sure that he was healing, doing well health-wise, and that he and his family were safe. Then, Joe wanted him to head to San Diego. He and Mark could work together by email and burner phone.

Hell, that's exactly how I worked with Jack Forest for years. Mark will just have to cooperate or I won't involve him. His life is too important to me.

☙❧

Joe got a call from Louise's parents, Ken and Antoinette "Tony" Harding around noon on Louise's cell phone. A Coast Guard support services truck, out of Miami, had just arrived and Ken signed for over ten large packages.

Evidently, Jack Forest stayed late that night and had everything that Joe requested. He'd packaged everything up, with the help of his team in Virginia, and made the Coast Guard ship that left for Miami at midnight. Neither Jack nor Joe were aware that a daily courier ship left every night from Portsmouth's Maritime Intelligence Fusion Center to Miami's COMMSTA Coast Guard Communications facility. Portsmouth was the Coast Guard Fifth District and the center for intelligence—other than Washington DC—for the Atlantic Coast. Miami covered the entire southeastern part of the United States and Puerto Rico.

Joe told Louise's father, Ken that he'd be there in ten minutes. He only wanted one of the two Super Sweep 2000s to bring down to the rear admiral's office later that evening. The rest of the equipment would be stored at the Dania Beach Station after it was moved from Louise's parent's house. In the meantime, Ken put all the equipment in a back bedroom that was used as an office. Before heading to Miami, Joe would use the Super Sweep 2000 and make sure that the Dania Beach Station was clean.

In the meantime, he called the rear admiral on Louise's cell phone. He asked him to step outside the office, preferable a few miles away and use a pay phone. It was lunchtime, anyway, so Barnes left and headed to the Bayside Marketplace in downtown Miami, only a few blocks from Coast Guard headquarters. Fifteen minutes later, Joe got a call from Barnes from a payphone outside the mall entrance.

Joe continued using Louise's cell phone while he was there. He thought he'd better give it back before leaving for Miami.

"Joe, I'm at the Bayside Marketplace at a pay phone. Before I go to lunch, let's talk. You said there was a leak in my office. Are you really sure?"

"Yes, I'm sure. I'd like to meet you tonight at 7:00 p.m. in your office. I want you to be alone while I set up and run the sweeping equipment. I met with Michelle Bower this morning and I'm meeting with Mark's men around 4:00 p.m. I need to head to Islamorada, right after our meeting, after we go over your office for bugs."

Joe wouldn't be back to Islamorada before midnight. He needed to pack for Julie's meeting up in Orlando at Hollywood Studios with Julie's attorney that Joe had promised to be at over the weekend. Everything was set, and Joe had to be there on time. It was the only weekend that they could meet. Disney's people would fly in from Burbank for the meeting.

Before heading to Miami, Joe wound up at the hospital and said goodbye to Mark. If the Dania Beach Station was clean, he'd have the men pick up the rest of the delivered equipment and store it at the Coast Guard facility. He'd tell them that after he met with them that afternoon.

He handed the cell phone to Mark to give back to Louise. "Tell her thanks," he said.

It only took a few minutes to get to the Hardings' house. Joe rang the bell and Louise's father opened the door immediately.

"Mark is doing well and it looks like he'll make a full recovery but it will take time," Joe told him. "The rear admiral is sending Mark and the family on an extended vacation to San Diego until he recovers. Both you and Tony should go as well because no one ever knows who'll be targeted in this kind of an investigation. I also want you to either stay with Louise and the kids or have another guard assigned at your house. It's better if you go to Louise's," he said.

They agreed and said they'd pack as soon as Joe left. Joe didn't think it was safe for them to be there by themselves so he said he'd wait and drive behind them as soon as they were ready. It was the least he could do.

Joe looked in the back room. All his equipment had arrived at once. It covered the entire floor and the bed. He grabbed the two Super Sweep 2000s and put both into the trunk of his car. He grabbed the rest of the equipment, put it into their guest room, and covered the stuff with a bedspread. He closed the shades in the house then Tony and Ken were ready to go to Louise's. Joe followed them and called Louise to tell the two guards to be ready to meet them at the front door. He told her that he gave her phone to Mark.

As soon as they arrived, the front door opened and both guards helped the Hardings bring in their suitcases. Joe waved and immediately left for the Dania Beach Coast Guard Station to meet with Michelle. It was earlier than he wanted to be there but he'd already called Michelle and asked her to clear the station for an hour. The only staff he wanted there was her and Mark's men who would help him.

He arrived, walked in, and went to Michelle's office. He'd left the sweepers in the trunk of his car, where they stay until everyone else left.

After the last person left, Joe went to his car, brought in the sweeper, and set it up, first in Mark's office, then Michelle's, and then they'd clear every room in the building. It took about ten minutes a room so they'd be done within an hour. Joe was methodical and set the machine to pick up everything he could, including bugs, phones, cell phones, data, and all electrical appliances in the building. The Dania Beach Coast Guard Station was clean. There were no bugs present anywhere in the building, or near the building, right to the telephone poles. Joe was very pleased that no one was listening in on Mark. The leak didn't come from Dania Beach and, more than likely, had to be at Coast Guard headquarters in Miami. He left the sweeper on in Mark's office to catch any future bugs once the investigation moved forward. He was sure something would happen.

After clearing the station, Joe and Michelle met with the three noncoms who would be helping Joe solve this investigation. He told them that Mark would be fully involved but from a distance. They already knew that Jack Forest was fully involved and had been on previous investigations, especially with the Russians. They were unaware of Jack's connection to the meth takedown in Nashville or the Mexican Mafia problem over a year ago. Joe wanted them to be on alert because he was unsure when he'd need them, but when he did, they'd have to leave at a moment's notice. He also mentioned that Michelle was the new Dania Beach Station commander and everything they did with Joe and Mark was to go to Michelle as well. There was to be no command confusion issues. They understood and they were all in. They loved Mark and they wanted to get to the bottom of the shooting as well. If this was an inside job, they wanted the bad guys out of the Coast Guard.

With that, Joe went to Michelle's office and called Julie. It was past 3:00 p.m. She should be out of school for the day and headed to cross-country practice. She was still the assistant cross-country coach and was guiding Lucy Talbot, Joan's daughter, to be the best she could be.

Julie specialized in positive motivation and breathing techniques. She was an All-Florida runner in her day and wanted to pass that along. Her new book, *Conch Town Girl,* was aimed precisely at girls like Lucy to help them achieve and create their own self-esteem and positive self-worth that would last a lifetime.

తుఎత

"Hi, Julie," he said. "Did I catch you at a bad time?"

"No, Joe. I just got out and I'm heading to cross-country practice. We've a big meet two weeks from Saturday, and, other than Lucy, we've a very new and young squad of girls. They saw how well Lucy did last year and it was quite a recruitment tool. Most of the new girls are ninth graders and a few eighth graders as well. Lucy, being a veteran now, is like the old lady on the team. There were only a few left from last year."

"Well, you've got your work cut out for you," he said. He went on to tell her all about Mark and how he was doing.

She knew about both Joe and Mark's incidents when he called yesterday. She asked if there was any progress and he said that he was moving forward but didn't suspect that they'd catch the carjackers in his case or the shooter in Mark's. They didn't need to know because they only reported into someone, probably the Colombians living in Miami, as he suspected. When he got to them, the other issues would be resolved. He asked her to be careful and either stay with Tillie in Key Largo or have Tillie, once again, move over to his officer's quarters with Julie in Islamorada. He said to call Joan and let her know in either case. Joan could set up surveillance at Tillie's, if needed, and her men could drive by a few times a day, very visible, to let people know that she was being protected.

Julie agreed but said it brought up another issue. She was, in fact homeless. She had no permanent place to hang her hat before the wedding. She was doing well. Joe just got a nice increase on his promotion to lieutenant, and she wanted to start looking at small homes in the area. She knew home prices were starting to rise and it just might be a perfect time to start looking. They were getting married in the spring so Joe agreed that his officer's quarters were too small for a permanent home and Tillie needed her space.

Julie had never owned anything before and this was a big step for her toward permanent independence. She then asked Joe a question that seemed out of the blue. "Would Tillie's old house be available for sale, now that the Russians have torn it apart and the new homeowners might be apprehensive about staying permanently? They live in Atlanta and this would be their retirement home."

"I'll think about it but it could be problematic. If the Russians come after us again," he wondered out loud, "wouldn't the first place they'd look be Tillie's apartment and her old house?" He thought that issue was done but in the back of his mind, he'd always been suspicious that if he let his guard down, it would come back to haunt him, and now him and Julie.

"I never thought about that, but you might be right. Perhaps we'd better look around somewhere between Key Largo and Islamorada, perhaps in Tavernier, just south of Key Largo and north of Islamorada. It's close to Coral Shores High School and the Mariner Hospital. Property values remain steady in that area and the school district is identified as one of the best in the nation. I'm not sure how long I'll remain employed at the high school with my promising writing career, but I do want to stay until Tillie hits age sixty-five and can get Medicare. Then her policy will kick in as supplemental so she'll be fully covered." One of the best deals Julie ever made was to have Tillie covered under her health insurance as a dependent.

Nothing was resolved but Joe and Julie both felt better that they addressed these issues now, rather than later. Julie was raised poor. Not in terms of love or family but Tillie raised her by herself since she was eight years old. A waitress's salary didn't go far, but they made it. Julie never wanted to be poor again and she'd take care of Tillie just like Tillie took care of her all those many years.

For as long as Joe had known them both, since he was a first year Coast Guard seaman, just turned nineteen, he knew that Julie would always be there for Tillie. Joe loved Tillie like his own mother and whatever Julie wanted was fine with him. He just couldn't believe his good fortune to have a beautiful, independent, caring woman in his life. Julie was everything to him. However, his thoughts had to return to the problem at hand or he wouldn't have to worry about homeownership or wedding plans. He had to remain alive to carry out either.

Julie also reminded Joe that her appointment at Walt Disney World's Hollywood Studios was coming up this weekend and he said he'd be there for her, along with her attorney, Jane Swanson. They were to fly out of Key West late Friday afternoon and fly back late Sunday. This was the only weekend she could meet with the Walt Disney Studios Division staff, who'd be flying in from Burbank, California to meet her along with Marshall Tillman the head of Hollywood Studios in Orlando. Joe told her he'd be there for her.

CHAPTER 7

Joe finally took off for Miami. It was around 5:00 p.m. so he had time to kill. It was less than an hour to get to Coast Guard headquarters, so he stopped at a McDonald's on the way and had a quick dinner. He had an iced tea, a Big Mac, and a large fries. He loved Big Macs. It didn't taste like any hamburger he ever had, but it was delicious. He'd been eating them since McDonald's opened in the Burgh in Troy.

He remembered going there after baseball practice at Knickerbocker Park when he was at Catholic High. It was only four blocks to Second Avenue, by the Hudson River. It was close to home and Joe's mother always wondered why he wasn't hungry for dinner. When he was older and she'd just been diagnosed with breast cancer, he finally told her what he'd done. He was on leave and they went out to lunch together, to McDonald's. He'd started to laugh.

"Why are you laughing?" she'd asked.

And he told her the truth.

She smiled. "And I thought you didn't like my cooking."

"No, that's not the case."

He laughed again about the mashed potato incident. *God, the potato incident is imbedded in my brain.* His mother remembered it as well, but to her it was less than a laughing matter. However, she did mellow out, especially when she knew her days were numbered.

At the time, Joe was sixteen and worked fulltime during the summer for his father, with grown men on a construction crew. He came home that night and, during dinner, he forgot where he was. He asked his mother to pass the "fucking" potatoes. You could have heard a pin drop. Joe turned to his brother and father and their looks told him that he was on his own. He turned back to his mother and apologized and said it would never happen again. It didn't, but he never forgot the incident and neither did his mother.

When Joe's father was in Albany Medical Center having a triple bypass, just a short time ago, the incident was brought up and neither he, his brother, nor his father, could contain themselves. Along with their versions of various movie quotes, in spite of the major surgery issues facing his father the next morning, it was as close as he'd ever gotten to his father and brother at the same time. They remembered the incident like it was yesterday, even though Joe's mother had died a few years ago. They all agreed it kind of kept her alive in their hearts. However, it still didn't stop the laughter to this day.

☙❧

It was closing in on 6:30 p.m. when Joe pulled into the Coast Guard parking lot and then into his assigned space. He still couldn't believe that he reported directly to the rear admiral. It was about a year ago, when he'd been out of the service for about four years, living back in Troy, a recent Rensselaer Polytechnic Institute MBA graduate, then working at the Albany Coalition for Families as the Director of Institutional Research and Grants. Now, a year later, he was a lieutenant in the Coast Guard, working directly for the rear admiral, in charge of all major investigations for south Florida and the Keys. It was a big blur, but now, dangerous as hell. Of course, shooting the son of the Mexican Mafia general and three gangbangers, all at the same time at the coalition's corporate headquarters, was a little dangerous, too. Joe thought that maybe danger followed him like a bad penny. If anything, it was one hell of a very interesting year in his life at age thirty-four.

He had the sweeper in his trunk, in a cloth bag that looked like a laundry bag. He walked up the stairs and was met by the front desk guard. Joe flashed his badge. The guard knew who he was and he was listed as having an appointment with the rear admiral at 7:00 p.m.

Joe walked up the stairs and into the rear admiral's office. Barnes greeted Joe at the door but, before he could speak, Joe put his index finger to his lips and the rear admiral nodded his head.

"Is anyone around?" Joe whispered.

The rear admiral shook his head. Joe proceeded to set up the equipment on his desk and started the task of seeking out any listening devices, in this office first, and then onto the suite of offices up and down the corridor, including Joe's own office a few doors down.

He started this counter surveillance probe with the five most desired sweep functions that he learned how to perform many years ago from Jack Forest. Joe started with the RF probe. He got an immediate read out that there were active bugs in the room and the printout stated that the incoming phone lines were bugged. Joe pointed to the phone and nodded to the rear admiral.

Barnes was now beside himself, knowing that his entire office had been compromised. He was certainly glad that Joe spotted it or he'd have gone on just as he had, not knowing a thing. He was compromised and now officially pissed.

Joe then tested all the AC outlets, using the very low frequency probe, for the phone lines and for any suspicious wires.

He found that the rear admiral's cell phone was compromised as well. Whoever did this could hear all of the calls and the things said near the cellular phone.

Joe aimed it at his own cell phone and picked up that it

was compromised as well. He'd thought that his was bugged when he came earlier to meet the rear admiral.

Joe knew at this point that, when he left the rear admiral's office earlier that afternoon, he could have and should have been a dead man. He and Mark were very lucky not to be killed, and Joe hoped it would stay that way. Everything the rear admiral said was now compromised. Joe's little speech in the office about the volume of space required to house all those bales of cocaine was also compromised.

After the sweep, the alarm monitor on Joe's equipment, that would be left in the rear admiral's office and well hidden, would guard against any new devices being brought in, any remote control activation, or someone tampering with the equipment. Next, Joe went from room to room and there was nothing there. Evidently, the only room bugged, thoroughly bugged and compromised, was the rear admiral's office. Joe set up the equipment and put it into the bottom drawer of the rear admiral's desk. He hid the device by putting a hole in the bottom of the drawer and plugging it in below the desk. It was as close to being undetected as he could possibly make it. He got the key from Barnes and secured the desk. He pointed to the door and nodded for the rear admiral to walk out of the building with him.

☙☙☙

They walked down the street, not speaking, staring straight ahead. Joe pointed to a small coffee shop at the next corner.

He went up to the counter, got two coffees, and brought both back to the table at the very rear of the store. Joe handed a coffee to the rear admiral and sat down.

Barnes looked like a truck had just hit him. "In all my years of service, I've never been so pissed off. I can't believe that this happened on my watch. Thank you for watching my back. I really don't know what to say. When I tell my boss in Washington that I've been one hundred percent compromised and screwed over by my own men, I believe my career will be long over."

"Well, it doesn't look good, sir. But I believe we can find out who did this, maybe not tomorrow, but quick enough that it can be straightened out and used as training lesson for future officers. If it can happen to you, sir, it can happen to anyone."

"Thanks for the kind words, Joe, but I'm afraid my days will be numbered."

"Sir, think about this. What if the thirty to thirty-five bales the FBI thinks are missing lead to the taking down of all the Colombians in all of south Florida? I mean what if it leads to completely shutting them down like we did with the meth dealers up in Nashville? That takedown took care of the delivery of meth to the entire southern eastern seaboard. This could do the same thing. Please don't give up, sir. My partner Mark was shot and I could have been killed. We don't want a target on our backs, forever. If this goes well, we can stop it in its tracks. They shot at us for a good reason, sir. They must have felt that we'd get too close and they were worried. That's a good thing. Not good for Mark or me, but good, nevertheless," Joe said. "I always wanted to use the word 'nevertheless.' It's a triple word score in *Scrabble* you know?" Joe smiled.

"Thanks for the laugh," Barnes said. "When we're alone, please call me Jake. This rear admiral shit is a pain in the ass. Nevertheless is a triple word score, huh?" he said with a smile.

"Sir, I mean, Jake, your office is bugged. If there's anyone listening in at this point, we can get to the source. Someone who has direct access to your office is the culprit. The problem is that it can be anyone from your assistant outside your office to the cleaning lady working at midnight. We won't know until we know. I'd suggest that we leave everything the way it is right now. Why let them know that we're on to them? Let's think of a plan that if anyone were listening, they'd follow it. Say, for example, I'm going to be on a certain ship at a certain time late at night waiting for a ship to come in loaded with dope. That could be set up so if someone took a shot at me, they could be taken down and dragged through a full interrogation. You could have a meeting with two of your staff and tell them one thing and then tell your assistant something else and see what happens. Someone close to you is screwing you, Jake. We need to find out whom, and quickly. We can still do the investigation but give different orders to different people and see where it leads. What do you think?"

"It's better than I have right now. From now on, we meet outside the office to plan and only talk in the office when we want the listeners to know what we're planning. You're right. Leave the equipment where it is and let's see where it leads us. I'm going to have to go to Washington on another matter and I'll tell my superiors about this problem. I've got a moral obligation as an officer in the United States Coast Guard. I believe they'll assist us in any way you deem necessary, Joe. When are you going to Orlando with Julie?"

"We're leaving early Friday night and we'll be back in Islamorada late Sunday night. I'll drive back to Miami early Monday morning."

Joe and the rear admiral made plans to meet at the end of the following week to start the ball rolling. In the meantime, Joe would start to develop a plan. He'd read everything he could on the seizure and security of drugs taken at high sea. He'd get all the names and ranks of everyone involved from the point of the original takedown to the point where the bales were placed under lock and key. He'd follow the paper trails from beginning to end. By the time Joe met with the rear admiral, he'd know as much about the processes involved as those who made up the procedures in the first place. Joe's main advantage was his photographic memory. After this review, he'd never have to look at the paperwork again to make a point. This was invaluable to him. During an investigation, you had to look like you knew everything that was going on, and, in Joe's case, he'd know the entire manual, from beginning to end. His saving grace was that no one could ever snow him about what he knew.

"Jake, before we leave, I think we need a couple of burner phones so we can talk next week without being compromised. Your phone and mine have bugs. The cell phones appeared to have bugs when I ran the scan in your office. We will talk on our cells regularly when we don't need to discuss our steps but use the burner for everything else."

"Will do. There's a phone store two blocks from here. Since I'm in uniform and you're not, go and pick up two phones right now. I'll wait around the corner." He handed Joe all the cash he had on him.

Twenty minutes later, Joe came back and handed a phone to Jake. "It's partially charged. Charge it fully and keep it hidden at all times."

He gave Jake back a hundred dollars in cash. They each had 1,200 minutes of prepaid time and a cheap burner. Joe put his cell number in Jake's phone and Jake's number in his. He made sure that all they had to do was press a "one" to get the other. "There will be no other calls made on either phone unless Mark or Jack get burners as well."

They shook hands and said goodbye.

"Keep your head low and be safe, Joe. I'm sure we can protect Mark until we get him away from here with his family. Are you sure Julie and her grandmother will be safe?"

"The guys in Islamorada will be watching Tillie, and Julie will be with me. When we get back, I think I'll try and get them both moved back to the station until this is solved. Those guys I can trust, even Jacob. I know he's pissed at me, but I don't think he'd compromise our lives. He's a good officer even if he's a little bit of a jerk. But then, aren't we all?"

"I hope being a jerk doesn't get us killed, Joe."

With that, they parted. Joe waved to Jake, turned around, and headed to his car to go home. He'd be at Key Largo to meet Julie in less than an hour and a half.

He was sure that Mark and his family would be protected. He wasn't that sure about himself, and he didn't want to worry Julie, but this was a big deal to her and he had to go. He'd call the chief of police in Orlando. Cal Roberts, the chief, owed Joe a big favor and Joe would ask him if he'd assign a few guys to watch their backs while they were meeting in Walt Disney World that weekend. It couldn't hurt. They were flying up from the Key West Airport to Orlando on a private jet supplied by Marshall Tillman, the head of Hollywood Studios. They'd get a ride from the Orlando International Airport right to Hollywood Studios in an Orlando Police car and they'd be staying there for the weekend and flying back Sunday night. It seemed like a plan. He called Julie and confirmed and then he called Cal for the favor.

Cal answered right away and told him that he'd have his detectives cover them all weekend. Joe felt a little relief.

CHAPTER 8

Joe made it back to Key Largo, going directly to Tillie's apartment. There was no cross-country meet on Saturday for Julie and that's why the meeting in Walt Disney World was scheduled for that weekend. They'd be meeting the Disney private jet at the Key West airport, about an hour away. The airport was just north of Key West, so they'd miss a lot of the weekend traffic that started around 4:00 p.m. Friday afternoon. The plane would leave right at 4:00 p.m. It took less than an hour to fly into the Orlando International Airport's private jet complex. They'd meet the Orlando Police who'd give them a ride to Hollywood Studios.

Joe had to meet with Joan and Jacob before leaving with Julie for the airport. Julie would meet Joe at the Islamorada Coast Guard Station and they'd leave from there, after Joe's quick meeting. When they got back Sunday evening, they'd stay at Joe's officer's quarters at the station and she'd head for school early Monday morning. She'd reverse her schedule and go to the Coral Shores High School for a morning meeting and then to the elementary school by noon. It would be hectic, especially since she had to be back at the high school for the afternoon cross-country practice.

"I'll tell you everything that's happened so far when we get on the plane," Joe told Julie. "I have to meet with Joan and Jacob. We need to leave from my office by 2:45 p.m. to ensure that we get there no later than 3:45 p.m."

"Sounds good, Joe. I'm packed and ready to go. I'll leave right after you and I'll wait in your office until your meeting is over. Do you need me to pack anything for you?"

"Actually, that will be very helpful. You know what I need better than I do. Please pack my one good suit, shoes, tie, and dress shirt as well. I'm sure there will be some kind of meet and greet event when we get there. No Coast Guard clothes this weekend."

"Got it. I'll meet you there."

Unknown to the rest of the station, other than Joan, Julie had her own key to Joe's officer's quarters. It was another wink-wink situation. Everyone knew that they were now engaged but Julie had had the key ever since she and Joe became a couple after Julie's father was sent to prison. Joe didn't want to take a chance on her or Tillie being in danger, so they could head to his place any time they wanted. Forgiveness always came before permission in the Coast Guard. Joan knew that and never said a word.

❦

Joe had a half an hour before leaving with Julie for the airport. He sat down with Joan and Jacob to discuss what had happened to date since his call for a meeting with the rear admiral less than a week ago. It became complicated because Joe would tell Joan everything but he wouldn't discuss his entire situation with Jacob. Jacob's last comments to Joe as he was leaving to meet Rear Admiral Barnes had left a bad taste in his mouth. Joe was through explaining his situation to Jacob but he still needed to trust him. If those responsible for bugging the rear admiral's office went after him, which seemed more than likely, Joe still needed to protect Julie and Tillie.

"What I'm about to tell you can't be discussed with anyone else," Joe told Joan and Jacob. "Do you understand? These are strict orders from the rear admiral, himself. If you need to check with him, it's at your own peril." He knew he didn't need to say it to Joan and she caught on that it was for Jacob's benefit.

Jacob nodded. "We understand. So, tell us what the situation is right now."

Joan simply listened. She knew she'd get the full explanation over pizza and beer at her place when Joe was ready. Jacob could have gotten the same treatment if he'd only gone with the flow. Joe and rules were never meant to be, if it meant those rules stood in the way of getting to the bottom of an investigation. He didn't cut corners but he knew the chain of command was a problem if you needed timely answers. Joe's father had told him many years ago that there were only two people he needed to deal with when he needed something. First, you dealt with the person waiting on you and, if that didn't work, you went directly to the owner of the company. Everyone else in between was there to stop you from going to the top.

Joe had various bosses in the Coast Guard but he went directly to the rear admiral if it was important. Jacob would never do that, could never do that, and couldn't understand how someone else could do that. That was why he never solved a case on his own and was thought of, not as incompetent, but not someone you wanted to cover your back when the chips were down either. As Joe mentioned to the rear admiral, he wanted Joan to retire as the chief of the Islamorada Station, not Jacob. He didn't want to hurt Jacob, but he also didn't want him in his way. That was made very clear the last time Joe spoke to Cramer.

"We're leaving shortly. Julie and I have to be at the airport for 3:45 p.m. for our flight to Orlando. We will be back around 6:00 p.m. Sunday night. I'll be leaving Monday to meet with Jack up in Miami. The rear admiral will be coming in from Washington at the end of the week and I need to fully inform him of how we will proceed. The cases down here can wait, all except our takedown on Tuesday afternoon. It's small and won't require much attention. It's a go-fast boat coming into Big Pine Key and our guys should be able to handle it. It's not outsiders but our own home-grown good old boys from Marathon taking a shipment of coke from there to Miami."

"We can certainly handle that," Joan said.

Jacob nodded sheepishly.

"Thanks, Joan. Thanks, Jacob. It's appreciated. Joan, can you keep an eye on things for Julie and Tillie while I'm gone? Especially, if you hear any internal chatter on what I'm supposedly doing. I'm sure the grapevine has been well oiled by now about the shooting on I-95 and Mark being shot in the doorway of the Dania Beach Station."

"Will do."

"Good. Can I see you for a minute afterward?" Joe asked Joan.

Jacob's eyes went cold but he said nothing.

Joe and Joan walked outside after Joe pointed a finger in that direction. "My cell phone has been compromised," he said. "Between you and me, I got a burner. If you need to call me, leave a message on my cell and say, 'Your report is ready.' I'll hang up and call you from my burner to Jeff's cell. I don't believe anyone is aware of that phone."

"I can't believe this is going on, Joe. How did you figure this out? What else do you want me to do?"

"I haven't figured it all yet. These are just guesses. As for what I need from you, first, we need to check all the phones to see if Islamorada offices are compromised. I don't believe the office has been compromised, but I believe it will be if this continues. Call Jack Forest and he'll over-night you a testing kit. Call Michelle Bower up in Dania Beach. You know her, right?"

"Yes, of course. We women, as few of us as there are, stick together."

"Well, that will change if I've got anything to do with it."

"Care to enlighten me?" she said.

"Not now, maybe later over a few beers when we get

back. Call Jack and tell him my phone is compromised and I've a burner. Tell him you need the sweeper for the Islamorada office. Either he can get the one to you we left at Dania Beach or he'll ship you a new one tomorrow. I need you to do the sweep at midnight when Jacob isn't around. It's not that I don't trust him. It's just that I don't want him involved. If you get a load of crap from him or anyone else, call me and I'll have Jake Barnes call you directly from Washington."

"Jake?"

He raked a hand through his hair and sighed. "Yes, Jake. It's a long story but even people at the top need someone watching their backs and he wants to be called 'Jake' in private, okay?"

"Yes, sir. Anything else, sir?"

"Bite me," Joe said.

Joan managed a small smile. She knew Joe so well. "Yes, sir. Bite me, it is, sir."

"I have to go." He kissed her and she told him to be careful and good luck to Julie at Disney.

☙❦❧

Joe went to his office, if you could call it that. Julie was waiting for him. She'd packed all his things in her trunk along with hers. He closed up his office and locked the door. As they were leaving, Joan waved to both of them and blew them a kiss. Joe didn't know what he'd ever do without Joan. She was now less than two years away from retirement and she'd be taking it as soon as she could. With her retirement and Jeff's growing income, they'd have a very nice life in the Florida Keys. If Lucy got a cross-country scholarship to the University of Miami, it would relieve a lot of the pressure that would build up from having two in college at the same time. One, anyone could handle. Two was considered a wallet-ectomy, leaving nothing to live on but the basics for the next ten years. Joe knew he'd be facing the same thing but he'd be that much older, not necessarily wiser.

They arrived at the private entrance at the Key West Airport, right on time. They beat traffic by only a few minutes. When they got back Sunday night, it would be the same situation going home. Julie parked right in front of the aviation building. She popped the trunk and Joe looked at what she packed. He thought he'd need the luggage carrier that they used to load the planes. She smiled at him as he unloaded everything.

"Julie, how long are we staying at Disney?"

"Just carry what you can, Joe. I'm young and energetic and I'll get what you can't carry." She then stuck her tongue out at him and smiled.

Someone at the front desk must have phoned the staff. Two young guys met them at the car with a luggage carrier and loaded their belongings onto the racks.

"Thank you," Joe said. "I wasn't sure we'd make our plane."

"No problem," one of the guys said.

Julie walked in with her pocketbook and a carry-on bag with all her *Conch Town Girl* contracts and manuscripts. Unlike Joe, who had a photographic memory, she really had to work at remembering everything she wrote and what she wanted to say when she got there. Joe taught her many years ago to prepare for at least fifty really dumb questions before a presentation. He told her someone would ask at least 20 of those same questions. She could then smile at the person and have a stock answer ready. He said it made you look a lot smarter than you really were.

They got on the plane and taxied out the runway. They took off in a matter of minutes. This was so much more convenient than flying out of Miami International Airport, which was a city unto itself. They'd be in Orlando by 5:00 p.m. and, hopefully, at Hollywood Studios to meet Marshall Tillman no later than 6:00 p.m. The staff from Disney's

Burbank movie studios would be there and dinner was to be at 8:00 p.m. at the administrative headquarters in the back of the theme park. They'd be staying in a suite, right in the same building that was set up for visiting dignitaries.

On the plane, Joe used his burner phone and called Jack up in Virginia and Michelle at Dania Beach. Both said that Joan had already called them. Jack was leaving the sweeper in Dania Beach and was heading down to Islamorada with his own sweeper the next day. "I'll do the search with Joan at midnight and, if we're discovered, I'll handle it as if it were an audit." He'd then have Jeff Talbot get him back to Miami on his go-fast boat and charge it to his Virginia Beach operation, if he needed to, so no one would be the wiser. "I'll stay in a hotel near Coast Guard headquarters and I'll meet you when you get back late Monday in Miami."

Joe told him about the condo around the corner from headquarters but Jack thought that it would raise suspicions as to why he was there. "The hotel would be better."

❧❦❧

The private jet landed on schedule and taxied right up to the private gate, in Orlando, where Joe and Julie were met by Cal Roberts and two detectives. Joe was very surprised to see him there and smiled from ear to ear. They'd head to Disney in Cal's private unmarked police car, followed by the two detectives, who'd accompany them for the entire weekend. Joe thought it might be overkill but it only took one mistake to ruin your life.

"Cal, I'd like you to meet Julie Chapman, my fiancée."

"Nice to meet you, Julie. I've heard nothing but nice things about you, not from this slug, but from my own wife, Estelle. Our daughter loved your book as well as Estelle."

"Thank you, Chief."

"Please call me Cal." He gestured to the two people with

him. "I'd like to introduce you to these two fine detectives, Archie Higgins and Trinity Hightower. Archie has been with us for fifteen years and a detective for almost eight. Trinity has just been promoted to detective this year. She was first in her class, if you've any reluctance because she's young."

Julie smiled. "Of course not, Chief. I'm glad not to be always surrounded by guys. This is refreshing. Thank you. It's nice to meet both of you."

"Nice to meet you as well," Trinity said as Archie nodded quietly.

Joe wondered if they knew why they were being guarded all weekend.

Cal turned to Joe. "They'll shadow you and Julie all weekend right up until you get on the private jet Sunday night. We called Marshall Tillman and they've room for both Archie and Trinity, right down the hall from you. They'll be as non-intrusive as possible. Joe, are you armed?"

"I didn't bring my weapon with me, hoping that I wouldn't need it. That was probably dumb but I just wanted us to forget about what I'm involved in. Can you understand that, Cal?"

"Of course, but Trinity has an extra weapon. She'll keep it loaded and be by your side when you're out in the open and not in meetings."

"Have you told Archie and Trinity why this is happening, Cal? I don't want them to think we're prima donnas and it's all for show."

"No worry. I told them about the bust here and in Nashville and what you did for us. They're also aware of your current assignment, but only that it's as dangerous, and that they need to be watchful at all times."

Joe shook Cal's hand. "We can't thank you enough."

They hopped into Cal's car, with Julie in the back and Joe in the front passenger seat. Their luggage was placed in the detectives' car, which would follow them west to Walt

Disney World. As they traveled the twenty-five miles, Joe told Cal exactly what he was involved in. He'd already told Julie on the plane. She knew that Mark was shot and would be leaving for California, with Louise and the kids, to recover. She didn't know that Joe had shot out the windows of two cars on I-95 N. She was soon made aware of the fact that someone would be hunting for Joe and Mark and that she and Tillie could be placed in danger as well.

They arrived at the front gate at Hollywood Studios and were directed to the administrative offices behind the theme park. Marshall Tillman was waiting for them as they pulled up. He introduced himself to Julie and Julie introduced him to Joe. Julie then introduced the chief, Archie, and Trinity. Marshall was already aware of the security situation and was prepared. They unloaded their luggage and everyone pitched in.

Everyone looked at Julie and the luggage.

"What's your problem, guys," Trinity asked. "A girl's got to do what a girl's got to do."

"Amen to that, Trinity." Julie laughed and they pumped fists with each other while walking in the front door. Trinity asked her if she could have a copy of her book to read while she was there. Julie handed her an extra book that she brought just in case the studio didn't buy enough.

"Thanks, Julie," Trinity said. "I'll read it as fast as I can while I'm here."

Joe thanked Cal and Julie gave him a kiss on the cheek. They turned and headed through the front doors of the administration building.

CHAPTER 9

As soon as Julie and Joe walked through the front door, Claire Murphy greeted them. Claire had started the ball rolling several months earlier when she handed Marshall Tillman Julie's book, *Conch Town Girl*. Even though her children were very young, Claire read about the book and recommended it to Marshall as a potential movie or television series after she read it cover to cover, twice. This was before she made the connection of Julie Chapman, budding author, to Joe Traynor.

Claire's father, Tom Jones, was Joe's first chief petty officer when he joined the Coast Guard so many years ago. Joe and Tom had a special relationship all these years. When Tom was murdered in Orlando a short time ago, the first person Claire called was Joe.

Joe solved his murder and Claire was forever grateful. She didn't want Tom's name muddied as a drug dealer. Joe made sure that it never happened, even though Tom was somewhat responsible for his own death. Tom was in over his head by personally investigating a drug dealer in his apartment complex. He paid for it with his own life.

Claire hugged Julie and Joe. "Thank you for meeting with us this weekend. I'm your 'hostess with the mostest.'" She laughed. "As you know Marshall is my boss, and I'm his administrative assistant for Hollywood Studios at Walt Disney World. I've volunteered to make sure that whatever you need, along with your guests, will be taken care of. Just let me know."

Julie hugged her back. "Let me introduce you to Trinity Hightower and Archie Higgins. They're detectives with the Orlando Police Department and will be with us for the weekend. As soon as we meet, Marshall, we will be glad to let you know why they're here. Marshall already set up the arrangements for all of us, or did you do that?"

"I did. I understand that the work Joe does might have something to do with it but, hopefully, everything will be fine. We've our own security staff on notice that there could be a potential issue during your stay. Marshall fully understands and is grateful that you came."

As they finished their quick introductions, Marshall came down the stairs to meet Julie and Joe. "It's a pleasure to meet you, Julie. Claire has told me so much about you. Is this Joe Traynor, whom I've heard so much about?"

"Guilty as charged." Joe shook Marshall's hand and introduced him to Trinity and Archie. They both looked a little overwhelmed at the circumstances, not from a security angle but just because they'd never been anywhere near the inner workings of Walt Disney World. They shook Marshall's hand as well.

Joe beckoned Marshall aside. "Before we go any further, I believe you're owed an explanation of why we have security. It's certainly not because of Julie. Can we speak privately for a few moments?"

"Certainly. Please follow me to my office upstairs. Claire, are you in on this too?

"Yes, of course."

They went upstairs after Joe told Trinity and Archie that his situation was classified but he said he'd give them the highlights after he met with Marshall. They said fine but wanted to stay outside his office, just in case. They took their responsibilities very seriously.

"By the way, my attorney, Jane Swanson, will be coming in from Miami later tonight," Julie told Marshall. "I'll have to give her a call and let her know what she has to do if she comes after the park closes at 10:00 p.m. She'll probably need an escort into the building if you're around. If not, either Joe or I can meet her at the gate."

"No problem. We will be up past midnight, anyway, with nothing to do but stay close to you until you go to your room for the night."

∽∾∽

Once they were seated in Marshall's office, Joe cleared his throat. "I'm in the middle of a major internal Coast Guard investigation that includes a multi-million dollar drug case, involving some of our own people and the Colombians, I believe. My partner Mark Silva, who Claire knows very well, was shot and seriously wounded in the doorway of his own station in Dania Beach. I had an altercation on I-95 N where I took out two cars of Hispanic gangbangers at the same time. Our rear admiral's office has been compromised. But I can't say anything else. However, Julie wanted to be here and I wanted her to be here. If needed, she can pack up with Tillie, her grandmother, at any time and head to Burbank. I didn't want her to miss this meeting. The detectives are aware of a situation but haven't been informed of the specifics. I don't believe that your Burbank staff, who are coming to this weekend meeting, are in any danger. However, I can't guarantee that, so I want to be open and honest with you."

"Thank you for your candor," Marshall said. "Claire has the utmost respect for your abilities in safeguarding our country. Her father, as I well know because I'd met him on a number of occasions, felt the same way. I won't lie and tell you I'm comfortable with the situation, especially with our staff being flown in for this meeting, but we want to be here as well. We believe in Julie's book and how it could affect young girls, forever. With that said, we will take care of ourselves and you and your detectives take care of Julie. This will work out just fine."

Joe was relieved as so was Julie. Claire nodded in agreement with Marshall and they all shook hands.

Marshall rubbed his hands together. "Our guests will be flying in around 7:00 p.m., arriving here at the park before 8:00 p.m. I thought we could have a light dinner, which will be brought in from our resort catering service, meet and greet, and get a good night's sleep. You must be exhausted as well. We will begin tomorrow at 9:00 a.m. with breakfast being served in our administration dining room, right next to my office, any time after 8:00 a.m. We will see you back here for drinks after you get settled."

Both Joe and Julie suspected that Marshall was more upset than he made out, but there wasn't much they could do about it. The meeting would take place, or not. They were there and they felt protected. Joe was frustrated about the whole thing but didn't want to let Julie know.

She knew Joe was upset but she kept it to herself. When she glanced over at him, he shrugged his shoulders as if to say, "Same crap, different day."

೧ல೧ல

After the meeting in Marshall's office, Joe and Julie, Trinity and Archie headed to their rooms. Archie and Trinity were on each side of Joe and Julie's suite. Joe gathered them into the suite for a minute and gave them the up and up on why they were being protected. Trinity's eyes lit up. Archie seemed calm and collected. Apparently, Cal hadn't let them know exactly who Joe was and what he did. He'd only told them to stay on top of the situation for as long as Joe and Julie were in town. Then they all went to their rooms.

Joe immediately looked out the window from his and Julie's third floor suite. The administrative offices were adjacent to the Streets of America/Backlot. The area known as the Streets of America was probably one of the most overlooked attractions in Disney World. Most visitors didn't even realize that it was not just a few streets that got you from place to place. If you were standing in front of some of the areas that were supposed to represent the streets of New York City, you could hear the city noises—traffic, pedestrians, and honking horns.

Joe thought he was in Manhattan, it was that realistic. "Julie, look. This is amazing. It's like New York City. Hear the traffic and sounds? Amazing." There was a brochure on the table explaining the scenes just outside their window. The brochure stated, *Take a look at the facades of the buildings—Chinese laundry and restaurant, complete with an old-fashioned telephone booth that's decorated with a little pagoda, just like you might see in Chinatown.*

Julie hugged herself. "I'm really getting excited and nervous, all at the same time."

"I won't lie to you, Julie. Me too. At least we can forget about my job and your Key Largo problems for the weekend."

"In that case, Mr. Traynor, perhaps we can take advantage of our free hour before we meet the Burbank contingency."

Julie closed the shades and turned down the light. She turned on the music from the stereo and found an appropriate channel. She then jumped into the king-size bed and pointed for Joe to get over there ASAP. Joe grinned from ear to ear. *Problems. What problems?*

✦✦✦

Before they went to meet with Marshall and his colleagues from Burbank, Julie called Jane to give her the phone number for Marshall as well as to make sure hers was in her contact list as well as Joe's number.

"I'm closing in on Orlando and will be at Walt Disney World around 9:00 p.m. I'll call you when I arrive."

"Sounds great. I'll make sure someone meets you out front and gets you situated. Your room is close to ours on our floor. The meeting starts at 9:00 a.m. tomorrow and will go as long as needed. You're welcome to stay overnight tomorrow and head out Sunday if you want. We're flying back late Sunday afternoon to Key West airport. I'll make sure your rooms has dinner and drinks when you arrive, if you miss our meet and greet."

"Thanks, Julie. This is all very exciting. You know, I don't have the experience you might need, but I'll have your back. If negotiations do get tricky, we're only a phone call away from my law firm who specializes in these contracts. I don't, but I'm learning. At least you got the lowest paid lawyer in my firm to bill you," she said, laughing.

"Just keep it that way until we're rich and famous and then I won't care. See you later," Julie said as she hung up and went to the door to go to the meet and greet.

❧❦❧

Marshall took Julie by the elbow and led her over to a group of people. "Julie, I'd like to introduce you to my fellow Disney people. You obviously know Claire, who started the ball rolling around here."

Claire nodded and smiled.

"This is Sharon Vincent, who works right here at Hollywood Studios as my general manager for operations," Marshall continued.

Julie shook Sharon's hand. "Hi, Sharon. Nice to meet you. This is Joe Traynor, my fiancée and business manager."

"Hi, Joe. Nice to meet you," Sharon said.

Marshall went on to introduce the Burbank contingency that included Marcia Manning, Vice President for Human

Resources for Walt Disney Studios worldwide, Edward Bell, Assistant Vice President for Motion Picture Production, Ricardo Gomez, Assistant Vice President for Walt Disney Studios Marketing, and Deana Finkle, Vice President for Hollywood Records and Disney Music Publishing.

Marshall gestured to the group. "All our Burbank guests have a great deal of input into the decision making at Walt Disney Studios. It may seem strange to have a full Vice President for Human Resources but Marcia carries a dual hat for diversity resources related services for the studio's employees, including recruitment, talent management, organization design and development, compensation, and HR administration. You fit under her umbrella of diversity resources, talent management, and compensation, Julie. There's also an opportunity if you ever wanted to pursue employment with us."

"Well, thank you. It's a pleasure to meet all of you. I look forward to our discussions tomorrow. This is Joe. He's my business manager and fiancée. My attorney, Jane Swanson, will arrive in a little less than an hour. These other two individuals are Archie Higgins and Trinity Hightower of the Orlando Police Department. They're both detectives and will be shadowing us for the weekend. Marshall can tell you a little about the reason why, after our get together, if you want."

After the introductions, they all headed for the dining room for drinks and a light late dinner. Archie and Trinity said they'd eat later and stayed close to the door, in the lobby, to wait for Jane and provide an added sense of security. They also noticed a Disney security vehicle parked right outside the door. Trinity went outside and introduced herself as an Orlando detective and told the security guard that they'd be there for the duration. She also told them about the arrival of Jane Swanson.

As everyone ate and became acquainted, they seemed to loosen up. Joe watched Ed Bell and Ricardo Gomez speaking to each other at the end of the table. They spoke Spanish. From the gist of their conversation, Joe knew that Ricardo thought Julie was "one hot tomato," as he so eloquently put it. Ricardo made a few other blatant comments in Spanish as well and Joe kept those comments in the back of his mind. He smiled. Never would he give up his cover to them without a valid reason. Claire seemed to be on a lower level and stayed by herself a little. Joe sat next to her to keep her company and she seemed grateful. Of course, Julie was the center of attention. It was her meeting and her time to shine. Joe wanted that to happen but, like any ordinary guy, he had mixed emotions. His father explained mixed emotions to his construction crew many years ago. He said at the time, "Mixed emotions are what you feel when your mother-in-law goes over the cliff in your new Mercedes." Joe chuckled to himself. Claire looked at him with a perplexed smile. He just shook his head. "I'll tell you later."

Jane arrived half way through the dinner, around 9:00 p.m. Julie gave her a big hug. They'd only met once before when Joe drove her up to sign all the paperwork when her grandmother, Tillie, was in the hospital. They needed wills and powers of attorney in case Tillie didn't make it. She did but now they were fully protected because of Joe's suggestion and Jane's actions.

Jane was a very good friend of Dan Simmons up in Albany, one of Joe's best friends. Dan took over the Albany Coalition for Families at Joe's suggestion after Joe broke up a Mexican Mafia conspiracy to drain non-profit agencies and foundations across the country. Dan suggested Jane, who went to Albany Law School with him and was now practicing in Miami.

To date, Jane had handled all the contractual obligations that had to do with Julie's new book.

Marcia seemed fascinated by Julie and said she read her book *Conch Town Girl* from cover to cover. She gave it to her young daughter, age thirteen, just like Marshall Tillman did for his daughters. Claire had read it first. She gave it to Marshall, who gave it to his teenage daughters, and it started from there. Marcia seemed to know all about Joe and what he meant to both Julie and her grandmother, Tillie. She was a little surprised about their engagement after all these years, but seemed to understand fully what Joe had always meant to Julie, and she to him.

The night broke up a little after midnight and everyone headed to their rooms. Marshall and Claire were staying over as well, along with Sharon, who said she'd be camping out in her office for the night. She did this a lot, depending on the seasons, the rush, and major events.

Claire and Marshall had rooms right down the road and would be dropped off by security and picked up at 8:00 a.m. in the morning for the return trip. Trinity and Archie took turns every three hours and stayed outside Joe and Julie's room. Julie didn't want them to bother but they insisted.

CHAPTER 10

Jack arrived in Islamorada late Friday night and was met my Joan Talbot at the dock. He came down on the mail boat from Virginia, first stopping in Miami for normal delivery, and then they went out of their way to drop him off. He was a fixture up in Virginia and whatever he needed, he got. It took about an hour and a half after their Miami stop and the cutter pulled into Islamorada.

Joan met Jack getting off the ship. Her husband, Jeff, would fill the cutter's fuel tanks so they wouldn't have to stop again before going back up to Virginia. The fuel was paid for out of the special account that was set up for miscellaneous donations. Jack was prepared to cover the expense but didn't have to. The funds came to the Islamorada Station from Joe. His various efforts over the last year had placed several hundred thousand dollars into the coffers of the station, all with the knowledge of Rear Admiral Barnes in Miami.

Jack gave Joan a quick hug. "Hi, Joan. Hell of a trip but sure beats flying in to God knows where and renting a car."

"Welcome to Islamorada, Jack. This is my husband, Jeff. He's in charge of the marina that houses this facility. He'll go fill up the cutter so they won't have to stop back in Miami. No flags will be raised if they head directly back to Virginia. Stopping in our maintenance facility in Miami Beach would raise a few eyebrows."

"Got you. Good point. Hi, Jeff. Nice to meet you, finally." Jack had spoken to Jeff several times, especially when Jeff piloted the go-fast boat a few months ago when Joe had the Russians renditioned out of the country. Jack was in on the rendition as well. Jeff met Joe in the port at Miami, hit the gas, and went as fast as the boat would go to meet the CIA out of the territorial waters of the United States. He got Joe back to Islamorada safely and nothing was ever mentioned about it again. Joe was forever grateful to both Joan and Jeff as well as to Jack. Next to Mark Silva, they were Joe's closest friends, especially after Tom Jones died.

Joan walked Jack to Joe's officer's quarters and he placed his bag inside the door. He had his equipment to do the audit of the facility in a separate bag. It was closing in on midnight and he wanted to work with Joan, alone, and not have anyone else wonder what they were doing. This was critical because, if Islamorada was compromised, the whole operation going forward would be as well. Jeff waved the cutter over to the fueling station with no one the wiser as to why Jack was there.

Jeff would bring Jack back to Miami the next day and Jack would get a taxi to the hotel where he'd meet Joe on Monday when he got back.

Joan and Jack walked through the front door of the station with Jack carrying his Super Sweep 2000, which would determine quickly if there were any problems at the facility. Once again, just like Joe had done in Miami, Jack started with the RF probe. The machine sniffed the entire building, room by room.

Jack got an immediate read out that there were no active bugs in the building and the printout showed that the incoming phone lines weren't bugged. Jack signaled to Joan that there were no bugs, as of yet. He then tested all the AC electrical outlets, using the very low frequency probe, for the phone lines and for any suspicious wires. He tested for unknown wires and cables to find any wired microphones. Joan's cell phone was okay as well. Jack aimed at his own cell phone and picked up nothing. This building was clean for now.

"Joan, I'll leave the equipment plugged into Joe's office with the door locked and the equipment hidden under his desk. As of now, everything looks okay and this will pick up anything twenty-four-seven from now on. Not to worry. We're on top of this."

Joan nodded. "Joe told me a little about what's happening and what happened to both him and Mark. Are we in danger from our own Coast Guard people?"

"I won't lie to you. I don't know. What I do know, as of right now, you aren't under any surveillance whatsoever. That's a good thing. If you become under surveillance, I'll know right away and I'll know who's doing it. This is state-of-the-art equipment. As far as being safe, you're safer here than anywhere else."

"Good to know. Please call me regularly and let me know what's going on. I know Mark and his family are being shipped out to San Diego. Joe told me. Where will Tillie and Julie be when Julie gets back from her meeting, along with Joe?"

"I believe they're safer at Tillie's apartment complex but if you can have some of your men swing by every now and then, it would be appreciated, I'm sure. They can also stay at Joe's quarters at the station as well. Play it by ear," he said.

"We did that with the Russians as you know and we will do it again. What do you want me to say to Jacob Cramer tomorrow? What if he finds out what's going on? What do I say?"

"Joe could tell you what to do better than I could but, in the meantime, if he asks, just tell him to call the rear admiral in Washington and that you're under strict orders. He may be pissed but if Joe completely trusted him, he'd be in the know. However, Joe told me that he's been acting flakey ever since Joe's promotion to lieutenant, so Joe will keep him in the dark for now. I know for a fact that Joe is working on something with the rear admiral that will give you greater visibility here. That's all I can say for now. Trust me, Joan. Joe has your best interests at heart."

"I know he does. I just feel awkward, under the circumstances."

Jack sighed. "Over the last twenty years, you've gone through chief warrant officers like popcorn. It may be your time to shine, and we all have your back."

"Thanks, Jack. That does make me feel better. Can I talk to Jeff about this?"

"Yes, and if he has any questions, I'll answer what I can when he brings me back to Miami. I'm not sure what I can tell him but I know that he and Joe are real tight and Joe would want me to reconfirm that he has both your and your family's best interests at heart."

With that, Jack gathered up his bags and left the equipment in place in Joe's office. A sign went on Joe's door that no one was to enter his office without clearance from Rear Admiral Barnes, directly. What everyone didn't know wouldn't hurt them. Nobody cleared it with Barnes, but Jack was sure he'd back Joe on everything he was doing.

♋♋♋

Joe and Julie got up around 7:30 a.m. There was a small breakfast bar in their room so Joe made coffee while Julie took her shower. Joe started making calls as soon as he took his first sip. He called Louise to see how Mark was doing. They were leaving from the hospital today and heading directly to the airport for San Diego.

Louise had already packed for the entire family and the bags were in the living room, ready to go. She'd called Jennifer and MJ's teachers and they already knew about Mark's condition.

Evidently, Michelle Bower had already taken care of that. Michelle had a checklist and went over it with Louise as soon as she found out they were going away until Mark recovered.

Louise didn't remember exactly what was discussed, but they would stop by and thank Michelle on the way. Joe gave Louise his new burner number and told her to call at any time. Her number was already in Joe's new phone.

Joe called Jack and was brought up to date. Jack was on his way to Miami in Jeff's go-fast boat and would meet Joe Monday night at the hotel room they'd share. It was a suites hotel, very similar to the Embassy Suites that Mark and Joe shared in Orlando during the murder investigation. Jack told him that there were no bugs at either Dania Beach or Islamorada, which was a good thing. It appeared that the only compromise was in the rear admiral's offices in Miami. At least they could now pinpoint the problems and, hopefully, who was doing the bugging.

Jack laughed. "I'm running out of equipment. I feel like the manager of a rental store."

"Your life would be so boring without us, Jack."

"Yeah, I know. I'll see you Monday night," he said and hung up.

Joe dialed another number. "Joan, it's Joe."

"Hi, Joe. Jack's on his way to Miami with Jeff. Is this the burner you're using?"

"Yes. Memorize the number and don't write it down. Do you have Jack's number?"

"Yes. He gave it to me last night."

"His is encrypted. My encrypted phone was compromised so I'm using this in the meantime. Are you all right?"

"I will be. I just feel a little weird with Jacob not in the know. Jack alluded to what you were thinking about and mentioning to the rear admiral. Thanks, Joe. I appreciate it. I hope it goes smoothly. I don't need to be in the middle with you and Jacob. I got less than two years to go."

"I know and we will work this out. Trust me."

They said goodbye as Julie finished in the bathroom. Joe hopped in the shower and, under two minutes, he was done.

Why do women take so long? They must have more moving parts. He smiled. She wouldn't appreciate his humor, especially with the meeting coming up shortly.

Julie and Joe met Trinity and Archie as soon as they opened their door and walked into the hallway. The detectives both looked tired. Joe knew at least one was outside their door all last night.

"Thanks, guys. We can't thank you enough. I hope you're hungry. They've got a buffet breakfast for us. Please just eat and don't worry about us."

All in agreement, they went into the dining room and picked up their plates. Joe had Trinity and Archie go first. They were appreciative. There were Eggs Benedict, an omelet station, bacon, sausage, ham, home fries and various waffles and pancakes. There were bagels, lox and cream cheese, as well as fresh squeezed orange juice right from Orlando orange groves. Trinity had an omelet, bacon, and a large orange juice. Archie piled his plate eight inches high and was smiling from ear to ear. Trinity stared at him.

"What?" he asked. "I'm hungry."

She shook her head and sat down when the waitress came over with a fresh pot of coffee. The four of them ate together and exchanged pleasantries throughout the meal. Julie looked pensive and Joe could tell she was nervous.

He quietly spoke to her. "Look, you don't have to impress anyone. If you don't like what they have to say, we can get up and leave. This isn't life and death, and you know exactly what I mean."

"I know, Joe. I'm nervous. This is my career. Not really my career, but you know what I mean. I want to do my best and have no regrets. This is big time and I'm not sure I'm ready for the main event yet."

"You are. So don't worry. Do you remember when I told you that I always got offered a job when it appeared that I didn't care one way or the other? I don't mean to be nonchalant, but it appears that you've got lots of choices and this is just one of them."

"Thanks for the pep talk, Joe."

"By the way, the two guys, Ricardo and Ed, think you're hot."

"How do you know that?"

"I'll tell you on the way home. It's funny how people underestimate others. They were speaking Spanish with a Mexican accent. They don't have a clue about my background. Let's just see what happens." He smiled at her. "They don't know how hot you really are, sweetheart."

"Don't make me blush here. I'll never forgive you."

He laughed and kissed her hand. "Yes, dear."

Archie and Trinity looked up and wanted to know what was going on. Joe laughed and whispered in Trinity's ear.

She smiled. "They don't have a clue. Do they?" She nodded to Archie and said she'd tell him later. "Thanks for the input, Joe. Most people would never say a thing but I guess you two aren't most people. I see why the chief wants us here."

The rest of the Burbank crew, Claire, Sharon and Marshall meandered in, got something to eat, and brought their food to the conference room where the meeting began.

Jane got there a few minutes late and apologized. She had a conference call that began at 7:30 a.m. that she had to take, involving one of her firm's best clients in Miami. They were closing on a multi-million-dollar property right in Key Biscayne on Tuesday morning and they needed Jane's input. She grabbed a Danish and coffee and sat down. She had her ruler-lined yellow legal pad out and ready to go.

Marshall began the meeting by reintroducing everyone. Julie looked at Ricardo and Ed and smiled her best smile at them. Joe chuckled to himself. *Here we go. Why would I ever underestimate her?*

Ricardo couldn't take his eyes off of her. Marshall turned the floor over to Marcia Manning, the most senior of the Burbank staff. She started by telling Julie, "I loved the book and we're interested in turning it into a movie or a television special, five-part mini-series. Either could be turned into a television series at a later date. We're here today to do our due diligence and wanted to understand how the book related to your actual life and where you intend to take it."

Julie advised them that she was given a three-book deal, approved by her attorney. The three books would be a trilogy aptly names *A Girl's Life*. Her first, *Conch Town Girl* had already been released, as they knew, and was doing quite well, moving up the non-fiction bestsellers list. She'd also been nominated for an award as a first time author. Julie, without missing a beat, moved into her Brown University background and support system.

"That's quite impressive for a twenty-four-year-old-author who's just released her first book," Marcia said.

At that point, the other staff members went through their presentations for motion picture production, marketing, records, and music. They took a break. Joe headed to the men's room and, as he passed Julie, he said, "They love you. You're everything they want and need. Let's see what they present to you as an offer. If you don't get an offer today, tell them that you won't be coming back for a second discussion without knowing their intentions. They need you. Let them know that. Make them blink."

"I'll see you in a few minutes. I need to speak to Jane and see what she wants me to do. I believe you're right. Let's see if she's on the same page." Julie headed over to Jane. "Can I speak to you for a minute in private?"

"Of course."

They went to the dining room so Jane could get something to eat. She'd had only a Danish and a sandwich since yesterday afternoon and was starved. "I don't do my best work fighting hunger pains," she said, smiling.

"Me neither. What do you think so far?"

"I think you'll have a long and prosperous career, if it's handled right from the beginning."

After telling Jane what Joe thought, Julie asked for Jane's opinion.

"Joe's quite astute," Jane said. "They may offer you a net profit offer for a movie. That means you'll never see a dime and they'll never show a profit. Up front, with no negotiations, you'll only do a gross sales percentage contract with a retainer in advance. We can negotiate the retainer but not the gross. They'll balk and you can walk. Hey that rhymes," she said and smiled. "Time is on your side, Julie. The Brown publishing deal that we negotiated will carry you a long way. One movie doesn't make a career."

"Got it. You do the talking, Jane, when it comes to that part."

They went back to the conference room and Ricardo began the conversation by asking who Jane and Joe were and how they fit in. They were told last night that the two detectives were there to protect Joe and Julie for the weekend, but they couldn't discuss why. Jane gave her background and how she came to be Julie and her grandmother, Tillie's, attorney.

Joe simply told everyone that he was Julie's business manager and that he had an MBA from Rensselaer Polytechnic Institute. Ed and Ricardo didn't have a clue about RPI but Marcia and Marshall knew that it was a highly recognized institution. Marcia had just read that the astronaut currently in space was an RPI graduate and, unfortunately, the general in charge of the US Army in Afghanistan, who was just recently killed in action, was, too.

"Am I correct, are you and Julie engaged?" she asked.

Joe nodded.

"Yes, we are," Julie said as she winked at Joe. She was now feeling as uncomfortable as Joe was in those situations.

Riccardo said something, at length, to Ed in Spanish. Joe turned to him and said in Spanish, "Please keep your remarks to yourself or you'll blow this deal. Do you understand?"

Ricardo appeared to be shocked and Ed was wide-eyed. Joe said, again in Spanish, "Julie is beautiful and I believe your remarks yesterday were sincere. Today, your remarks are unwarranted and, if I were you, I'd simply excuse my-self from the table, Ricardo. Ed you can stay and let Ricardo know what happened after he leaves. Thank you."

Ricardo excused himself from the table and closed the door behind him. Marcia turned to Joe and asked him if eve-rything was all right.

"Yes, of course." Joe said.

"Why did Ricardo leave the room so suddenly?" she asked.

"You can ask him later if you wish. Perhaps we can con-tinue this meeting?"

Everyone was a little on edge but, after a few minutes, they were back on target. They were down to negotiations and Jane stepped in for this discussion. They were just about ready to discuss the basis for a contract when Marcia said that perhaps they could eat lunch and start fresh this afternoon. Everyone agreed. As they were heading to the dining room, Marcia asked Joe if she could speak to him for a minute. He nodded and told Julie that he'd be right there.

"Joe, are you all right? Can you explain to me what hap-pened in the room a while ago with Ricardo?"

"Yes. Ricardo was out of line and made comments that I didn't appreciate, being Julie's fiancé. Perhaps, I should give you my background. I'm an MBA graduate from RPI. I'm also a lieutenant in the Coast Guard Intelligence Divi-sion, in charge of all investigations for South Florida and the Keys. I speak both Russian and Mexican-dialect Span-ish. Your friend is very lucky that I didn't respond more violently to his remarks. As you may be aware, I'm the low-ly Coast Guard, first year nineteen-year-old who showed up at Julie's school for Career Day. Right now, I'm in charge of a very important internal investigation for the Coast Guard down in Miami. My partner was shot up in Dania Beach and I took out two cars full of Colombian gangbang-ers on I-95 N, just south of Fort Lauderdale. The Orlando detectives are here for me, not Julie, but she could be hurt, hanging around me. You people are fine as long as I keep a low profile. We're flying back to Key West tomorrow night on a private jet and I'm back to work on Monday. Poor Ricardo doesn't have a clue. Perhaps you might tell him that not everything is as it seems. And, real life is a lot more dangerous than the movies. No matter what language he uses, he should keep his crude remarks to himself."

"We're all sorry, Joe, and this will never happen again. I'll personally talk to Ricardo when we get back to California. I think you scared him half to death with your Spanish remarks. We didn't understand the significance of what you do, and thank you for doing it. I mean that from the bottom of my heart. We want nothing but the best for Julie, and I believe we can do that and give her the success that she's entitled to after all these years. I promise you, I'll do everything I can to make this work. By the way, let me reiterate once again, you scared the living crap out of us with the banter in Spanish and the glare in your eyes. Our production team could never teach that to an actor. I guess you have to live it." She finally smiled. "Looking for a job?"

"No. Thank you." Smiling, he escorted her to the dining room.

Ed stopped him and apologized as well.

Julie studied Joe. "You okay?"

"Yes, and, now, you'll be, too." He then went on and explained to both Julie and Jane what happened with Ricardo in the room and what Marcia said afterward.

Marshall came over and asked Joe if everything was okay.

Claire, who'd seen Joe in action with her father's investigation, wasn't surprised by anything Joe did. She knew it was to protect Julie, just like he'd protected her and her family when the chips were down with her father's murder.

She whispered in Marshall's ear all about Joe and what he was made of. "I think Ricardo overstepped his bounds and fell into Joe's bad graces," she said. "I'll ask him later, but I suspect whatever Ricardo said really upset Joe. Ricardo should watch his step. He has no idea."

After lunch, Marcia and her group discussed the fact that they wanted to pursue the movie rights to Julie's first book *Conch Town Girl,* as well as obtain the movie and television rights to her trilogy, *A Girl's Life.* Ed Bell started talking about net revenue contracts and Jane immediately told everyone that, unless the contracts included a deal for gross sales, no contract would be signed.

Ed began his sales pitch but Marcia held up her hand. "Let's end this on a good note and work on a deal that Julie, Jane, and Joe will be comfortable with. Julie, when we get back to Burbank, I'll meet with the contract people and hammer out a contract that you'll be proud to sign and we will be proud to offer. I believe that a movie should be the first effort and then we can take it from there. What do you think?"

Julie looked at Joe and Jane and they both approved. She turned back to Marcia. "Yes, let's move forward. Call me whenever you need me. However, you know that I'm a teacher's aide and a counselor at Coral Shores High School as well as an assistant track coach for the girls. It's a three-hour difference, so if you call me at 5:00 p.m. your time, it'll be 8:00 p.m. my time, and I'll be home. Jane will be in on all the appropriate calls. Is that okay, Jane?"

"Yes, of course."

Marshall wrapped up the meeting. Since it was early and they planned on a celebration dinner at 7:00 p.m., they had time to visit the park. Marshall secured them a guide and a park vehicle to drive them around as special visiting dignitaries. There were a few shows that Julie had already mapped out, just in case they had time. They asked Archie and Trinity to go with them and they agreed.

Claire had to go home but would be back for the dinner. That was the same for Sharon and Marshall. Everyone from Burbank wanted to go as well, all except Ricardo. Evidently, Marcia asked him to head back to Burbank that evening. Joe was reluctant to see him punished but, as he knew growing up, you got what you paid for. Perhaps this little life lesson could reform his decision-making process for the rest of his life.

They had a great time that afternoon, visiting all the sites that Julie wanted to see. They even went over to the Magic Kingdom and Epcot for a few hours, all on Marshall.

The dinner went well. Marcia, once again, apologized for Ricardo's poor behavior. They said no problem. Marcia also mentioned that Julie's check, upon signing the contract, could be in the mid-six figure range to start.

Julie was worried that she'd have to head to Burbank and that made Joe nervous as well, especially with his problems now under way. But he thought everything could be worked out if it was worth it. Marcia also mentioned that if either or both wanted to work for Disney in California, it could be arranged. Joe mentioned that his friend Mark's sister, Jennifer Silva, was in the movie business in Hollywood as a well-known cinematographer. Marcia said she knew the name but had never met her. She wrote it down in case they ever ran into each other.

☙❧

Joe and Julie made the plane after a pleasant ride with Trinity and Archie back to the Orlando airport. Both of them said that if they ever needed shadowing again to please call them because they had a great time. All four became good friends. You never knew when you needed someone and it was good to know Joe had others beside the chief in Orlando on his side. They were all thankful that there were no incidents and everyone was safe and sound.

They landed at the Key West Airport right on time and headed home. Julie would stay with Joe and leave for school early in the morning. She knew she wouldn't be seeing him for a while.

He was headed to Miami and points unknown on Monday. Julie went directly to Joe's officer's quarters. Joe headed over to speak to Joan for a minute. He wanted to catch up on Jack's visit and see if he'd found anything at the Islamorada facility.

CHAPTER 11

Julie left Islamorada at 7:00 a.m. and headed to Coral Shores High School in Tavernier, about seven miles north. From there she'd head to the Key Largo school, another thirteen miles north of Tavernier. Back and forth, back and forth—it started to add up. She had to be back at the high school in the afternoon for practice of the girls' cross-country team. She also knew that everyone would stop and ask her how her meeting went up at Walt Disney World over the weekend. This was a big deal for a local girl, and Julie's comings and goings were now a hot topic, ever since her book came out, to very favorable reviews.

She pulled into the faculty parking area and gathered her folders for her morning meetings. The first was at 8:00 a.m. with Gary Myers the high school principal. He'd been the principal ever since Julie started at the school when she was fourteen years old in the ninth grade. Julie also dated his son Billy for a short time. He took her to the prom and they remained good friends over the years, knowing they were heading in different directions. Both of Billy's parents loved Julie and wanted their friendship to be more, but it had never materialized.

"Good morning, Gary."

"Same to you, Julie. How was your trip?"

She expected to be questioned, but not the first question out of his mouth. "It went very well. They're putting together a contract for my review that will address various avenues, including possible movie and television opportunities. It will be a while before I receive any kind of indication on what they're thinking."

"Well, that's great, but you know we don't want to lose you, Julie."

"I'm trying to get them to develop something right here in the Keys, or at least up at Walt Disney World in Orlando. They were talking about going to Burbank but I'm not comfortable with that. Especially, since Joe and I are engaged and planning a spring wedding."

"Am I invited? I hope so," Gary said.

"Absolutely. You, your wife, and Billy, of course, are all invited, if he's around. How's he doing?" She was trying to change the subject with little success.

"Billy's doing well. Not as well as you but he seems to have found his stride. It looks like he and Amanda may be a permanent thing. We'll just have to wait and see."

Amanda Byrnes had been in the same class as Julie and Billy, and he'd been going out with her ever since they graduated from high school. They went to separate colleges in Miami and stayed there after graduation. Billy worked for Time Warner Cable as an on-air production manager for their cable news program. Amanda was a manager for customer service at Baptist Health in downtown Miami, right around the corner from Billy. Neither Gary nor his wife liked to advertise that Billy and Amanda had been living together for the last two years. But Billy had told Julie the last time he and Amanda were back for a visit. Billy had been following Julie's success. Amanda seemed to be a little overprotective the last time they were in town but, since Julie got engaged, that seemed to satisfy her.

The meeting with Gary today was to review the status of all the seniors, as to where they were headed after graduation. Julie, through her friend Maddy's assistance, developed an Excel program that tracked the student's last ten years. The program included where they went to college, if they graduated, where they went to work, and updated all their social media accounts so graduates could continue to follow current student activities and continue to connect them to the school. Julie had also summarized all the scholarships won by the students, including her own scholarship to Brown University. She made the list of scholarships available to all high school students, even to ninth graders, so they could start thinking about their future outside of the Florida Keys. If Joe hadn't done that for Julie when she was in high school, she'd never have had the opportunities that were now becoming a reality. The counselors who Julie had back then were part time and usually teachers getting a small stipend to help out. Julie was the first full time career counselor in the district. She knew that Gary Myers and the new superintendent concocted the job, but it would pay dividends far greater than anything they'd pay her for the position.

She also downloaded every scholarship application at every Florida college and university, so as not to miss out on any opportunities for their students. She started a website where students could ask about various colleges they were interested in and she'd set up the connection directly to the college's online scholarship information.

That would have been great for Julie if she'd had this back then. It was a painful process that she, Tillie, and Joe went through to figure out where she wanted to go to college after graduation.

Gary patted her on the shoulder. "What you've created for us is remarkable. Please thank your friend Maddy for her help as well. When is she coming back to do the update for the grant renewal for next semester?"

"As soon as she can. We still have a lot to do."

"Really? I didn't realize that. Why don't you give me an update?"

"Sure. I can do that." Julie took a deep breath. This was her baby, after all, and she was immensely proud of what she and Maddy had accomplished for this financially strapped school district. "Well, our fifth grade class is already up and running and connected to Maddy's third grade class up in Wakefield, Massachusetts. Every student, teacher, principal, and all the teacher's aides in the grant have iPads and have been working together. The kids just love the programs and hands-on activities. Before long, every student at the Key Largo School will be involved. We're working on a new grant that could put an iPad in every high school student's hands, and the cost of textbooks could potentially be eliminated. When we looked at the annual budget for the entire district, books were well over six figures annually. When you buy that many iPads, under a grant, the costs go down by almost thirty-five percent. All you have to do is update the software for new curriculum, unlike buying new books for every year's update. It costs pennies on the dollar."

Gary chuckled. "I think we need to switch you over to the administration side next year."

"No way. You guys can handle that. We just want everyone in our schools brought into the twenty-first century. Even you, Gary," she said with a laugh.

"I used to be able to put you into detention for those remarks, Ms. Chapman," he joked.

"Must drive you crazy working with former students who gave you a hard time, huh?"

"As a matter of fact, yes. But I'll let that remark go. Thanks for everything you've done. Don't you have to head out to Key Largo?"

"Yes. I'm running late. I have to meet with Jan and Mrs. Black at 10:30 and then be back at the high school for practice. I'd better head out. Thanks again."

She ran from the office to her car. This schedule was getting crazier and crazier. She'd no idea what she'd do if she actually signed a movie contract. She had to keep telling herself to slow down and smell the roses. She didn't want to burn out before she even got started. She tried to make up for all those lost years living with Tillie, just Tillie and her against the world. If she got there on time and had her meeting, she thought she could meet Tillie for lunch at her apartment. Julie was excited to tell her everything that happened over the weekend. She also wanted to tell her about Joe's investigation so Tillie wouldn't be worried. Tillie seemed to be the last to know and her life had been in danger almost as much as Joe and Julie's. The Russians even knocked on her door a while ago. Thank God she was at work. Her sixty-fifth birthday was coming up soon and Tillie wanted to be able to tell everyone that she finally made it to retirement. That's if she could make it to age sixty-five.

eɔeɔ

When Julie headed out early that morning, Joe had to do his laundry, repack, and meet quietly with Joan, before meeting with Jacob Cramer. All before heading up to Miami. He got his wash done and put everything in the dryer. He had to wait for everything to dry, but started packing his other clothes. He mostly needed his civilian clothes, because most of his work would be dirty—climbing around warehouses and generally running around. He had his two dress uniforms packed in a separate garment bag with his polished shoes. He wore his old steel-toed work boots that he used when working for his father many years ago. They fit like a glove and served the purpose for comfort and protection.

He packed everything he could until the dryer went off, packed what he'd laundered, and then went to see Joan at her private family quarters.

She knew he'd be over before his formal entrance into the Islamorada Station to meet her and Jacob together.

"Hi, Joan. How did Jack do?" he asked upon arriving at her home.

"Fine, Joe, and how are you?" she said, smiling.

He laughed. "Sorry. Let me start over. Hi, Joan. Boy, do

you look beautiful today. How are you? How's the family? How was your weekend?"

"Why, thank you for asking, Joe. We'd a wonderful weekend. Your friend Jack came over and we entertained him before Jeff took him back to Miami. How was your trip?" She shook her head, laughing. "You'll never change, will you?"

"Probably not."

He walked in to Joan's living room where they had coffee.

"Jack went through the entire building and we couldn't find any bugs," she said. "He said we're bug-free."

"Good to know. Did he leave the equipment in my office and did he teach you how to use it so you can continue to monitor everything?"

"Jack said to leave it on and he can monitor everything himself simply by calling in on his phone which he programmed to read the sweeper. He said he'll discuss it with you when you get up to Miami."

"Okay, let's go meet with Jacob. I want to make sure that he understands the situation that we're in now. How much do you think I should tell him?"

"First, do you trust him, Joe? I'm getting the feeling that you don't. Not that I blame you, but that should be the deciding factor. I don't think he'd ever say anything to anyone, especially after that little discussion last week with the rear admiral."

"I guess I have to expand my inner circle a little. I trust you and Jeff implicitly and, of course, Mark, and his staff, and Jack. I don't trust anybody else, but that's just me. Of course, I also trust the rear admiral but I don't know who's spying on him in his own office. That we will have to find out."

They both walked down to the station administration offices and into Jacob's office. Joe thought that he'd play it by ear, for now, and see where it would lead him.

Joan simply listened while Joe gave Jacob an overview

of the situation, without giving up all the details. He told Jacob that he'd be away for a while, since this was a direct investigation for the rear admiral. He also mentioned that if Julie and Tillie felt unsafe, he'd hope that they could use his officer's quarters while he was away.

"I hope you understand the seriousness of the situation, Jacob," Joe said, looking Jacob in the eyes.

"I'll do whatever is requested of me. And I'll maintain contact with Julie and Tillie. They'll be protected by the Islamorada Station staff."

"Thank you both," Joe said and headed for his office.

He'd worked on his plans on the plane on their return from Miami on Sunday. The hour flight didn't give him much time, but he'd been thinking about everything he needed to do as far as the investigation went. He also need-ed to think about protecting those around him who could suffer the consequences if he forgot something. He had made his outline, line-by-line, date-by-date, and would fill in the blanks later. He wanted to do one more surveillance scan in his locked office before heading out. He also needed to call the rear admiral and Mark to make sure they were on their way to San Diego—Mark and the entire family, in-cluding Louise's parents.

He already sent a text to Jack. He'd be waiting for him at the hotel later in the day. Finished, he left his office and headed for Miami. He made the trip in a little over an hour and a half, and pulled into the Suites's hotel parking lot. Jack had already registered Joe's car as his own vehicle while they stayed there and listed Joe as a guest, under an-other assumed name. Jack gave himself another name as well. He had passports and driver's licenses, including cred-it cards, already set up for this purpose.

He's a jack-of-all-trades, Joe mused. He went right up to the room on the tenth floor and knocked on the door. Jack asked who it was. Joe answered, using his assumed name and then asked for Jack with the name Jack was currently using.

Jack let him in and shook his hand. "I see you made good time. I ordered lunch for you. It's over on the table, along with a few bottles of water in the refrigerator."

"Thanks. Let me get my things in my room and then we can eat lunch and talk."

Joe unpacked his bag and hung his uniforms in the closet. He'd be wearing his everyday civilian clothes and work boots for the foreseeable future.

As they sat down and began to eat, Jack gave him the lowdown on the Islamorada office. He gave Joe his new identity cards and began to discuss what needed to be done. They had a lot to tackle. They had to decide if they'd focus on the leaker first and find out who bugged the rear admiral's office, or track how the bales of cocaine wound up in the hands of the Colombians, if that had even happened. They'd assume that it had, to start the ball rolling.

Joe didn't think his friends at the FBI would lie to him. They might have lied or not told the rear admiral everything, in case they thought he might be part of it, but when Joe showed up at their office and told them that he'd be in charge of the investigation, everything they said appeared to be true—as far as he knew. When Joe told them that the rear admiral was a straight shooter and, more than likely, not involved, they'd believed him.

That had led to more openness and honesty. As Joe found out before, the FBI, Homeland Security, and the Coast Guard didn't always see eye to eye. Since Joe carried all three credentials, he could see all the sides involved, and everyone he'd met in all three organizations trusted him. Mark held the same trust, but he was out of this action for now. Jack was a known quantity but only as an outsider, helping Joe and Mark. That would soon change.

Jack studied Joe for a moment. "Speaking of Mark. How the hell is he doing and did he get to San Diego with his family?"

"To the best of my knowledge, I believe everything went off fine. Mark, Louise, the kids, and Louise's parents landed in San Diego. Mark, Louise, and the kids will be staying with Mark's mother, and Louise's parents will be staying with Mark's sister who lives right down the street. You remember Maria and Bill Fernandez and their daughter Cristina, don't you?"

Jack nodded. "I only met Maria at Mark's fortieth birthday party last December. Nice family, though."

After lunch, Joe decided to call Mark at his mother's house. Joe had previously called their other close friend, Mike McGreevy, who was stationed in San Diego. Mike had told Joe to give him a buzz when they got in and he'd head over to see them. Joe called Mike again after his call to Mark and let him know they'd arrived.

Mike's first love was the sea, and he wound up as a boatswain mate and master seaman, serving on a Coastal Patrol Boat out of San Diego. His vessel, *The Haddock*, was an eighty-seven-footer with one officer and ten enlisted men. Mike's ship actively patrolled from the United States and Mexico borders, to Los Angeles and offshore up to 200 nautical miles.

Her primary missions included search and rescue, homeland security, and law enforcement. Mike was second on this vessel and he'd seen plenty of duty chasing drug boats, illegal immigrants, and other internal homeland security issues, none of which he could discuss. Mike was also involved when the Mexican Mafia was taken down. At Joe's request to the FBI, at the time, Mike had led the charge into the offices of the National Child Welfare Associations headquarters in San Diego, where two of the Mexican Mafia team member graduates had remained and were in the process of training more sons and daughters to continue the world-class rip-off of the Association.

Chapter 12

After Joe finished his calls, he and Jack decided to map out exactly what they needed to do to solve both problems. The first was to find out exactly who was bugging the rear admiral's office and if it had anything to do with the missing bales of cocaine. Joe believed it did because of the two separate shooting incidents that almost cost both him and Mark their lives. It could only have happened because the rear admiral's office was bugged, and it gave the Colombians time to set up the simultaneous assassination attempts.

The second problem was to uncover exactly how the thirty to thirty-five missing bales wound up in the hands of the Colombians. They needed to know how it happened, who was involved, and then they'd follow the trail to take out whoever it was responsible and make sure it didn't happen again. At least not on their watch or the rear admiral's. Joe had a great respect for the man.

Joe looked up from his notes. "Well, first, how do we find out who's bugging the rear admiral's office?"

"I think that's the easy part. You swept the offices and found the bugs only in the rear admiral's inner office only. Since you left the bugs in place, we can follow everything that comes from that. If someone starts listening again, there will be an electronic trail that will lead us to the source. Proving an individual's involvement directly with that source may be a problem, but at least we will have a source to start with. From there we can watch everyone closely and see where it leads us."

Joe sighed. "I guess that's about the best we can do for now. However, I want to come up with a situation that I can discuss with the rear admiral so if someone was listening, we can set up whomever it is. Say for example, I tell the rear admiral that I know who took the drugs and I've got an informant that I'll be meeting with that night. We can get guys in place and see what happens."

"That may seem like a good idea to you, Joe, but you're placing yourself in needless danger. We don't need you to be a guinea pig. Don't do it unless we absolutely have to."

"Maybe we won't need to, but let's keep it as an option."

Jack made a note on his legal pad. "Now, as far as the bales of missing cocaine, how should we proceed?"

"First, do we have all the equipment we need? We should be wearing our vests everywhere, just in case. We won't bring that up in the rear admiral's office. I don't want anyone to know that so they shoot for our heads, instead. Just a feeling I have."

Jack handed him a list. "I brought down everything you asked for. We're waiting on the small surveillance drones we'll use to watch the entire perimeter of the warehouse first. Then we can get the big flying drone, if we need to follow anyone. I'm getting the security tapes twenty-four/seven for both inside and outside the warehouse, since the day the big bust took place a few months ago and the bales landed in the warehouse."

After reading the search-and-seizure-at-sea manual from cover to cover, Joe and Jack put their heads together to come up with some scenarios on how the Colombians could have gotten the bales of cocaine from the Coast Guard.

"I don't know if it's even true," Joe said with a sigh. "Just because the FBI told Homeland Security that it's true, doesn't make it so."

"Me, neither, but we have to assume it is to start."

"Yeah, but as I told the rear admiral, everyone doesn't have their own set of facts and truths. There's only one truth with different interpretations. I think we should write down questions that need to be asked. Then we'll compare and see if we come up with any matching ones."

"Good idea. Must be why you're the boss," Jack teased as he starting writing.

Joe came up with the following list of questions: Did the cocaine that was seized, bagged, and tagged at sea even get to the warehouse? And was number of bales seized exactly the amount written up? Had a daily inventory been taken and were any bales actually missing? When bales went out for destruction, did those bales, the exact number, actually get destroyed? Did the destruction tags brought back match the inventory tags for amount, weight, size, and code numbers that were originally issued when the bales were seized? Did every bale seized have the exact same number that was issued originally and did they carry that number all through the process? Had anyone tested what was actually in the bales when seized, when inventoried, and when shipped out of the warehouse to be destroyed? Had anyone ever tested the destroyed package material to see if the packages actually contained cocaine? How could the bales be missing, when each weighed approximately fifty-five pounds and was the size of a small overstuffed chair, at three feet by three feet? Did the warehouse have the physical capacity to actually store all the seized bales?

Jack's list contained pretty much the same questions.

Joe chuckled and patted him on the back. "When I first met with the rear admiral, I suggested that the room had to be a certain size to hold 130 bales. Unfortunately, that explanation was probably picked up by the bug. It still doesn't change the fact that, if 130 bales were seized on that one big raid, in sheer size, alone, the bales equaled 1,170 cubic feet of space. I did a quick calculation, at the time, in my head and told him that the storage area holding the 130 bales had to be a minimum of a room that was equivalent to twelve feet high, fifty-five feet long, and twelve feet wide. The actual dimensions of the bales, when stacked on top of each other, were nine feet tall, nine feet wide and forty-five feet long. You need three feet all the way around the huge pile just to get to it. We, at least, need the floor plans to see if it was physically possible to hold all the seized bales."

Jack scribbled a note. "I'll make sure we put that in our write-up."

"Has anyone questioned the chain of command to see if they actually understood the procedures and have actually read the manual?" Joe continued.

"All good questions, Joe. Let's check them off as we review where we are." Jack picked up his own list. "As usual, you have twice as many as I do, but at least mine are pretty much the same as yours. The ones I have, anyway."

"Be that as it may, let's go over them anyway. They may spark ideas, even if they are similar to mine."

Jack shrugged. "I'm a technology guy and, as such, I'm more concerned with the computerized inventory system and cameras. Your questions are more of a logistical nature than a technology-based audit list."

"So give me the list and stop stalling."

As Joe read over the list, he saw that Jack was more interested in the barcoding system that issued the barcodes for each bale seized at sea. Were those barcodes done at random? Did the codes come out like at a customer counter at the local deli?

Joe looked up from the list. "What difference does it make if the barcodes are issued in order or randomly?"

"Issuing bar codes in order is more suspect than randomly issued ones. The random count means that the inventory specialist has to audit each bale separately in the warehouse, rather than simply counting up to 130 bales that should have been there."

"Oh. Makes sense." Joe went back to the list.

Were the barcoded bales in the warehouse the exact same barcoded bales that were tagged at sea, minus those bales that were sent out for destruction? Could the destroyed bales be audited back to the original barcode issued at sea? Did they have an exact timeline from seizure to destruction?

"Well," he declared, handing back Jack's list. "I think that, together, we've covered most of the situations that could lead to missing bales. The one question that I asked and you apparently never thought about was the actual contents in the bales. The manual never addresses the actual testing of the content of each bale on a rotating schedule. If a bale was tagged with a barcode at sea, warehoused for any length of time, and then destroyed, the actual paperwork would match completely if the manual was followed precisely by all those authorized and in control of the product. However, if the question came up in court, whether or not anyone actually checked to see what each bale contained, no one could testify to what was in the bales. If we don't know that the bales actually contained cocaine, how can we ever hope to prosecute?"

Jack blinked and then stared at Joe for a long moment. "That's one hell of an insight. I'm interested in the paperwork procedures and computerized audit trail, but I never thought to question what was in each bale."

"No offense, Jack, but that was the first thing I thought about. Everything would be accounted for if the paperwork showed that nothing was missing and that bales were in the proper custody from beginning to end. If those bales, even those sitting there in the warehouse right now, didn't actually contain cocaine, we could have a 100 million dollar problem when all the paperwork says we're in complete compliance."

"That's one hell of a theory that needs to be tested. What should we do at this point?"

"Obviously, we need to see if there's been any movement in and out of the warehouse over the last several months, ever since the big haul came into port. I'm not talking about bales taken out to be destroyed. I'm sure the bales were destroyed. We just don't really know what was in each bale that was destroyed. We need to check the camera angles to see if everything has been picked up, all day long, twenty-four/seven. We need to do our own audit on the premises over the next couple of weeks to see if what we pick up as activity matches what the cameras outside and inside the building pick up. First, let's look at the actual camera tapes since the big haul came in. Let's see if the camera angles show access and egress points. Let's see what the cameras pick up right outside the room that holds the bales. We can look for any hidden spots, depending on time of day. If the cameras are moved or adjusted during the day, it might point to some clandestine activity. Maybe then we can pick up what's going on. I've already asked the rear admiral to get the drones back. The one we used to pick up the package at the Biltmore a few months ago would be big enough. The cameras on the drones include analog closed-circuit television cameras that record pictures or videos as analog signals. We can use the large armed drone to follow any suspects moving in and out of the area."

"Sounds like a plan," Jack agreed. "I figured to be here at least a week or two because of the situation. I have to make a few calls to Virginia to make sure my staff continues to finish what we were working on. They think I'm on vacation in the Keys. Let's keep it that way. I'll not go near headquarters here, so it won't get back to my office. However, if we need some more stuff, I'll have to call them. Where are the drones going to be housed?"

"The last time we housed them at a small airport near Fort Lauderdale. However, for the first week, the drones will simply hover or sit outside the warehouse on a building nearby. If we have to follow anybody, if we discover something, then I'll use the armed flying drone and the smaller drones can go right back to where we placed them a few months ago. I need to call the rear admiral and tell him what we discussed. Do you have anything else to add at this point?"

"No, this is a good first step," Jack said.

Joe picked up his cell phone calling burner phone to burner phone. "Rear Admiral, it's Joe."

"Hi, Joe. Didn't expect you to call so soon. How was your trip? How did Julie make out up at Walt Disney World?"

"She did fine, Jake. They're sending her a contract to review. We have to wait and see what it contains, and how much time she has to spend on it, to see if it's a good deal or not. I've got mixed emotions about her leaving for Burbank, if that's the case. She's got the same feeling as well. She has to finish the next two books in her trilogy *A Girl's Life*. She wants to continue at the school, as well. We'll just have to see how much she can put on her plate at one time. Also, she and Tillie could be in danger if this investigation continues, and I believe it will. We'll just have to wait and see on all counts."

Joe went on to explain what they planned on doing to get to the bottom of things.

"I'll be back by Friday," Jake told him. "I'll continue to be in my office as if everything's normal. Any discussions we have will have to be outside in person or on the burner phones outside headquarters."

"I understand, sir."

"Thanks for everything. I talked to my admiral and told him exactly what was happening. He wasn't pleased, to say the least, but said it certainly wasn't my fault. But I disagree. It happened on my watch. It's my fault."

"There will be plenty of time later to play the blame game, sir. Let's get the problem solved and then go seek truth, justice, and the American way."

"Truth, justice, and the American way, huh, Joe?"

"Yes, I'm quoting from my old man. Seems to be getting to be a habit of mine," Joe said. "I'll see you Friday."

"Say hi to Jack and thank him for me."

CHAPTER 13

Joe and Jack now had a pretty good idea on how to attack the investigation. First, the bugs in the rear admiral's office would be fairly easy. The hardest part would be to find out how the Colombians got 30 or so bales of cocaine when all the audit paperwork points to the fact that everything is fully secured in the warehouse.

Just to be sure on the first situation, Joe checked the chain of command structure for the US Coast Guard Seventh District, headquartered in Miami. The command cadre consisted of Rear Admiral Barnes who served as commander. He was responsible for all Coast Guard operations in the Southeast United States and the Caribbean Basin including Florida, Georgia, South Carolina, Puerto Rico, and the U.S. Virgin Islands. The seventh district encompassed an area of 1.8 million square miles and shared operational borders with thirty-four foreign nations and territories.

Second in command was Captain Bert Jennings who was also the chief of staff. His office supported the International Maritime Organization engagements and provided legal advice to the operations directorate on the Coast Guard's maritime safety, security, and stewardship missions, including drug and migrant interdiction, homeland security, search and rescue, pollution response, port and vessel safety and security, Outer Continental Shelf regulation, fisheries law enforcement, counter-terrorism and piracy initiatives, Arctic stewardship, and environmental protection. This position was more operations based and the commander's duties were more administration and strategic planning.

The third in command at headquarters was Command Master Chief Petty Officer George Pagan. His primary responsibility was to advise the commander of the US Coast Guard Seventh District on issues and initiatives pertaining to all Coast Guard members and their families throughout the district. His job was personnel based and handled all those issues surrounding the members and their families.

Both Joe and Jack were quite impressed by the credentials of all three individuals whom ran the seventh district. All three had over twenty years of service, with the rear admiral having over thirty years. Neither felt that the second or third in command had anything to do with the bugging of the office or the cocaine problem. As they read the chain of command pages in the manual, they also noticed that there were a number of direct reports right under the top three in command. Under the command cadre, in addition to the top three, there was the chaplain's office, civil rights office, legal office, and public affairs office.

Following the organization chart, there were several other divisions and subdivisions reporting directly to the top three. Those other divisions included planning and force readiness, prevention, resources, response, and security. Within each of those divisions were operations units, planning, facilities, administration and personnel, quality assurance, incident management, the command center management, intelligence and security for the entire seventh district. Under each area was listed the individual in charge of that unit and all relative phone numbers, both landline and cell. If the bugs continued to operate, and nothing was done to stop the flow, it might lead right back to an identified unit in the seventh district.

It might be hard to prove that an individual was personally responsible but at least it would isolate the areas where the bugs originated.

Joe explained his thinking to Jack, adding, "It would seem to me that not everyone in this organization would have the access, or even the skill, to place state-of-the-art surveillance systems in the rear admiral's office. Also, for someone to know what Mark and I looked like and where we'd be, he or she had to have access to personnel records online. After I spent time with the rear admiral, whoever was listening, had to have immediate online access to send out to the Colombians so they'd be set up and prepared to take both of us out. They could have followed me easily enough from the rear admiral's office, but to know about Mark, and be set up to kill him in less than three hours, means there was a definite insider involved. Who'd have access to those files and also access to bug the rear admiral's office?"

Jack considered this a moment. "Someone who would have online access to personnel records and pictures of members. To set up bugs, someone had to have access to the offices. The offices showed no signs of a break-in, from what you said. So someone had to have keys. They had to set up this high-tech surveillance system and that requires them to know what they were doing. If I were to guess, there has to be several individuals involved. My best guess would be personnel, enforcement, security, and maybe even intelligence."

Joe sighed. "I'm not involved with anyone in the intelligence unit here in Miami. So, I don't know anyone. The personnel staff reports directly to the master chief. The other units are operations and they report to the chief of staff. The only other one who could be involved would be the rear admiral's chief aide, Warrant Officer Al Cummings. He's very protective of the rear admiral. That's good and bad. I've had words with him previously when I was first assigned to work with Rear Admiral Barnes. The only other issue is that when someone is that protective, there may be other reasons for that, a smokescreen perhaps. So I guess we'll have to look into it."

eঞেঞ

They were both tired. They went around the corner for dinner, stopped at a 7-11, and got a twelve-pack of beer and snacks for the night. Jack would get the camera videos from the warehouse by late in the morning. He didn't want to ask for the videos, so he had to go through his own back channels and say they were performing a video audit on all cameras in the seventh district.

From what Jack had found out, there were six cameras outside the warehouse. Two cameras were directly related to the loading dock and the other four were located at the four corners of the building. He'd also get the camera feeds from the inside as well.

Neither Jack nor Joe knew what they'd be looking for, exactly. They hoped that a forty-eight-foot tractor trailer showed up and the camera had picked up guys loading bales of cocaine into the back of the truck.

No such luck, Joe thought. They were hoping maybe they could catch someone and put the capture of the "World's Dumbest Crooks" on cable. Probably no such luck there, either.

eঞেঞ

Before heading off to sleep early, Joe called Julie, and Jack called back to Virginia to see how things were going without him while he was on "vacation." Joe thought he slipped in a call to his new girlfriend, Shelly, but Joe would never ask him about it. "Hey, Julie, it's Joe."

"Really? I wasn't sure." She laughed. "What's this number?"

"It's my burner phone number."

She'd wondered what the number was that showed up when the call came in. "Okay, I'll put the number into my phone, so I'll have it."

"No!" Joe exclaimed. "If anyone compromises your phone, my burner will get picked up."

"Oh. Yes, I see. I'll write it down, memorize it later, and then destroy the paper."

"Great," he said with relief. "Thanks."

"You have a minute, Joe? I want to bounce something off of you."

"Sure, I have all night."

"I've been thinking. I'm not really sure that I want a movie made right now for *Conch Town Girl*. Let me tell you why," she hurried on when he started to protest. "We left Hollywood Studios on a positive note, in spite of the jerk they sent back to Burbank. When Ed Bell started talking net profit, my ears perked up. Jane said never make a deal unless it was based on gross sales only. The percentage on net didn't matter because studios notoriously never showed a net profit. I'm not as concerned about making money as I'm about having control over my book. I'm now finishing the second book and I still owe the publisher a third one. I already took an advance on both. What if the first book got turned into a movie that didn't coincide with the goals of books two and three? What if it even compromised my position with my editor? I know Marcia said she'd come up with a contract that we both could be proud of but what if I'm not ready for a contract right now? What do you think, Joe?"

"Well, first, I think you're very wise to move ahead cautiously. As I said to you up in Disney, you don't have to do a thing you don't want to."

"I'm also concerned about having the movie made in Burbank. I went to meet Marshall Tillman with the understanding that he wanted the movie made at Hollywood Studios in Florida not Burbank. He wanted to resurrect the studios that made Disney famous. However, I didn't think he was very happy when Marcia mentioned Burbank as the site. Joe, I don't want to spend any extended time away from home, especially since we're getting married in the spring. I think this whole movie business is premature."

"Let's see what Marcia comes up with. In the meantime, call Marshall, or better yet call Claire Murphy and let her know what you're thinking. You may be on the same page as the Hollywood Studio people. But at twenty-four, you've got all the time in the world."

"What if I turn them down and never get another contract? I can hear them all the way from Burbank, 'You'll never work in this town again!'"

"Why do you torture yourself? I thought I was the anal-retentive one. So you've told me, many times."

"I know. I know. I'm getting ahead of myself."

"Why don't you write all this down on paper? That helps me when I'm not sure what I want to do. You want to complete your technology project for the elementary school, the high school, and the entire school district. You like being a teacher's aide. You like working at the high school and you love being an assistant girls' cross-country coach. Am I right?"

"Yes."

"Your first book is doing exceptionally well. Your editor is thrilled with you and Brown University is using you as a recruiting tool for the university. You don't need the money. You banked both your advances and you're living off your salary at the school. We're getting married, and what's mine is yours. It's always been yours and Tillie's." He paused, sighed. "I'm sorry, I really didn't need to tell you that."

You're right," she said with a sigh of her own. "I'm actually sitting pretty right now. I'm already overwhelmed and I don't need to be more overwhelmed. I'll wait for the contract. We can both look at it together and then send it up to Jane for her review. But as of right now, there's a ninety-eight percent chance that I won't sign it. Thanks for the feedback."

"You're welcome. Now I need to tell you a few things, in case things get harry up here in a hurry." Joe told her exactly what she and Tillie needed to do if they found bugs at the Islamorada Station. "Joan will circle the troops and have both you and Tillie stay at my officer's quarters. Someone from the station will follow you to school and back. However, they can't stay twenty-four-seven. There just aren't enough people for that kind of coverage."

"We've been through this before, Joe, and we can do it again. I think my father put both Tillie and me on high alert forever. It's not a lot of fun to constantly look around, staring over my shoulder, but we have to do what we have to do to be safe. I'm well aware of that. It's not your fault, Joe. So don't worry about it."

"I love you, Julie. You know that, right?"

"Of course, and I love you, too. I miss you already. Just get your investigation over with and come back safe and sound. The movie business can wait."

CHAPTER 14

Both Joe and Jack got up early, had coffee in the suite, made a few calls, and headed down the street to the diner for breakfast.

Jack tapped his notes with his pen. "By the time we get back, my staff in Virginia will have all six outside camera feeds and the inside ones as well. From there, we can review each one for the last several months until we see something that raises our interest."

"Sounds good, Jack. How's your new girlfriend, Shelly? Did you call her last night? Is there anything you want to tell me? Will we be switching wedding locations in the spring?"

"You got all that from one call? Wow. You're one smart dude. No, I'm not getting married. Yes, I called Shelly because I haven't talked to her in a week because my two best friends got their asses handed to them and I had to help out."

"If that's the way you see it, Jack," Joe said, smiling.

They both ordered bacon and eggs, home fries, toast, coffee, and Jack had orange juice. "I'm not paying for the juice, Jack. That's on your tab."

"Paying? Have you actually ever paid for one thing that I've done for you over the last decade or so? Huh, Joe."

"If that's the way you see it, Jack," Joe repeated. "I kind of like that line and I'll be using it from now on."

Jack sighed. "Can hardly wait."

When they got back, they used the hotel's WiFi connection and both loaded the camera feeds into their laptop computers.

"What exactly are we looking for, Joe, or better yet, what're you looking for?"

"It would be great if we see a forty-eight-foot tractor trailer pull up to the dock with 'Colombian Enterprises' printed on the sides. Other than that, I think we need to isolate differences in camera angles over the time period. If one camera doesn't change during the time, it probably means no one goes in or out and nothing has happened at that camera position. If there are changes, we need an explanation. I think it might be that simple."

They started reviewing the feeds with the obvious outside cameras aimed at the two docks. They went through all of them for the last two months. If nothing happened over this period, whatever happened previously would be harder to pinpoint. Most likely whatever evidence there was would probably be gone. The two docks showed normal traffic during the day and nothing over the last shift. Shifts included the morning from 8:00 a.m. to 4:00 p.m., the second shift from 4:00 p.m. to midnight, and the third shift from midnight to 8:00 a.m. The Coast Guard trucks came in several times during that period, and it was quite clear that Joe and Jack were viewing the delivery phases and the destruction phases.

Every truck was clearly marked and every face was identified as a member of the team. Joe had gotten names and pictures of everyone involved, from the original pickup at sea and delivery to the warehouse to the final destruction back at sea.

As soon as a truck appeared, Joe went to his personnel file and matched the faces in the video to the personnel records. Before the rear admiral left for Washington, he got that information to Joe so he could study those who were involved in all phases of the program. As soon as Joe saw a person on camera, he remembered the individual and pulled each file. All of these team members appeared to be clean— on the surface. The delivery and destruction times and dates matched the paperwork and the actual camera time stamped and dated activity.

So far, so good. Joe raked a hand through his hair. "I don't think that the normal operations and the comings and goings of the teams are the problem. From all appearances, all that activity seemed to be accounted for."

Jack nodded. "I agree up to this point. However, if bales were missing or not accounted for, either physically or fiscally, there must be another method used to move such a large bundle of product. Don't you think?"

"Yes. Let's keep going. We still have the sides, the back of the building, and the inside to look at."

They reviewed the cameras on the south side and the back of the building with the same results. Nothing was out of the ordinary over the last two months. There were no windows on the south side and only one back door. There was no egress or back road that anyone could use to come in and out. The only outside spot left was the north side, which had full access to all the roads, the parking lot, was close to the docks, and had a side door with an alarm.

Joe and Jack watched the camera feeds for the north side for the same two months' worth. During the day, there was normal activity. Some of the guys took their breaks there and had a smoke. It had a lot of activity, in and out. This seemed to be the main door, other than the dock area. It also appeared that the alarm was off during the day and set only at midnight. There was the same size internal crew with a warrant officer, an inventory clerk, and two armed guards for all three shifts, including the weekend. Joe thought that maybe complacency had crept in and he'd find out that this place wasn't as tight as it appeared.

As they both watched the north side and particularly the door, Jack noticed that the camera angle appeared to change around dusk, every night at the same time. He played the video back and forth several times. "Why do you think they move the camera angle every night at the same time?" he asked Joe.

"If you notice, you can't see a thing on the camera because of the glare and the setting sun. It's very clear that they move it at the same time, every night. Perhaps we should look at the timer on the camera and see if it's preset."

Jack made a call and found out that was exactly what happened every night. The camera was shifted at 7:00 p.m. every night for one hour. "This could be a pretty good time to start moving product if you can't see the door from the outside for an hour. How long does it take to move a few bales every few nights? Ten or fifteen minutes if it's set up like clockwork."

Joe shook his head, confused. "What good would moving the outside camera angle do if the inside camera is still aimed at the door? We should check that out next."

They pulled the inside videos and ran the camera aimed at the north side door. Jack pointed to his laptop monitor. "That inside camera is moved at the same time, 7:00 p.m., every night as well. What do you think that means? I'll check and see if that's automatic as well."

It was also on an automatic timer.

"I think we might have found our problem. If both inside and outside north cameras are moved at the same time every night, someone could pull up and load or unload anything during that hour. The only problem would be that everyone in the facility at that time would have to know this to make anything happen. It's not like the two guards go on break, or the warrant officer is in the bathroom, or the clerk is having lunch. Once or twice, sure, it could happen. But every night, having open access to millions of dollars in cocaine? Has to be a joint effort. Now, I truly wonder if what was in the bales was really cocaine. I wonder if what's been destroyed was cocaine. That you won't know."

"You'll know what was destroyed if we test the destruction material that held the bales together," Jack retorted. "The bales would have been waterlogged but not the entire bale went into the water. We need to pull the audited bags that were used to match the destruction paperwork, which made everything legitimate. Perhaps, they weren't always destroying bales of cocaine. We need to get into the warehouse early in the morning, sometime very soon, and start testing the bales. But I'd wait until we do more surveillance using the drones. When are they coming in?"

"By the end of the week. I better call and tell them to get the armed drone as well. We may need to fly it if we see any activity outside the north door. We could follow it just like we did in Nashville and find the Colombians' well-hidden warehouse."

享

Joe called the rear admiral right after they reviewed all the cameras, including the rest on the inside. Those showed nothing of importance. There were no cameras inside the locked vault area that held all the bales. There was no alarm on the actual vault that had to be set. It was simply locked and tagged after every daily audit. It was crimped and sealed.

Anyone inside could cut the tag, re-band, and crimp a new seal with the same audited tag reattached. After this investigation was finished, it was clear that the people in charge of and involved with this process had to be removed and new audit procedures needed to be put in place. What may have worked previously, through sheer luck, wasn't the same as having processes and systems in place that ensured that they had full control over this operation.

I'll recommend the change to the rear admiral at a later date. "Jake, it's Joe."

"Hi, Joe. What's up? I'm heading into a meeting in two minutes. It this important?"

"Yes. When you get out of your meeting, please call me on my number." He gave the rear admiral a code "Irish" which meant use the burner phone.

"I'll call you in ten minutes. I'll make an excuse to leave for a few minutes but I have to be in the meeting at the start. I'm being called. I have to go."

Barnes called back in twenty minutes. He was being grilled about the very subject that Joe wanted to discuss. He'd told his admiral and boss that if he could be excused, he might have some answers. "Sorry, Joe. Couldn't be helped. Skipping out on a meeting where you're being grilled doesn't look good, you know. What do you have?"

"I won't give you the good news and then the bad news. We've only bad news and probably worse news. This is all conjecture, at this point. Jack and I believe that we found where product has been leaving the warehouse between 7:00 p.m. and 8:00 p.m. on a regular basis. We also believe that the entire second shift, all four men, have to be involved for this deception to take place. We're installing the surveillance drones on the north end of the building at the door where we believe product is being moved. I also need the flying, armed drone in case we have to follow someone to see where the product is being moved. We believe the Colombians, with help from our own guys, have this down to a science. We can't prove anything until we have surveillance photos, but we now have a very good idea of what's happening. As far as your office goes, we believe the second shift is in cahoots with at least two or three others who have to be in personnel, security, or the intelligence department here in Miami. As you know, I'm not in this intelligence unit, thank God."

"What took you so long? It's been almost a week since I called you, you know?" Jake said with a grim chuckle. "I hate the bad news and worse news but it looks like maybe we can contain it and find all those responsible. At least, I'll have that to hang my hat on above the noose that will be dangling from my throat."

"I don't think the noose is yours alone, sir. Whoever set up the audit manual and rules and regulations surrounding the capture, inventory procedures, and destruction of drugs should be shot. It's not you is it, Jake? These manuals have more holes than a block of Swiss cheese. Someday, we'll have a beer and we'll show you how lax their measures were."

"Those procedures came right out of headquarters here in Washington. What worries me is the fact that we use those measures everywhere we have facilities like this in Miami. I wonder if that's how the officer in California was able to become so addicted. If he was bright at all, he probably bypassed every security measure in the system. We didn't catch him for over three years. No one brought up the fact that the audit manuals were inept. When I go back into the meeting what do you want me to say at this point, Joe?"

"Just tell them, if you can, that we're on top of the situation and we're setting up a sting operation to clearly identify the culprits. Tell then we understand what's been happening, and we think we can get this straightened out within a month at the latest. I'm worried about the timing. We need the drones here as fast as possible. Perhaps a direct call from you to Texas will move them faster. They're good guys and we know them, so I don't want them mad at me, but we need to move fast. As far as your being bugged, that will happen when you get back and we use your office to set up another sting so we can catch them listening. From there, we can trace it back to the source. That will isolate it but may not identify an individual. We might have to sweat an entire unit to find the culprit. This is no small operation."

"What about the Colombians?"

"I don't believe we, as the Coast Guard, have any jurisdiction but Homeland Security and the FBI should be able to intervene. I can set something up with Paul and Terry at the FBI here in Miami and we can take it from there. Or, perhaps, your contacts in Homeland Security may be able to move more quickly if we're able to follow a vehicle back to a site. We can have the drones continue to monitor the ins-and-outs over a week and see what the activity brings us. Then we will understand the magnitude of their local operation and be able to take it down. That would be textbook, just like what we did in Nashville."

"Thank you, Joe. It's nice to have someone who's competent in these areas, who is actually on my side. I don't need yes men. God knows you certainly aren't one of those. Where do we go from here?"

Joe explained that they needed to do a full investigation on all four second-shift warehouse staff to see if they were moving sizeable amounts of money around. If they were wiring funds, Jack could get all the money back as soon as he got the information that he needed. Joe told Jake that he'd be using three or four of Mark's men up in Dania Beach to follow the four guys in the warehouse. These were the same guys he used before.

Michelle Bower was aware of the entire situation and had their backs. Joan had their backs in Islamorada as well. He might need some other help doing surveillance, where the second shift crew lived, to follow their comings and goings. He said he'd fly the main drone from the small airport south of Fort Lauderdale just like he did for the Russians, as soon as they spotted anything outside the north door at the warehouse."

"How long did it take you to decide how you were going to proceed, Joe?"

"Just a day or two. We've done this before, sir, just never following our own men. It's sad but it has to be done."

"Can I speak to Jack?"

"Sure." Joe handed his phone to Jack. "The rear admiral wants to talk to you."

"Yes, sir. What can I do for you, sir?"

"Thanks for being Joe's long-time friend and thanks for being on our side. I'd hate it if you were on the other side," Jake said, chuckling. "When, and if, this all over, I'd like to thank you personally for everything you did at the drop of a hat. It's appreciated, Jack. Not that you need it, I'm sure, but a letter of commendation will follow."

"Thank you, sir." Jack handed the phone back to Joe with a smirk on his face.

Jack never got too excited about anything, but Joe could tell that he was pleased by his conversation with Jake.

"I'll see you on Friday," Jake said. "Try not to get killed."

"Please stop saying that, sir. You're making me paranoid."

"You, Joe? Never." Jake laughed and hung up.

Joe and Jack had a lot to do and very little time to do it. The rear admiral's world would come crashing down on his head if they didn't get the bad guys as quickly as they could.

Being a good guesser didn't make the lack of evidence go away. Their guesses had to be one hundred percent correct and they had to prove it. Joe also had to make sure that Julie and Tillie were safe. From the last call, Julie seemed upset. She tried to hide it but he could tell. He wanted to get home and be by her side while she made the right decision about her future. It would affect him as well.

CHAPTER 15

The drones would be in from Dallas late Tuesday afternoon. The drone technicians were schedule to launch from the Broward County Airport at 320 Terminal Drive in Fort Lauderdale. Mark had set it up a long time ago for the Russian sting, so the same technicians from before knew exactly where to go and how to set up their equipment. Joe and Mark had started flying drones to catch drug runners several years ago, when drones were in their infancy. In the Keys, they used the Key West Airport when flying south of Key West.

The small surveillance drones would take off at 6:30 p.m. and hover over the warehouse's north corner first from 7:00 p.m. to 8:00 p.m. when the outside and inside cameras were shifted for that hour. After 8:00 p.m., the drones would be set up at each of the four corners of the building for the rest of the night, leaving when dawn came. The larger armed drone would fly from the time that the technicians picked up anyone coming or going from the north door. If a van or truck pulled up during that time, the large drone would follow it to its destination point, taking pictures along the route of the license plate and any individuals leaving or entering the vehicle. The larger drone could stay up for over twenty hours at a time.

The smaller drones used for surveillance only would be up for no more than twelve hours at a time. They'd all fly back to the airport and be serviced, if required, before they were re-launched.

Now that the drones were set up, Joe needed to concentrate on how he'd confront the second shift team if, in fact, the drones picked up any activity. It was a sit-and-wait process. The drones might never pick up any activity and then Joe would have to fall back on Plan B. Plan B didn't exist at the moment. Plan B would probably be a simple confrontation and interrogation but that never went smoothly when you'd nothing to back it up. Simply threatening the four individuals at the warehouse with a court martial and jail time probably wouldn't mean a thing to these individuals. They had millions of dollars riding on this and a simple investigation would surely not get them to give up everything. Besides, reading the manuals, Joe had to figure out what was a court martial offense. The Coast Guard didn't have military police like the army or marines.

First, he looked up the court martial procedures manual and found out that those serving in the United States military did so under the implicit understanding that service members might be subject to military court hearings in lieu of civil court hearings. Due to the fact that a court martial sentence could not—and did not—legally exist within a civilian setting, a court martial existed solely under the jurisdiction of military law. Individuals in the service of the United States Armed Forces were subject to their respective adherence to the Uniform Code of Military Justice, UCMJ, which was a code of legislative protocol with regard to legal matters applicable to service members enlisted in the armed forces. Judge Advocate General Corps, JAG, served as the judicial body responsible for legal oversight with regard to service members enlisted in the United States Armed Forces. JAG Corps not only oversaw the court martial process, but was also responsible for upholding the maintenance of the protocols and parameters expressed in the UCMJ. Stipulations for the enactment of a court martial sentencing existed within the expanses of the UCMJ. Offenses resulting in a court martial were Absent Without Leave, AWOL—the un-lawful desertion of a service member with regard to their respective commitment to the United States Armed Forces and individuals deemed to have abandoned their positions might be tried by military court and subsequently court mar-tialed; Treason—the act of treason was defined as an act of sabotage, disloyalty, or sedition committed by a citizen, or citizens, directed at the specific country or nation to which that citizenship belonged; military rape—within the scope of military law, this nature of rape was the illegal and un-lawful engagement of a sexual act involving military per-sonnel and, similar to civilian rape, military rape was non-consensual, typically taking place through threat, force, or exploitation, and might be punishable by court martial.

As Joe read further, he learned what the general public knew—that anyone in the military could be court martialed for a military offense, but they could also be tried for ac-tions such as robbery or murder that would be considered crimes in civilian courts. *Trafficking in stolen bales of co-caine and selling them to foreign nationals for millions of dollars would certainly fall well within any of the above conditions.*

He was a little concerned about using Mark's men from the Dania Beach Station for the investigation and takedown without Mark being present. The Russian intervention was rather clandestine, but approved. This investigation would have more political overtones and much more legal scrutiny because they were dealing with United States citizens *and* members of the military. The Colombians, if found, would be a different issue. They'd be imprisoned or deported, or both, and handled through the FBI and Homeland Security.

Mark and his family were safely tucked away in San Di-ego. Michelle Bower was very capable, but involving her in the takedown of Coast Guard personnel might raise eye-brows when all was said and done. He'd definitely use Mark's men, but in more of a surveillance capacity, instead of a direct confrontational approach. He thought about using

Frank Cortez, the chief warrant officer in charge of the Port Canaveral Station who was indispensable in dealing with the Warlocks biker gang in Orlando. Joe noticed that Frank had three criminal investigators on his staff for the northern Florida region.

One was a criminal investigator IV, another an actual detective, and one was serving as a police officer at the station. The demographics for northern Florida were much different from the greater Miami and Keys areas, but those officers might fit perfectly into this investigation. In addition, they were geographically removed from the Miami area by over 300 miles and, since two of the three were older and retired from north Florida police departments, now serving in the Coast Guard, it would be a better fit. He could trust Frank implicitly, and he knew that the rear admiral had faith in him as well. Frank had also received a commendation for his actions while helping Joe and Mark in the takedown of the meth operation serving the entire southern eastern seaboard.

Joe decided to call Frank. Jake said he could have all the staff he wanted.

"Hi, Frank. It's Joe Traynor. How are you?"

"Hi, Joe. I'm fine, but what about you? I heard about Mark. Didn't hear much about you but knew you were probably in the middle of something."

"That's why I'm calling. I'm working very quietly on an investigation for the rear admiral. That's why I'm using this burner number."

"I was wondering what that number was and then I recognized your voice."

"I need to see you and pull you and several of your investigators into a very sensitive investigation." Since Joe didn't have time to go up to Port Canaveral, he decided to give Frank the gist of the problem. "Tell me about your investigator, the detective, and the cop."

"Perhaps you may, or may not, be aware, but we're constantly recruiting good cops into the Coast Guard. We don't have military police like the army and marines so this is what we do to bring in qualified men and women. The investigator IV provides me with support for Coast Guard law enforcement and intelligence missions. He conducts both criminal and personal background investigations, collects and analyzes intelligence information, and provides personal protection services to our high-ranking Coast Guard officials and other VIPs up in Jacksonville. His name is Warren Anderson. He's forty-six years old and retired from the Orlando Police Department. He knows Chief Cal Roberts very well. The detective, Jeremy Lock, just retired from the Jacksonville Police Department after twenty years and is forty-two years old. The cop is Jean Gold and is a lot younger at thirty-two. She got tired of the routine and wanted a change. She's from Atlanta, Georgia."

"What kind of assignments do they get involved in?" Joe asked. "I have to be very specific in what I need down here. I'm about to take down four Coast Guard members, immediately, and several insiders in the lower command levels fairly soon. We could probably use their help as well if we catch up with the Colombians, but that would be up to the FBI and Homeland Security folks."

"Assignments we've given all three at various levels of participation have included criminal investigations for crimes relating to Coast Guard missions, interagency law enforcement and liaison operations, investigations into felony violations of UCMJ, protective services operations, and law enforcement information collection. All of these came from the greater Jacksonville to Port Canaveral areas. To enlist in this program, they all attended the Direct Entry Petty Officer Training Course, called DEPOT if you haven't heard of it. They were all graduates of their basic police or criminal investigator academy and had to serve as a law-enforcement officer with a minimum of three years' experience. In addition, once they joined the Coast Guard, they all took correspondence courses and on-the-job training which provided the majority of their required Coast Guard additional training. All three received additional training at the Federal Law Enforcement Training Center in Glynco, Georgia."

"I guess all three are well qualified for what I have to do. You and I can do the interrogations, starting with the first four at the warehouse."

"Where do you stand right now? When would you need us?" Frank asked.

Joe went on to explain that they'd pulled the camera feeds and had isolated the times he thought were crucial. "The drones will be flying so by the end of the week, so I'll need your team in place then."

"Who do I need to clear it with?"

"I'll call the rear admiral and have him call your commanding officer to free the team up. He'll be back by Friday and I want everyone to get together to go over every detail and that includes the rear admiral. The meeting will be at the Broward County airport up in Fort Lauderdale late Friday night."

℘℩℘

Joe and Jack went up to the warehouse area to park and see if anything would happen the first night. Joe doubted it, but you could never tell. The phones in the rear admiral's office wouldn't show any signs of someone listening since Jake wouldn't be back until Friday. Joe needed to think of something they could talk about on their bugged cell phones to see if there would be any chatter or activity that would lead them to the listeners. He hoped the bugs were tied in with the stolen bales, but you never knew until it happened. He also needed a plan to go in and audit the actual bales of cocaine. He felt that Jack lent enough credibility with his title and stature up in Virginia to serve as an auditor and, backed by Frank's team, go into the warehouse during the morning only, for a surprise audit to take samples from each of the bales to see if they actually contained cocaine. They'd also take samples from the disposal bags, which were brought back and matched to the disposal paperwork. There should be traces of cocaine on each bag.

The rear admiral would bring in the warrant officer in charge of the day shift at the warehouse and tell him the ramifications of what would happen if he and his crew told anyone else serving on the other shifts. He'd make it clear that there were going to be several court martials, and those crewmembers could be the first if they let the cat out of the bag. Between now and Friday, Joe would have Jack do a complete financial investigation on each member of each shift to see if there were any unusual financial events. In total, there were three shifts per day with four crewmembers and three separate shifts on the weekend staffed with other teams only working one day a week.

Those weekend crews wouldn't have enough time to set up an operation like this. At least that was what Joe was hoping, at this point. Jack would still do an investigation on each and that totaled twelve individuals during the week and twelve on the weekend or twenty-four to be done by Friday. It was daunting but doable, or so Jack claimed.

They had plenty to do before Friday.

Nothing happened that night at the warehouse between 7:00 p.m. and 8:00 p.m. The cameras were moved at that time both inside and outside, automatically.

CHAPTER 16

It was late Tuesday night, around 11:00 p.m., when Julie got a call from Marcia Manning back in Burbank, California. It was around 8:00 p.m., her time, and she forgot about the three-hours' time difference. Marcia was just leaving her office and emailed Julie a first draft of a contract for the movie and television rights to *Conch Town Girl*.

"Julie, it's Marcia Manning from Disney. I'm so sorry for calling you so late. I completely forgot about the time difference."

"No problem, Marcia. What can I do for you?"

"I just put a first draft of a contract into an email attachment for your review. If you look now, if you will, it should have arrived. I just wanted to make sure you'd gotten it before I went home."

"Just a minute. I have to turn my computer back on. I had just finished a chapter for the second book and I was headed to bed. Got school bright and early every morning. I have to be there by 7:30 a.m. It doesn't leave much time for anything else." Julie turned her computer back on and saw the email from Marcia, which had the attachment labeled *Draft Contract*. "I got it. I'll print it out and read it tomorrow. I'll call you when I'm done."

"That's great. I'm glad it went through. Please read it thoroughly and, if you've any questions, please call me as soon as you can. We're all very excited about this opportunity. I believe the contract is fair and reflects our faith in your book. Good night, Julie. Thanks."

Marcia hung up and Julie decided to print out the contract so she could read it as soon as she got up. She wouldn't act on it until both Joe and Jane read it carefully and they all agreed upon a plan of action. As of now, Julie was reluctant to sign anything, regardless of the signing bonus.

After printing it out, she skimmed the contract, thirty pages of it, and went to the back where the compensation clause was placed. She immediately read that she'd be getting $300,000.00 upon signing the contract. Not bad, she thought. She wondered if she had to sell her soul to get it. She chuckled to herself. She and Tillie had already given up the $300,000.00 they found in Tillie's attic. It was split between her church and the Coast Guard. Neither Julie nor her grandmother wanted any part of it since it was drug money stolen by her father.

Julie immediately checked to see if her contract was based on gross sales. It was. So, it was worth the trip to go up to Miami and review the entire package.

⌦⌫⌦

Julie got up at 6:00 a.m., same as always, and had a quick breakfast with Tillie before Tillie left for the breakfast shift at the Waffle House. No longer having to drive, she walked the two blocks, door to door, from her new apartment. She really loved the setup.

Julie showed her the draft contract. "I'll review it with you tonight or tomorrow. I want to get a hold of Joe and Jane to see if I can drive up after school. Leaving at 2:30 p.m. from the high school, it will take at least an hour and a half, if traffic isn't bad. And it shouldn't be at 3:00 p.m. It's the after work rush hour traffic that's bad. If I can meet Joe and Jane around 4:00 p.m., we could have the contract reviewed by 6:00 p.m. and then go to dinner, if Jane's available."

Joe would take the time if she came up. Julie knew him like a book. Maybe she'd bring an overnight bag since he was staying at the Hampton Inn and Suites right at Brickell Plaza, one block from his office. "I'll call you and let you know what's going on as soon as I know," she told Tillie.

Julie knew Joe was hiding out at the Hampton Inn with Jack because of their investigation, instead of at the condo around the corner, where he usually stayed. The hotel was less than a mile from Jane's law firm, also located on the same street in Miami. Jane was an associate at Clyne, Roberts, and Lynch Law Firm at 800 Brickell, Penthouse One. She'd been there a little over two years but was well thought of by the partners. She was partner material and they all knew it. She was in the contracts and intellectual properties protection division at the firm. This was one of their main bread and butter practices, along with a few other growing divisions, including mergers and acquisitions, employment issues, general corporate governance, litigation management, immigration, and real estate. The firm was a well-known well-established law firm with good connections. It had over 200 employees and room for growth.

Julie picked up her cell phone and called Joe's burner. "Joe, got a minute?"

"Sure. What time is it?"

"It's around 6:00 a.m.," Julie said. "I got my draft contract emailed to me late last night. I printed it out and I'm sending it to you and Jane, by email, as we speak. Do you have time to meet me at Jane's law firm at 4:00 p.m. today? It's important to me, Joe, or I wouldn't ask."

"I know. Have you called Jane?"

"I'm doing it right now on her cell. If she says yes, is it a go? Do you want me to stay over tonight and leave in the morning? Traffic isn't bad at 6:00 a.m. heading to Key Largo."

"I'd love nothing better. Call me right back after you speak to Jane. I'll move my schedule around. The 'birds' are flying, but I don't have to be there. It's nice to be in charge for a change," he said.

"I'll call you back." She then called Jane. She didn't pick up so Julie left a message. "Jane, sorry to bother you so early this morning but I got my preliminary draft contract from Marcia Manning late last night. I emailed it to you. Can you make time to see Joe and me around 4:00 p.m. today? I'll drive up after school if you're available. Maybe we can go to dinner right afterward. I'll stay over if you can make the time."

Then she hung up and got herself together to leave for school. Just as she was leaving, the phone rang. "Hello?"

"Hi, Julie. It's Jane. So you already got the preliminary draft contract, huh?"

"Yes. Can you make time?"

"I'll have to move things around but I'll make time and, if you can eat at 7:00 p.m., I'll meet you and Joe as well. I've a 6:00 p.m. mortgage closing right in my office. We can go to the Plaza and get something to eat right after. Nick will be free as well. Can he come?" Nick Snyder was her husband and a neurologist at Jackson Memorial Hospital in Miami.

"Sounds good. We'll see you this afternoon at 4:00 p.m."

Julie would read the draft contract during breaks and at lunch to see what it actually said. She'd then call Claire Murphy and let her know of her preliminary decision before meeting Joe and Jane. She'd also ask if Marshall received a copy of the draft contract. If he hadn't, Julie would be upset, since it was his recommendation, along with Claire's, that started the ball rolling. Claire might have a good handle on the situation and let Julie know what Marshall thought of the contract before her 4:00 p.m. meeting. That was if he'd gotten a copy. Armed with that knowledge, she could better react with either a counterproposal or simply telling the Disney people that she was going to pass at this time.

Julie knew that Marshall was a little upset when their meeting broke up in Orlando. He wanted it filmed at Hollywood Studios not at Burbank. This contract wouldn't help him and she wondered if she turned it down, would it give Marshall more leverage if there were further negotiations?

✺✺✺

Joe would have to hump today to get some of things done that he wanted to accomplish before 4:00 p.m. He also needed to be very careful while running around during this investigation. Mark was safe but Joe and Jack could very well still be targets of the Colombians. If the drug lords didn't want the investigation to move forward, they could very easily try to stop it once again. That was why Joe wasn't hanging around the headquarters office until the rear admiral came back from Washington. Joe was also worried about this afternoon's meeting with Julie. If he were being followed, she'd once again be in danger. He'd ask Michelle if she had some guys up in Dania Beach who could follow them for the night.

Jack had spent all day doing the financial investigations on the second shift team. He and Joe also selected a few individuals from personnel, security, and intelligence, just to get a feel for the people they could be dealing with. All the second shift team members had excellent credit. Two of them had substantial transactions in and out of their savings. They'd a few CD's as well. None of the funds were exceptional, so perhaps they had cash transactions with the Colombians. Wire transfers would show up, but these members were probably smarter than Jim Butler, the crooked Orlando detective who wired all his funds to a bank in the Cayman Islands. As far as Jack was concerned, he might have well placed a sign on his back, "Need Cash, Call…"

Jack got a JAG warrant, went to every bank in Miami, and checked out the safe deposit boxes. The warrant officer in charge of the second shift had a box at a bank right down the street from his house on the west side of Miami, near Coral Gables. Jack would get another warrant to open the box after they had all of them charged, if they got anything from the drones. Neither Joe nor Jack thought a woman would be involved in this kind of mess, but you never knew. Maybe one of the non-military staff members in personnel or in security had a boyfriend involved. Three of the four on the second shift, all men, weren't married.

Jack pulled financial records for everyone in the personnel, security, and intelligence units in Miami. Three records stood out. A young lady in personnel had just made several deposits into her savings account over the last two months. Each deposit was less than $5,000.00 but there was over $50,000.00 that had moved in and out of her account recently. Two people in security had safe deposit boxes but no substantial cash transactions. He needed to open the their safe deposit box as well.

So, for the present time, Joe and Jack would concentrate on Elana Martinez, the personnel clerk, the four crewmembers on the second shift at the warehouse—especially the warrant officer, the two members of the security unit that had safe deposit boxes, and of course whoever picked up the other end of the phone or listened in on the bugs when the rear admiral came back.

Joe and Jack headed up to Dania Beach to speak to Michelle and her crew. He asked Michelle if she had some men who could follow them for the evening until morning when Julie would leave. Joe wanted them to watch over him and Julie after the meeting at Jane Swanson's. Michelle said sure. Joe had full use of her staff until this investigation was completed. She knew what Mark meant to Joe. He meant the same to her.

Jack would retest the station for bugs, and then the team, together, would call Mark and his family to see how they were doing. Joe wanted to talk to Mike McGreevy as well to make sure that Mark was well covered. The Colombians could certainly reach Mark in San Diego, as easy as they could in Miami—probably even easier.

After the meeting, Joe and Jack headed to the airport to meet the technicians. Michelle followed them in her own car. Joe knew the two staff and would make introductions so that if he weren't around, they had someone to contact in an emergency. Michelle said her guys would be around the lobby when they arrived. Julie didn't know them, but Joe did. Joe also asked Jack to make himself scarce a little later.

Jack laughed. "Why? You got plans?"

"I'd do the same for you, Jack," Joe said with a grin. "That's if I ever get to meet her."

"I'll check downstairs at the front desk and tell them I need a separate room for one night. I'll try to get one on the same floor in case there's a problem. Just don't go banging on the walls all night."

Joe laughed. "I'll try to contain myself, Jack. I can't make any promises for Julie. She's a lot younger, you know. I've got no control over her."

"Sure, Joe. Whatever."

CHAPTER 17

Julie got to Jane's office around 4:00 p.m. She'd been there previously so she knew exactly where to park. Julie was a little nervous about meeting Joe. She wouldn't lie to him. It was just that she'd seen enough danger, caused by her father, and didn't want to deal with more criminals. She'd meet Joe at Jane's office and then move her car to the hotel parking lot at the Hampton Inn.

Joe would leave the meeting by a different route and meet up with her later, just in case he was followed. When she left in the morning for Key Largo, she'd have Jack walk her down to her car, just to be safe. Joe had told her that, at this point, Jack was completely off the radar. No one even knew he was in town, except for the team and the rear admiral.

Julie walked into Clyne, Robert, and Lynch and was greeted by the receptionist at the front. "May I help you," she asked.

"Yes. I've a meeting with Jane Swanson at 4:00 p.m. I'm Julie Chapman."

"Yes, Ms. Chapman. Ms. Swanson told me to show you right to her office as soon as you arrived."

"Has Joe Traynor arrived yet?" Julie asked.

"Yes. He's already arrived and is in Jane's office."

Julie thanked her and was told Jane had a new office right down the hall, second door on the right. She proceeded down the hall, walked into the room, and smiled at Jane and Joe. Both were seated at a conference table. "Nice office. I see you moved up in the world, Jane."

"You could call it that but I didn't get any big bucks to go along with it," Jane said, smiling. "Please make yourself comfortable. I read your contract several times since this morning. Joe said he read it as well. So, we're ready to go."

"Great. As you know, I'm reluctant to sign anything at this point but here is another email I got during the day from Marcia. She wants this wrapped up quickly. She said she'd never seen a book be grabbed up this quickly before. In the email, she wrote that the movie was already greenlit, whatever that means."

"It's a film and television industry term. To 'greenlight' is to give permission or a go ahead to move forward with a project. The term is a reference to the green traffic signal, indicating 'go ahead.' In that context, to greenlight something is to formally approve its production financing and to commit to that financing, thereby allowing the project to move forward from the development phase to pre-production and principal photography. The power to greenlight a project is generally reserved to those in a project or financial management role within an organization. Evidently, Marcia Manning has a lot more power than we could ever have guessed."

Joe listened attentively. He wasn't sure why he was at the meeting, other than as moral support. He knew that Julie wanted to make the right decision and he thought he knew what that decision would be right now. She was going to wait until her three books were finished. He wasn't one hundred percent positive, but once Julie made up her mind, that was it. She'd been like that since the day he met her when she was ten years old. He remembered her saying, "Can I come visit you on your boat?" That was the beginning of their life-long commitment to each other. She made up her mind then, and she'd go through her own process and make up her mind about this as well.

"Have you been involved with movie contracts before?" Julie asked Jane.

"Not like this, but I've done a lot of work in the intellectual property area. I knew you'd ask that question so, if you don't mind, I asked one of our main partners and my direct boss, Sidney Clyne, to come talk to us for a few minutes."

Jane called Sidney into the office and he arrived moments later. He introduced himself to Julie and Joe. "I'm very happy to have you as a new client, Julie. I haven't read your book but I will and I'll give a copy to my wife as well. Unfortunately, we don't have any children. We will dote on Jane's when she decides to start a family."

"Not for a while, Sidney."

Sidney gave Julie and Joe his background and told them about the people he dealt with in the entertainment world, without naming names. He said that was confidential just like her name would be held confidentially. Miami was an entertainment center and he dealt more with professional athletes rather than stars but he had several under contract and two authors who had movie contracts.

That was good enough for Julie.

"Back to your greenlit question," he said as he took a seat at the table. "What it means is that they want to go right to contract. In most cases, probably ninety-eight percent of cases, the producers option a book. That means they purchase the right to buy certain rights to intellectual property, not a complete contract for your book. A typical option fee is five to ten percent of the cost of the rights. In this case, the producers are Walt Disney Motion Pictures Production with full financing for the *Conch Town Girl* project and have it already greenlit. Since this project is already greenlit, they have provided a legally binding guarantee to purchase the film rights. This language is at the end of the proposed contract. Most of the thirty pages in the contract have to do with the chain of title. The chain of title simply means that once purchased, they write the script and own the rights to the derivative work, while you, as the original rights holder, own the underlying rights. This lineage is the legal chain of title. This lineage can become cloudy if the underlying rights are divided. In many cases, producers may purchase the rights to specific countries or they may purchase ancillary rights such as merchandising rights. Is that all clear, Julie?" he asked with a smile.

"It's clear as mud, Sidney. That's why I wanted to meet with Jane and Joe today. You're a welcome addition."

"I only had a few minutes to scan the contract but this is as good as gold. There are no funny provisions that I can see. There's also a significant financial consideration. To pay $300,000.00 initially says that they believe your book, turned into a movie, will be financially rewarding all the way around. However, there are pitfalls, like with everything. They'll have their own screenwriter and they'll adapt your book to the screen. You have no final say about the end production. They've got full control over this movie from the beginning to the end. They also have rights worldwide. If you don't want it to go to China, you've got no control. They're good, smart people who've been doing this for a long time." He paused a moment. "I see you got a percentage of gross, not net, sales. That means they are very serious. But, Julie, they still have full control."

"How will this contract affect my next two books?"

"I've read your original contract with the book publisher. Jane did an excellent job in protecting your rights. That's one reason why you now have the ability to sell your movie and television rights. She had you keep those rights, rather than assigning the rights to the publisher. Also, your contracts for each book are independent of each other. You signed a contract for all three books but you've separate movie rights for all three, along with the auxiliary rights."

"What would happen if I signed this contract and then the movie went in a different direction than what I'd envisioned and then messed up my trilogy *A Girl's Life*?"

"That would be a problem down the road for you. They can do what they want, when they want, and how they want.

You can put in language that you have final say but that wouldn't really mean anything, because it could take years to sort out and could affect your career as a writer."

"That's what I'm afraid of at the moment. What would happen if I turned them down for now with the understanding that once I complete all three books and all three are published as a trilogy, then I'd go ahead with a contract for the entire project, for all three books?"

"Actually, that's not a bad idea. What do you think, Jane?" Sidney asked.

"I believe that it might be the best approach for you now. You're nervous about the future right now. You've got contractual obligations for your books and you're getting married. Perhaps this might be the time to ease the pressure, back off, and then move at your own pace. Disney may not be happy, but that's their issue. You said you were going to call Claire Murphy and Marshall Tillman today. Did you get a chance with everything that's happening?"

"I talked to Claire on my break this morning. She knows that Marshall wasn't happy. He wanted the television or movie production to take place at his studio but he had limited say over that. Perhaps, this could give him more ammunition. I really didn't want to go to Burbank and give up everything I have here but, according to this contract, I don't have to do anything but take the money and run. Do I?"

Sidney shook his head. "You don't have to do a thing. The more wildly popular your books become, and I mean books, not one individual book, they'll come clamoring back, I believe."

"Joe, you've been more quiet than usual. What do you think?" Julie asked.

"Well, first, you should do what's in your heart, and I don't believe, at this moment, this is in your heart or in your best interests. I may be one sided but I don't see the upside at this time, other than getting a check for $300,000.00. That's a lot of money to turn down, but we're doing fine and I think you should wait. You've got my complete support and you know that. Please do what you need to do."

Julie took a deep breath. "I believe you're right. I think I needed to hear it from all of you. All those in favor of turning the contract down at the present time to revisit it later, please raise your hands," she said, laughing. "It's not like we haven't turned down that much money before. You know?"

"I know," Joe said.

"Inside information?" Jane asked.

Sidney appeared curious as well. Behind closed doors, Julie told both Jane and Sidney what had transpired with her father and how they turned over the same amount to the Coast Guard and her church, less than a year ago.

"Wow," Sidney and Jane said at the same time.

"That took a lot of courage, Julie," Jane said. "This would appear to be a lot easier than what you already went through. Tell your story completely and then revisit the movie business."

"I concur," Sidney said.

Julie excused herself and went into Jane's office to call Marcia Manning with the bad news.

扣扣扣

"Hello, this is Julie Chapman calling for Marcia Manning."

"Please hold and I'll connect you," said the switchboard operator.

"Marcia Manning speaking," she said.

"Hi, Marcia. It's Julie Chapman. How are you? Do you have time to talk?"

"Of course, Julie. Fire away."

"I hate to tell you, but I'm not going to sign the contract that you sent me. I'm just not ready at this point. I'm reluctant because I've got too much on my plate at the moment and I have two books left to complete the trilogy that I owe my publisher. I think that this contract is premature, at best. If I go ahead now, it will interfere with the next two books, and we could be on two different paths. For that reason alone, I'm unable to sign in good faith."

"Julie, please tell me that this has nothing to do with Ricardo Gomez's behavior in Orlando. The look on Joe's face was frightening. I offered him a job to train our actors in intimidation techniques."

"No. I couldn't believe the way he acted. Joe was a lot more polite that I thought he'd be. If Ricardo had said what he said in English, I wouldn't have wanted to be him. But since it was in Spanish, Joe took it easy on him because I didn't know what he said at the time. Joe told me later and I wasn't happy, but no, that's not the reason that I can't sign the contract. Also, Claire Murphy who's very close to Joe, as you know, and Marshall Tillman seemed to have been left out of the process, even though they were the initiators of the events that followed."

"I can revisit that if you want, Julie, but it seems that you have more issues than just that."

"I do. I want to ensure that my three books are taken as one tale. That's the way I planned on writing it and that's the way I'd like it portrayed. I just read that the most important thing that a novel and a screenplay have in common is the story. The forms of both are different but the underlying principles and structures are the same. The story should be the heart, regardless of media or genres. The article stated that if you planned to write novels or write, direct, or produce stories on film, it was important that you learn as much about the story as you can. This story isn't complete until the trilogy is done. For that reason, I'm reluctant to sign now."

Marcia sighed. "I guess you really thought about this. Did you review it with Jane?"

"I'm in Jane's office, as we speak. I met with her boss, Sidney Clyne, one of the partners and someone with a lot of experience in this area. Joe was here as well. All of us agreed that this was the step I needed to take at the present time."

"Well, I'm very sad to hear the news but I understand your concerns. What if I get back to my people and I call Marshall and Claire as well? Maybe, we can agree to agree down the road. I don't want to lose you, Julie. So I'll reluctantly back off for the moment and give you time to continue your books, if you promise to keep me informed all along the way."

"I'll certainly do that, Marcia. Thanks for your understanding and consideration. I believe, for now, this is for the best. I'm glad I didn't hear, 'You'll never work in this town again.'"

"I've actually seen that used by a few unscrupulous people here and it never worked. So please don't put me in your book as saying that," she said and started to laugh.

"You got it. Thanks, Marcia. It's appreciated." Julie hung up, feeling as if a load had been lifted from her shoulders. She went back into the conference room and gave all three the thumbs up. All of them wanted to know what happened. She told them and finally felt happy.

ↂↂↂ

Julie went to the hotel in her car and parked in the lot. Bypassing the front desk, she went up to the room and knocked on the door. Jack opened it up. She gave him a big hug and put her overnight bag on the chair. Jack took her coat and she told him what had just happened. Joe was walking back, armed, of course, but taking several twists and turns, in case he was followed.

Jack nodded. He would make himself scarce until morning, when he'd meet Julie at 6:00 a.m. to walk her to her car so she could make it to the Key Largo School on time.

All in all, Julie felt a lot better and more relaxed than

she'd been in a long time. She was sure she'd get a lot of questions at school about her books and the movie rights. She'd tell everyone that everything was moving forward. She just didn't know the timetable at the moment. She was more concerned about Joe, Jack, and Mark than she was about her own issues. She'd had to resolve those issues before she became overwhelmed. Now she'd be fine, as long as Joe was okay. She'd have to live with it until he came home to her.

Chapter 18

Julie made it back to school right before the first bell. She had to meet with Jan to discuss this week's plan. They were right on target in meeting the learning standards, which was a surprise because of the children in their classroom. They'd been behind last year but now, with the new technology-infused lesson plans, the kids were catching on. Hands-on learning was always better with at-risk children. Giving each of these students an iPad to do their lessons was a godsend. Letting them take the iPads home was a little dangerous, but a few lost or stolen iPads was a small price to pay.

Julie had vowed that she'd personally buy new iPads for any children who lost theirs or had the iPads stolen. She'd take the money from her contracts. She still wondered what she'd do with the $300,000.00 if she got a check from Disney for the sale of her movie and television rights. At $300.00 each, she could buy a 1,000 iPads and give them to half the district's students. She could never envision simply taking the money and placing it in a bank account for a rainy day. What a terrible way to live your life. The more you had, the more you had to protect it. The more you had, the more people wanted you for your money. Tillie was right. She couldn't live that way and neither could Julie.

"Hi, Julie. Welcome back," Jan said. "How did your meeting go?"

"If I tell you, will you promise not to say anything? I'm feeling a little strange and I don't want to have to continue to explain myself."

"I promise."

"After meeting with my attorney, her boss, and Joe yesterday afternoon, I called Marcia Manning in Burbank and turned down the contract."

"Why? Are you nuts? You're kidding, right? Tell me you're kidding, Julie."

"No. I'm not kidding. Fortunately, or unfortunately as the case may be, I didn't want my trilogy screwed up by having them make a movie on the first book, instead of the trilogy. When the screenwriter is done, I'd have no control over the results. If the movie went in one direction, it would ruin my next two books. I owe two books to my publisher. I didn't think that was fair to go ahead and not be able to do the best I could. It was that simple."

"I'm afraid to ask but was it for a lot of money?"

Julie laughed. "Yes, it was a lot of money. However, if it's there now, it could still be there later. Marcia understood and said she'd back off until I completed the trilogy. So all is not lost. I haven't completely lost my mind, Jan."

"Oh, well. There goes my hanging on to your coat tails for dear life," Jan said.

"You can still tell everyone that you knew me when I was poor and not famous. It's just continuing for a while."

"Big deal." Jan shook her head and gave Julie a big hug and a kiss. "Let's go get the thundering herd back on track."

Julie was back into her daily routine. The only problem was that Joe wasn't back to his. When he went on an investigation, it was always dangerous, and she never really knew when—or if—he'd be back. It was like being a cop's spouse. Never knowing if you'd ever see your loved one again. She was back at the high school helping to start the iPad program with the ninth graders. It wasn't beneficial starting with the older students because they'd have graduated by the time the entire plan was in place. At least the ninth graders had four years in the new technology-based curriculum to catch on. When they went to college, they'd be on an even par with their more affluent peers throughout the world, not just in the United States.

Julie also had three scheduled appointments with seniors who wanted to understand financial aid and the college experience. Julie had all the information at her fingertips plus her own experience to rely on. The kids really looked up to her. They knew that she had their best interests at heart and that it just wasn't a job to her.

She took a few moments to say a prayer of thanks to the Lord for helping her, hopefully, make the right decision to avoid the movie business right now. She really had too much on her plate. When she finished her next book after cross-country season, she could then be in a better position to articulate what the third and final book would look like and where it would end up. Like most writers, especially Brown University writers, she'd learned to reach out for the ending before moving straight forward. The term was Imagineering. It meant to reach out as far as you could to envision what your end result would look like without viewing any of the linear impediments along the way. If you had a three-year plan or even a five-year plan, you could review your destiny backward and then envision what you needed every step of the way, based on your end result. There were always impediments but those became known more clearly when you worked backward. Some called the process Reengineering. Julie learned to create fishbone diagrams that looked like a fish with no flesh, just the bones. The bones became labeled steps of things that could occur, frontward and backward. You could then isolate the problems and attack those issues when they arose, labeling each step so it became visible. It was a very helpful tool. Joe showed her the process that he'd learned in his MBA program at Rensselaer.

☙

After cross-country practice, Julie arrived at Tillie's around 5:00 p.m. She was still living with Tillie for the time being. It was close to her first stop at Key Largo School in the morning.

Some things never changed. Tillie still woke her up and made her breakfast. She was getting a lot better, though. She wasn't lecturing Julie anymore. It was almost like a truce. Tillie knew that she'd better treasure the time she had left with Julie since she'd be getting married and moving in with Joe. Now, it was hit or miss with her staying with Joe some nights. But as long as Joe was away, this worked out fine.

The phone rang. "I'll get it," Tillie said.

"Hi, Tillie. It's John Traynor. How are you?"

"Good, John. How are you feeling? Are you better?"

They'd both had concussions in the not-too-distant past. Both were in critical condition but both survived with their memories, long-range and short-range, fully intact. It was touch and go for a while. Both were placed in induced comas, which saved their lives. They seemed to be kindred spirits now.

"I'm doing great and back to work almost full time. Not because of my health but because I don't want to work so much anymore. I could get used to retirement. How about you?"

"I'd go crazy being a hundred percent retired. I only do the breakfast shift now and I come in for dinner once in a while. I love it here. It's close to everything, including my work, my friends, and church, of course."

"That's great to hear," John said. "Can I speak to Julie? Is she there?"

"She just walked in a few minutes ago. I'll get her." Tillie handed the phone to Julie. "It's John Traynor."

"Hi, John. How are you? Are you looking for Joe? He's on an investigation and won't be back for a while."

"Actually, Julie, I'm looking for you. Do you have a minute?"

"Of course."

"I know you were thinking about getting married at St. Patrick's Cathedral in New York City and holding a ceremony down in Key Largo at your church the following month. Is that still the plan? Joe told me that the last time we spoke. It's been a while."

"Yes, that is what we planned. And I just saw Joe in Miami yesterday, John. He's in a critical investigation for the rear admiral. He and Jack are undercover for now. You know about the shooting, of course?"

"Yes. He called Peter and me as soon as it happened from the hospital when Mark was in surgery. I take it they're both okay?"

"Yes, of course. Mark got shot but Joe seemed to have taken out two cars with gangbangers on I-95 N heading to Fort Lauderdale. He really can't talk about it, though."

"Well, here's why I'm calling you. I don't believe that you know of our Catholic Church connections. Getting married in St. Patrick's is no easy feat. As a matter of fact, there's a three-year waiting list for weddings, even for small ones. Joe asked me to check into something. Perhaps you didn't know that the bishop of the Roman Catholic Diocese of Albany is a very close friend of mine. He actually grew up in Lansingburgh, right around the corner from me. His parents were very close friends with mine and I played baseball with the bishop. He went to an all-boys high school and I went to Catholic High, the same as Joe."

"I didn't know that," Julie said.

"So I just saw my friend the bishop this week at the cathedral in Albany. He invited me down for lunch with a few of our old friends. We'd a great time and I mentioned your preference of getting married at St. Patrick's. He knows Joe, of course, and he watched his baseball career at Catholic High. He actually showed up for a few of Joe's games. You know about Joe's specialty of picking off runners on first base, don't you?"

"He told me about it. Not much, you know Joe."

"The bishop was fascinated by Joe's prowess in those tight situations and saw him pitch a lot. As a matter of fact, Joe would never tell you, but his major recommendation for MIT was the bishop," John continued. "The bishop is a close friend of the new cardinal in the Roman Catholic Archdiocese of New York. He called his friend and asked if you could be married on May sixteenth next year at noon at Saint Patrick's Cathedral. That's the date that Joe told me. Is that all right? The cardinal said it was approved. I told him there would only be about thirty guests. Is that right, too?"

"Is it all right? I love you, my favorite future father-in-law," Julie said, jumping up and down in the kitchen. "Are you kidding? That's great. I'm so pleased and I know that Joe will be, as well."

"I hope Joe will be pleased. He asked me, of course. That's the first thing he asked me to do since he went to college and I called the bishop for the recommendation. It's only been about sixteen years since his last request. By the way, not to take away any thunder from Pete, but you might be attending another wedding next summer as well. Don't say anything to Joe. But I just had to tell someone. I love you, Julie Chapman. I love Tanya Fields, as well. My boys are the luckiest guys around, I'll tell you."

Julie was so pleased that she was bursting at the seams. She ended her call to John, thanking him over and over again. Evidently, someone that she had prayed to had answered all her requests. Every Sunday, she'd light a candle to St. Jude and say the Rosary at mass. She'd then request that God and her favorite saints would watch over her family, and now Joe's. She was beside herself with joy for the first time in quite a while. Joe would be so pleased. All her stress seemed to leave her body and left her in a sudden state of joy.

"What're you so excited about? Tell me," Tillie said. She hadn't seen Julie that happy since she came home that day a long time ago after meeting Joe at Career Day when she was ten years old. She couldn't contain herself then and she couldn't now.

Julie just hugged her and then told her what happened.

Tillie was as pleased as Julie. She hadn't been to New York since she and Julie flew up for Joe's mother's funeral. That had only been to Albany, not to New York City. "Who're the thirty guests?" she asked.

"Let me get my list." Julie went into her room and got out her pad. "First, there's you, Tillie. Then there's Joe's father, brother, and Tanya Fields, Pete's girlfriend. There will be Mark and Louise and the kids. That's four more. Jack, Mike McGreevy, and Sean O'Neil, Joe's original Coast Guard team. Tom Jones, unfortunately, is deceased, but we're inviting Claire and Brian Murphy, not the kids. That's thirteen. There's Maddy and her fiancée, Kevin White, and her parents. That's four more. Now seventeen. We're inviting Dan Simmons and his girlfriend, Jane Swanson and her husband Dr. Nick Schwartz. There's, of course, Joan and Jeff Talbot and Lucy is in the wedding. Jeff, Jr. is in college and will be in the middle of final exams, then. I also want Jimmy Smith, our cross-country coach and his wife, and Jan Marino and her husband as well. We're also inviting Rear Admiral Jake Barnes and his wife but we're not sure they'll make it. That's thirty right on the nose. We still would like to invite Johnathon Mills and his wife. He was so kind to Joe when Joe worked in Troy at the Education Consulting group. I probably should invite my dean from Brown University and my publisher in New York City. I'm sure we can use their apartment that week so that will certainly help. We'll invite our pastor, Fr. Schmidt, of course, but I doubt he'd come. He could assist with the ceremony if he did. I want to ask him personally now that we know the date. He and the church volunteers were a tremendous help to you when you were in the hospital and even when you got home."

"I could never repay them for their kindness, Julie."

"I guess the list will be around thirty-five now, if those

people come that we wouldn't expect to attend. We're also having a ceremony down here in Key Largo on Saturday, June twentieth for your friends, my friends at school, and for all the volunteers at church. When I invite Fr. Schmidt to the New York City wedding, I'll check the date for the St. Justin Martyr Church schedule. We will hold the reception right at the church hall. There will be around 125 people, hopefully. I almost forgot, Tillie. I turned down the movie offer from Disney for now. It was a lot of money, but I wasn't comfortable where we were at this time. Marcia Manning said they'd hold off for now. I hope she meant it. If not, we will see what happens when I'm finished the trilogy."

Tillie put her arm around Julie's shoulders. "You've got so much going on, that should be the last thing on your mind. By the way, what's going on with Joe? He was closed mouth when I talked to him the other day."

"There's an ongoing investigation that could include several internal Coast Guard officers and enlisted men who could go to jail. He can't say much but I know he's in danger. Mark was shot, and you knew that, but Joe was almost killed on I-95 N near Fort Lauderdale. You know Joe. He anticipated it and took out two cars of gangbangers before they lifted a finger. I really don't know how he knows."

CHAPTER 19

Joe spoke to the rear admiral on their burner phones, early Friday morning. Jake was coming back to Miami from Washington DC later in the afternoon. Joe told him that they were meeting the drone team at the airport near Fort Lauderdale at 8:00 p.m. that night. The rear admiral would call Joe when he arrived in Miami and two of the four men from Dania Beach station would follow him from the airport to headquarters on Brickell. They'd wait around until he was ready to leave for Fort Lauderdale a little after 7:00 p.m.

"Don't use your office phone or talk about anything sensitive with your staff until after the meeting tonight," Joe reminded him.

He was sure that the rear admiral's top two staff members were fine but he hadn't cleared his assistant at this point. "The drones are in place but nothing has happened at the warehouse this week."

He knew that a fresh start on Monday could prove the difference. Whoever was listening in on the wiretap in the rear admiral's office might become complacent and start up their plan once again. This time, Joe and the crew would be waiting. It was clear to him that it was the second shift because of the simple camera maneuvers between 7:00 p.m. and 8:00 p.m. every night. It wasn't the outside cameras that made Joe suspicious. It was the inside cameras that made all the difference. To Joe and to Jack, keeping that north side door unprotected told them everything they needed to know. Having no cameras in the actual locked area that held all the bales showed a total lack of concern for the security of the confiscated cocaine. At $825,000.00 a bale or fifty-five pounds at $15,000.00 per pound, at wholesale value, Joe thought they should have come up with better security than they had. Following a ten-year-old security policy without updates and new technology equipment to oversee the protection of the secured material was unforgiveable negligence.

Joe got to the Broward County airport a little after 7:00 p.m. He wanted to be there early to meet with the drone team first and then be there when the rest of the team members and the rear admiral showed up. Joe had learned from his father that if you took ownership of anything, you were the first to arrive and the last to leave. No questions asked. He parked and walked into the same hangar that they'd used previously for the Russian investigation. The same two technicians from Dallas turned around from their computer screens and waved to Joe as he walked into the small hangar office. Everyone would be meeting later at the two picnic tables in the hangar.

Michele Bower was coming. Joe trusted her implicitly. There were two other men from Dania Beach who worked previously with Joe, not including the two assigned to follow the rear admiral.

In addition, Jack would be there. He had other assignments on the financial side that he wanted to complete before he got to the meeting. He rented a Hertz car during the day for the next week. He knew that he and Joe would be doing different things. He didn't want anyone to know he was around so he certainly couldn't ask for a government car. He covered his own bills, just like all the other times. If he needed money, Joe would provide everything he needed. He knew that but wouldn't ask. That was just the way he was. He was the same as Joe in personality but even a little more intense. He had to be. He was the inventor and implementer of clandestine stuff. He had to keep everything close to the vest.

Frank Cortez and his three key team members would also be there. The investigator, the detective, and the police officer would all come down separately because they'd be assigned to separate people who they'd have to follow. Those people being followed were the members of the warehouse second shift, the personnel clerk, and a few individuals in the security office. At this point, they hadn't pinpointed who was responsible for bugging the rear admiral's office but they had a pretty good idea what kind of skills were required to pull it off. The first wave included staff from personnel and security. They'd work their way through the rest after those investigations were completed.

Everyone had arrived on time, including Jack. The rear admiral was last and was followed in the door by the two men from Dania Beach. "Joe, did you have me followed here?"

"Yes, sir. Your office was bugged and I didn't want to take a chance that you might be followed. Did you ever see the shadows behind you?"

"No, I didn't. That's good and bad. I'm glad they were there, but I'm mad that I didn't pick them up all the way from Miami to here."

"Sir, they're trained for that. You're not."

Everyone sat down at the picnic tables. Joe began an overview of what had happened to date and made everyone swear a pledge to the rear admiral that nothing would be repeated that was discussed at this meeting. Never. Joe introduced the two drone technicians and discussed what they'd be doing and how they'd function as part of the team. The main part was for them to manage the surveillance drones at the corners of the warehouse and stay alert if there was any activity, especially from 7:00 p.m. to 8:00 p.m. during the weekend. Joe didn't believe that the weekend part-time crews were involved. He told the team that if there was any activity at all, the large drone would be immediately launched and would follow any vehicles that were caught on camera. The drone was launch-ready and would be at the Miami facility within four minutes of launch time. In addition, the surveillance drones would feed all their information into the armed drone so that timing would never be an issue. The main drone would have the GPS coordinates. It was flying so high that no one would ever know it was there.

Michelle stared at him with her mouth open. "Joe, that's amazing."

"Your own guys, led by Mark, saw it happen in person when the drone took out the Russian limousine."

The men just nodded in agreement. One said, "It was a thing of beauty. It was like watching your kid's video game. It happened so fast that everyone was stunned, even though we knew it could happen."

Joe gave everyone his or her assignments for the next few days. "Things can change on a dime. So be prepared if our plans get screwed up." He turned to Jake. "Rear Admiral, do you have anything to say to the team members?"

"Yes, Joe. I do. I'm very proud of all of you, especially you, Michelle, for jumping right in to take Mark's place. Your men are the best and have already proven it before. Frank, thanks for bringing your team. Your team's criminal investigation and good police work experience will prove invaluable, not just in stopping the leak, but in closing down the second shift and, hopefully, the Colombians at the same time. I also want you to know that Joe and Jack, who are running this investigation, have my complete support. I've never seen such loyalty in all my thirty years in the Coast Guard. I take full responsibility for the problems we're facing and I want you to know that I'll go to any length to fix this. You've got my word on that."

They all clapped for the rear admiral and he shook hands with everyone in the room. Then everyone left for their assignments while the two drone technicians went back to their office. Joe and Jack stayed behind to talk to the rear admiral. Joe needed to make sure that he knew exactly what he needed to say and do while acting like nothing was going on during the next few days.

Jake nodded in agreement. "Joe, and, Jack, I can't thank you enough for what you've already done and are doing to end this nightmare. How is Mark, by the way? His family?"

"They're doing fine, sir. Mike McGreevy and his crew are watching the family twenty-four-seven. I was worried about them going to San Diego because it was that much closer to the Colombians. However, Mike has assured us that they're fully protected and will be until this over. Mark is recovering but has a ways to go with physical therapy on his arm and shoulder before he's back to fully functional. He's a little worried that he'll be forced to retire. He needs the money, sir. He's got two kids who'll be in college before long."

"I'll call Mark tonight on the burner and assure him that won't happen. He literally took a bullet for me and I won't forget that, Joe. I know you took a bullet up in Albany as well. How could I ask any more of you than what you've already done?"

"Thanks, sir. But let's start the ball rolling. We need a plan to get the listeners off their asses so we can pinpoint where they're located. Jack, tell him how it's done, will you?"

Jack went through the steps on how he'd trace the bug back to its source. Then they left the building and took three separate cars back. It might have been a little extravagant, but having someone wipe out all three at one time in one car could severely curtail their activities. Joe remembered what he told the rear admiral when asked why he shot up the two gangbangers' cars. Joe had said it was easier to report his findings if he was alive.

CHAPTER 20

J ack had gone through a list of over thirty names who could have potentially been involved in either the bugging of the rear admiral's office or the theft of cocaine. They still hadn't proved that the bales came from the warehouse on MacArthur Causeway, but they were pretty sure, after reviewing the camera angles and discovering the switch indoors and outdoors at the north end of the building between 7:00 p.m. and 8:00 p.m. The drones were hovering over the entire facility with a focus on that end of the building. If, and when, anything transpired they'd be ready.

After the financial investigation, Joe and Jack had decided to hone in on a handful of staff who not only had access but the experience, capability, and connections required to pull off this operation. They had Saturday and Sunday to continue this end of the investigation before the rear admiral got back to his desk and started to make calls that could be traced by Jack. On Monday, tracing the bugged calls back to the source was paramount to the investigation.

So far, the persons cleared were Captain Bert Jennings, second in command, and Petty Officer George Pagan, third in command. The rear admiral was also investigated, just to be even-handed. He'd have the most to lose if he was involved.

Joe and Jack decided that none of the three were involved. They also looked into the rear admiral's administrative assistant and warrant officer, Al Cummings. He was a pain in the ass but his issues stemmed from feeling a little superior and better than those coming in to meet with the rear admiral. *He's clean but still a pain in the ass.* Cummings had no in-the-field experience but was inherited by Jake from the previous retiring rear admiral.

Next, they scoured all the units reporting into the seventh district. A full investigation was done on everyone in security, personnel, and administration. Not only were financial records reviewed, but also cell phone records, landline, and emails were all checked. There were some unusual findings. In the personnel department, Elana Martinez, age thirty, Hispanic, single, with no children, had been making a few large deposits into her account over the last few months. Not over $5,000.00 each but ten deposits between $3,500.00 and $4,500.00. There was a cash transaction for $4,250.00 on the exact day that Mark and Joe were attacked.

Elana had been in the department for eight years, had an associates' degree from Miami Dade College in business, was a civilian employee, and lived in North Miami Beach. Her office was at 100 MacArthur Causeway, the same location in a complex with security, other administrative offices, and the warehouse holding the bales of cocaine. She'd also had emails to Andy Marino, the district security manager who was located one building away. Phone records, including cell and landline, showed over twenty calls to Andy within that week and one of her emails had two attachments on that exact day. Jack had some work to do to get the attachments but he was working on it.

Joe thought the attachments might be pictures and information on both Mark and himself. If that were the case, it would be a real break. The rest of the administration and personnel unit appeared to come up clean with no major indicators of any involvement. Joe had to shake his head on several of the files that they'd reviewed. Cases of arrests for DWI, child support, restraining notices, and public intoxication popped up. "Don't they ever update these files to see if those working for them still meet all the qualifications—like no arrests?" Joe asked Jack.

Jack chuckled. "You'd be shocked what I've come up with over the years on things people do that no one knows about. You've no idea the kinds of human frailty I uncover. It would shock you."

"I'll bet it would," Joe said.

They went back to their review. "Andy Marino is district security manager for the seventh district," Jack said a few minutes later. "Lo and behold, he's also located in a different building at 100 MacArthur Causeway. He's Hispanic, age thirty-five, divorced with one daughter, age five. He started as a guard at age twenty-five and has ten years of service. He has an associates' degree from Broward County Community College in public administration. He lives in Hialeah, which is just a little northwest of Miami. He received the emails from Elana. Those calls and emails were recorded on his computer and equipment. Look on the chart and you'll see that we have all the phone numbers traced."

"So either they're lovers or in cahoots, or both," Joe mused.

"Looks like it, anyway."

"We will need to trace any calls or emails from his office to anyone outside the Coast Guard. It would be nice if we ran his call list through the computer white pages website and Colombian Drug Cartel popped up. You know? That could tie the bugging of the rear admiral to the theft."

"What're you on, crack, Joe? Huh? Shall we move on, you poor misguided public servant?" Jack shook his head and continued. "We also checked his bank accounts. There are none locally but he has two safe deposit boxes at a bank near his home in Hialeah. We will need a court order to get those opened. I also discovered that he opened an account in the Cayman Islands and transferred several thousand dollars into it in the last few weeks. There wasn't much, but I need to go into that account to see what's transpired over the last several months. It's like we're eighty-five percent done with everything but nothing ties until we get that one hundred percent on something. It's like freaking Sudoku, where one number leads to another. I'm hooked, you know?"

"I'm well aware of that, Jack. Well aware," Joe commented with a grin.

"Shall I go on?"

Joe cleared his throat and stifled a laugh. "Yes, sir. I really have been paying attention, sir."

"Next. Dwayne Bullard is the command security officer for the entire seventh district. He's Caucasian, age forty-two, married for fifteen years, and has two daughters, ages thirteen and eleven. He joined the Coast Guard after receiving his BS degree from Nova University in criminology. He's been with the seventh district for twenty years in Miami and is eligible for full retirement. He may just be retired after this fiasco, even if he wasn't involved. He should have been more vigilant. He lives in Coral Cables, in the same house for the last ten years, and is one hundred percent clean, as far as his financial records are concerned. He had one disciplinary action in his jacket—for harassment over ten years ago. He's been nothing but a model employee since."

Jack paused for a quick breath. "Let's discuss the second shift, which seems to be our main focal point. There are four men assigned to that shift. Let me give you their background. Colton Gilley is the chief warrant officer in charge of the warehouse for the second shift. He's Caucasian and a good old boy redneck, who likes to go to bars around town. He's thirty-eight years old with a high school diploma and he's a graduate from the Miami Police Academy. He spent six years as a Miami cop, is divorced, and has a son, Neal, age fourteen, who lives with his mother in Fort Lauderdale. He's been with the Coast Guard for twelve years. Neal is a ninth grade high school student. Let's say Mr. Gilley's jacket shows a preponderance of hothead encounters. He's been disciplined three times but never had any other complaints. His bank accounts are another matter. He only has a checking account that receives his paychecks automatically. He leaves a hundred dollars in the account to keep it open. That's the minimum balance required. That tells me a lot. That tells me that he's hiding his money from his ex-wife."

"The scumbag," Joe quipped.

"The clerk in charge of all the paperwork processing and shipping is Grant Akers. Mr. Akers is of mixed heritage, Caucasian and Cuban, is thirty-four, married for two years for the second time to Felicia. They live right in Miami. He started college at Miami Dade College and dropped out after his first year. He bummed around for a while, working as a cashier in a local supermarket. Evidently, he had a family friend in high places and got this job three years ago. His first wife left him after a beating and he was locked up but released after she dropped the complaint. He's deposited about $20,000.00 in several accounts in the last year. I'll bet, Joe, that this has been going on for some time and what we found was a really good thing for these bastards, except somebody got greedy."

"I'll bet you're right, Jack."

"The next two individuals are the armed guards, securing the facility on this shift. The job doesn't require a lot. They're paid very well but, in fact, are no different than mall cops with guns. The training they received lasted six weeks, less than twenty-five percent of a police academy standard. Who approves this shit, anyway? I'm really starting to get mad. Our administrators have guys who barely got their GED guarding eighty million dollars in street value cocaine. As a matter of fact, Rico Fejos, Hispanic, age twenty-six, barely got out of high school at age nineteen. He lives in Miami, not married, and has no kids. His career isn't going anywhere. These are the same people who're recruited to join the gangs in Miami. They've no experience, are uneducated, and are given an assault weapon."

"Wow. Who's last?"

"Last is Jevon Carter, African American, age twenty-three, single, and just got his GED. He lives in Homestead, in a not-so-nice area. He's been here three years as well. He came on board at the same time as the clerk, Grant Akers. That's our crack warehouse team for the second shift. I never did a deep search on the other shifts but how could they be any different? There's a huge problem. Maybe, Petty Officer George Pagan has been here for a long time, but it appears that his knowledge of personnel, job descriptions, requirements for service, and simple common sense, may be missing. I think we found our next retiree, Joe."

Joe rubbed at the back of his neck to ease the tension building there. Not that it helped. "I think we've enough to go on now. Let's concentrate on the people we just reviewed. On Monday, we'll trace the bugs, if possible, and match the end with these phone numbers. We can also do a GPS search on the end if none of these phones are used. Then we can go to the location, dial the number, which no doubt will be a burner number, and then walk in as the phone rings. Sound like a plan?"

Jack grinned. "Good starting point."

"I think they'll get careless on the second shift. And $825,000.00 a load is nothing to sneeze at. I'll bet they do at least one more shipment out and then you'll go to the warehouse as a surprise audit and check each bale to see if the bales actually contain cocaine. I believe there's a switch involved. I don't know how, at this point, but if they're caught, not on camera but by our drone surveillance, we will know what they're doing. We need to audit all the ins and outs, since these 130 bales went into inventory. We need to check each empty bale bag to see if the bales that were supposedly destroyed actually contained cocaine. At least we now have a very good idea as to what's going on."

CHAPTER 21

Joe called Julie on Sunday night as Monday would be a big day. He wanted to know how she was doing after turning down the movie contract. It was fine to do mental gymnastics and make yourself believe that you were doing the right thing, but it was still hard to turn down a lot of money after you'd worked so hard. At least Julie knew her priorities. At twenty-four years old, her priorities were a lot straighter than his. He seemed to go from one crisis to another, every single day. He constantly put himself in harm's way. Why did he do that, especially now that he was marrying the love of his life? After this investigation, he needed to sit back and think about their future together, a lot more than he had. He'd been running from day to day since he came back to the Keys to be with Julie after Tillie almost died. There hadn't been a day gone by that didn't have some kind of trauma. It would be nice to plan a week out in advance that didn't have anything to do with criminals, drugs, and flying bullets.

"Hi, Julie. Do you have time to talk? Sorry I'm so late. I just got done working and I thought I'd see how you're doing. I miss you," he added.

"Hi, Joe. Everything here is fine. I was just finishing the next chapter in book two, the middle years. Let me fill you in on what's transpired since the meeting with you, Jane, and Sidney. Your father called me about the wedding."

"Really? What did he say?"

"Was it supposed to be a surprise, Joe? Did your father blow it?"

"Evidently."

"We'd a nice long chat. He even talked to Tillie at length. He seemed very pleased. I think he likes me more than you, his own son."

"What a shock. I ask him for one favor since I was eighteen years old and he blows it. Nice."

"We got St. Patrick's Cathedral for May sixteenth at noon. Our second wedding in Key Largo will be scheduled in June if Father Schmidt approves, and I believe he will. I also think we can get the publisher's apartment in New York City from that Wednesday before the wedding until the following Saturday. I can do a little justification for using the publisher's apartment by handing her my third and final book in the trilogy. Wouldn't that be great? All our hard work would be done and we could enjoy ourselves for the first time in a long time."

"That's terrific. I'll call my father and thank him. I wish he told me first but no harm—no foul. It's nice to have friends in high places and I mean very high places. It doesn't get much higher than the bishop and cardinal."

"You got that right. I'm so pleased. I'm also glad that I took the movie business off my plate. I couldn't handle all that pressure at the same time. It will also give us time to look for rings, like you wanted. I know I put it off but now I've got no excuse. I'd also like to start looking for a small house near Islamorada or even in Key Largo if there's anything affordable. I heard you about buying Tillie's old home. But it holds too many bad memories that I don't want to be stirred up again."

"What the hell? Do you have a check list or something," he said, laughing.

"I learned from the best."

"You haven't seen Jack in action. He makes me look laid back, for God sake. His lists are ten times longer than mine, if you can believe it. Mark's a breath of fresh air compared to Jack. Mark goes with the flow. Nothing ever bothers him. He's the exact opposite of Jack. Yet, we're all good friends. Who'd have thought?"

"Speaking of Mark, Louise, and the kids, have you talked to them?"

"Actually, not for any length of time. Mike McGreevy has been filling me in on the family. The Hardings are fine as well. Toni and Mark's mother get along great."

"Joe, I have to go. I promised Tillie that I'd go through a bunch of wedding items with her. I know she's giving me away since I don't have a father or mother, but I was thinking of making her my matron of honor along with Maddy as maid of honor. I haven't asked her yet, but what do you think? I'm whispering because she's in the backroom changing the bed."

Joe laughed. "I think that would be great. As I was lectured to by Mark, I should just agree to everything and my life will be wonderful. If I don't, he said it could be a living hell."

"Mark is a very smart man. Bye, Joe. Call me when you get a chance. I love you. By the way, Lucy is ranked number one in Florida in girls' cross-country. She's come a long way."

"Bye, Julie. I love you too. Tell Lucy that's great. Please say hello to Joan and Jeff as well. I really miss everybody. I still want to talk to you about my career in the Coast Guard after this operation. I can't keep running around getting shot at with no plans for the future."

"I agree, Joe. Let's talk about it when you get back."

With that, they both hung up.

⌘

Joe spoke to the rear admiral around 11:00 p.m. on their burner phones. They set up a plan to talk on their bugged phones early Monday morning. In addition, they devised a phony plan, whereby the rear admiral would meet with his staff and discuss plans for moving and consolidating several offices and the warehouses over on MacArthur Causeway. He'd give his direct staff duties involving the potential moving of personnel in those areas, including personnel, administration, safety and security units, the port management staff, and the warehouse affiliated personnel. "I'll simply tell my staff that after meeting with the admiral in Washington DC, it was decided that we need to cut costs across the board and consolidate our facilities in the greater Miami area."

Joe laughed. "If that doesn't shake the crap out of everyone, nothing will."

Neither one could think of a better plan to get the troops riled up. The only other plan would include forced retirements or pay cuts for the civilian staff. If this phony plan generated movement, Joe would expect that the investigation would generate good results by the end of the week.

It hinged on the drones picking up movement outside the warehouse between 7:00 p.m. and 8:00 p.m. and tying back the bugging devices to the source. More than likely, the second shift would increase their activity if they knew the warehouse was going to be shut down soon.

Getting the Colombians would be a completely different matter. If the drone found where the pickups went, then they'd have to contact the FBI and put into place several different layers of investigative services, including Homeland Security, the FBI, and maybe even the Miami Police Department.

"These are happy consequences," Joe told Jake. "It's like having a problem with too much money. It's a nice problem to have."

〜❧〜

Rear Admiral Jake Barnes met with Captain Bert Jennings and Petty Officer George Pagan, with Al Cummings taking notes. During the meeting, as planned, Joe called the rear admiral on their bugged phones as they discussed the potential shut down of various facilities and other cost-cutting measures.

As the call was taking place, Jack had his line connected to the Super Sweep 2000. During the conversation, the machine picked up line static and started tracing it back to the source.

The static ended and the machine, attached to Jack's high-powered computer, showed the ending coordinates and telephone number of the bug, simultaneously.

Jack gave Joe the "okay" sign, and Joe ended the call rather abruptly. Joe had already coordinated with the rear admiral that if he brought up the *Miami Heat* in the discussion, it meant that Jack got the GPS coordinates for the source and the telephone number at the other end.

The rear admiral immediately told Joe that he was in a meeting and would talk to him later. He gave no indication to the staff at the meeting that anything was going on, other than that he was very abrupt with Joe. Al Cummings smiled at the exchange.

The rear admiral noticed his little smirk and made a mental note of it. Joe was right. Al Cummings wasn't Joe's biggest fan. *Little does Mr. Cummings know that Joe's in the process of saving his ass.*

Joe turned to Jack "What did you get?"

"I got the ending coordinates and the cell number which is 786-210-9010. I just went to my source codes for phone numbers and it's a burner number. That's fine because the GPS coordinates say that the cell phone is located at 100 MacArthur Causeway. As a matter of fact, it looks like the call went to the security office. Can't tell who made it but that's where it went."

"What do you know, Jack? That's where personnel, administration, safety and security are located. With the heads up about closing the facilities, I'll bet we see a lot of calls generated from that location. Can you stay on top of all of them?"

"Actually, no. But I can call my guys up in Virginia and run all the phone calls through my system up there. If the burner number shows up anywhere else, we got them. By the way, I just looked at the call sheet for those we suspect. That phone has called Elana Martinez twelve times over the last two weeks. She called that number back the same amount of times. There's no mistake. There's a definite connection."

"Is it premature to go over to MacArthur, dial the number, and see where it rings?"

"Do you want to do that now or wait and see if we get any activity at the warehouse?"

"I honestly don't think we will get a better shot than this anytime soon. If we hear the ringing on the burner, all we have to do is pick up the person closest to the phone. However, as soon as we do that, we need to pick up the personnel clerk, Elana Martinez. We can have Frank and his team bring her up to Port Canaveral and put her in a separate interrogation room. We'll do the same to whoever is in security. They've got lockup facilities up there, and they'll be sufficiently isolated to keep them away from the second shift guys. The security guy can be court martialed, but I'm not sure about the civilian. I downloaded court martial procedure. You can court martial a civilian employee working for any branch of the armed services, but only if they're working outside the continental United States. We need to bring in the FBI as soon as we can and they can determine if her actions are local or federal crime based. What do you think?"

"Sounds like a plan."

"Let me call the rear admiral on his burner. We've got a code that I let it ring twice and he'll go outside and call me back as soon as he can."

A few minutes later, Joe's burner rang. "Joe, got your beep. What's up?"

"We got the GPS and burner number. We will pick up Elana Martinez on the way and have Frank and Jean Gold bring her up to Port Canaveral. I'll take the other two, Jack, and two of Michelle's men and go to the security office where the GPS coordinates say the phone is located. The other two of Michelle's men will stay on the second shift guys for the day.

"Do you need me to come with you?"

"Not at this time, sir. Hang loose, though, I've got a feeling that things will be coming to a head very shortly."

"Call me when you need me. Thanks, Joe."

Joe and Jack headed to the MacArthur facility. He called Frank and told him to pick up Elana Martinez at her personnel office and to use Jean Gold so there would be no sexual harassment charges. "Don't say a word. If she doesn't cooperate, put her in cuffs and drag her out."

Frank was on board. Joe told him to send the other two guys to meet them outside the MacArthur Causeway Coast Guard gate in twenty minutes.

CHAPTER 22

Joe and Jack met Frank's two team members at the gate. Two of Michelle's men were also called in to action. The other two were still following the warrant officer and the clerk on the second shift. They believed the two armed guards were involved but were following the lead of the higher ups. It didn't mean that they weren't dangerous, however. They all walked in, separated by a few minutes. One of Michelle's men stayed at the front door of the facility and the second covered the back, in case someone took off after the confrontation. Frank and Jean Gold were next door, all ready to take custody of Elana Martinez as soon as Joe called.

Joe and Jack stood outside the security office door and Joe dialed the burner cell number that was picked up by Jack. They were anxiously waiting, hoping for the best. If the phone didn't ring, they'd have to bluff their way through, which could prove fatal for any conviction.

A phone inside the office rang. Joe looked at Jack and the two investigators and nodded. "Let's go." He opened the door just as Andy Marino answered the burner cell. *Thank God.*

Marino turned around with a puzzled look on his face. "Can I help you, gentlemen?"

With guns drawn, Joe said, "Are you Andy Marino, district security manager for the seventh?"

"Yes, I am. Who are you?"

"Mr. Marino, you're under arrest under the United States Military Code for so many illegal activities, I don't know where to begin."

There was no reading of any Miranda Rights. Joe took a napkin out of his pocket, went to Marino's desk, picked up the burner phone, and placed it carefully into an evidence bag. Andy Marino was seized by the two investigators and placed in handcuffs behind his back. They'd immediately send him up to Port Canaveral and lock him up. He was military all the way so Joe could be in on the grilling along with Frank's staff. Marino kept protesting that he didn't know what was going on. At the same time, Dwayne Bullard walked into the office. He was the command security officer for the seventh district and Andy Marino's direct boss.

"What's going on?" he demanded.

"Mr. Bullard, you're to report directly to Rear Admiral Barnes's office, immediately. You aren't to talk to anyone about what's happening now. Do you understand me?"

"I still don't know what's going on."

"Do you need an escort to the rear admiral's office, sir? You're on suspension as of this very moment."

When Bullard just stood there, his mouth open, Joe pulled out his burner and called Jake.

"Yes, Joe. What's happening?"

"We caught Andy Marino with the burner phone but Mr. Bullard just walked in and is standing next to me. Can you please tell him to come to your office and that he's suspended until further notice?"

"Put him on the phone."

Joe did.

Bullard appeared to be all ears and his eyes went wide. "Yes, sir. Immediately, sir. No, sir. I'll come to your office on my own, sir. Yes, I'll take a different route from normal, sir."

He gave Joe back his burner phone, turned around, and

headed out the door. Joe called Michelle's two men and told them to follow him in separate cars and watch him go in to the rear admiral's door.

Joe then called Frank. "We caught Marino with the phone so pick up Elana Martinez and bring her to Port Canaveral."

Next he called Paul Philips and Terry Owens at the Miami FBI office and briefly told them what was happening. He asked them if he could meet with them in one hour.

They both said yes. They'd be waiting for him.

∾∾∾

Joe wanted the arrest of the two kept as quietly as possible. He believed that Bullard would keep his mouth shut until further notice. He appeared to be scared to death. If anything, there would be a reprimand in his jacket for not knowing what had happened under his watch with his own assistant in the office right next door. Perhaps, another retirement was going to take place very shortly. Jake Barnes called Joe as soon as Bullard arrived at his office. Joe asked him to please keep him under wraps and have him sent home on vacation for at least a week. "Jake, I think we need to discuss a few potential retirements, including your own staff member, Petty Officer George Pagan. I don't believe he has a clue about all the personnel issues under his authority. It's a mess, from everything we uncovered."

"What's next, Joe?"

"Everything is hinging on the cameras and the surveillance at the warehouse. We hope something happens tonight or at least this week. I'll bet they heard about the potential facility closings and may speed up their activities. At least that's our hope."

"Thanks, Joe. I'll go read the riot act to Bullard."

∾∾∾

Jake Barnes studied the man seated in front of the desk. "Mr. Bullard, do you know why you're now sitting in my office?"

"No sir. I don't," Bullard said.

"Your direct report, Andy Marino, with the help of Elana Martinez in personnel, have been spying on my office and, in fact, can be charged with attempted murder of two Coast Guard officers. In addition, we believe that those two are part of a team that's stolen millions of dollars in cocaine. All on your watch as head of security for the seventh district, I might add."

"I'm sorry, sir. I had no idea. I promise you that I've been totally unaware of any of this. I realize how it looks but I had nothing to do with this."

"We actually believe you, but you can't stay in a key position in charge of all security for this district after this happened on your watch. I'm just as responsible, if not more, for not knowing either. As they say, ignorance of the law is no excuse. You're being put on indefinite suspension. You've been a very good Coast Guard member for a number of years. You're closing in on retirement and you might want to visit that opportunity. This may be your only voluntary shot at it. Until then, you're to call me daily from your home and let me know if anyone has contacted you about any of what I'd just told you. Do you understand me?"

"Yes, sir. I understand you implicitly. Again, I'm sincerely sorry about this. I'd like to be given a chance to correct it, but I understand if you don't want me involved."

"You're dismissed. Make sure you call me every day by noon, and before that if anyone calls you."

"Yes, sir. Thank you, sir."

Jake was really pissed off and could hardly contain himself. Shaking his head, he sighed.

"Boy, do I look like a fool. If it weren't for Joe and his team, I'd be in deep shit."

❦

Joe went to FBI headquarters immediately after making his calls. It was only ten minutes away. He hopped in the car, a straight shot up I-95 N, exit 2B, to Second Avenue in North Miami Beach. Paul Philips and Terry Owens were waiting for him in their conference room.

"Hi, Joe. How have you been? Busy I suspect," Terry said.

"Very busy, too busy, you might say. I need to tell you what's happened to date and I need your help." Joe went through every day's events since he met them in their office only a short time ago. It seemed like a lifetime but everything was now moving fast. He explained about the warehouse and the miss-aimed cameras inside and outside the warehouse and how they traced back the bug to the second in command in the security office. He explained Elana Martinez's role and how Mark and he were almost killed because of it.

"We can court martial our own members of the service but Elana Martinez, as a civilian employee, is a different situation. She could be court martialed if she worked outside the continental United States for the Coast Guard or under martial law. However, neither of those conditions is applicable. This is either a federal case, involving the FBI and Homeland Security because of the issues of dealing with the Colombians, who're non-citizens residing legally or illegally within our borders. Or it's a local matter for the Miami Police Department. I don't want to involve INS, because deporting them means they'll come right back on the next drug ship. I don't want the Miami Police Department involved unless we have to. Colton Gilley, the chief warrant officer in charge of the second shift at the warehouse is an ex-Miami cop."

Joe paused to take a breath and make sure they followed him so far. "Both Elana Martinez and Andy Marino were taken to the Coast Guard Port Canaveral facility to be interrogated. They won't interrogate Martinez unless an FBI special agent is part of that. In fact, I want both male and female agents, just in case a sexual harassment claim is made." Joe sighed. " I really hope a truck shows up tonight, especially since we put a fake claim out that they'd be closing the facility shortly. I'm hoping they'll take the bait. We've had the drones stationed at each corner of the warehouse since last week."

"Joe, what happens if a truck shows up tonight? What're your plans?" asked Terry.

"If a truck comes, the surveillance drones will notify the drone crew at the airport and they'll immediately send in the armed drone. It will take less than ten minutes to get there. It will hover at 1,000 feet and follow the truck to its final destination. By the time it gets there, we will have the plate number, registration, ownership, and location of the final stop. We will wait a day or two, do surveillance on the facility, and take pictures of anything moving in and around that facility. We will get the blue prints and building plans, just like we did in Nashville, and come up with a plan of attack. When I say we, I mean the FBI and Homeland Security. We can shut down our own warehouse, but this new location with the Colombians is out of the Coast Guard's jurisdiction. We will be glad to help with the takedown and cleanup duty, but we can't lead the charge. Can you start gathering troops together just like we had to do in Nashville? It's fairly similar in nature to what we did to close down the meth distribution center in Nashville."

Terry shook her head. "This is larger than our office in Miami, Joe. We'll contact Washington and have a full team prepared in two days. Can you hold off until then?"

"The only problem is if the second shift gets any inkling of what we're doing. Remember, we already took into custody two people and sent the commander of security home. Tomorrow, if we get any activity, Jack will be going into the warehouse on the first shift. The chief warrant officer on the first shift will be meeting with the rear admiral at a location to be determined tomorrow morning. Jack will test every bale in the facility as well as the packaging remnants from the destroyed bales. Those remnants are matched with the destruction paperwork and kept under lock and key in a safe in the warehouse. We will get full access to everything. What I suspect, and have all along, is that the destroyed bales and even those sitting in the warehouse may not all contain cocaine. I've got a feeling and I don't know for sure, but I think there's been a switch in bales. We can't find thirty or thirty-five bales of cocaine missing anywhere. All the paperwork matches and they've done a daily audit since forever. However, I don't believe anyone has ever checked the bales from the date they were seized to the date they were destroyed or those still kept in the warehouse. That seems to be the missing link."

"How the hell did you figure that out, Joe?" Terry asked.

"To Jack and me, it seemed like the only logical conclusion. That's why our plan headed in that direction. When we saw the changing of the cameras, inside and outside, at the same time every night, we thought that was the key. The other key was the non-inspection of the actual material. Someone knew that and took advantage of a flaw in the auditing system. There were several calls from the warehouse to Andy Marino's burner cell phone, always between 8:10 p.m. and 8:30 p.m. after the cameras went back to their normal position. The calls were only on the second shift's hours."

The meeting ended after an hour. Joe had to meet Jack and the team and he only had a few hours. Hopefully, something would happen. Terry and Paul thanked Joe for stopping in and said they'd do their part to end this nightmare. Joe thanked them and headed back to the hotel for a quick bite and to meet Jack before heading out for the night.

CHAPTER 23

The technician sitting in the airport hangar outside of Fort Lauderdale beckoned Joe over to his workstation. "The surveillance drone, sitting on the building near the north end of the warehouse, just picked up some activity. We're moving in the armed drone and it will be there in less than five minutes. It will hover overhead and take pictures of everything happening. Get to your computer and, as soon as all the surveillance data comes in, we'll send it to you. If there's real activity, the armed drone will follow the vehicle until it stops and will remain in the air for a full twenty hours, if needed. As soon as it stops, we can reprogram it to fly around the area where it stopped, at 1,000 feet, and continue to take pictures of all activity until we have to bring it back for service, sometime tomorrow. So cross your fingers."

"Will do, and thanks."

Joe and Jack headed back to their hotel and prepared their computers to accept any and all transmissions that would, hopefully, come to them, and soon. At 7:45 p.m., Jack's computer started chirping. Evidently, a vehicle left the building at 7:45 p.m. and was picked up by the flying armed drone. As soon as the emailed video attachment came in, Jack hit the view button. The screen opened up like a movie and in the picture was a white Ford panel van. It didn't look too new but it was in good condition. As soon as it pulled up, two obvious Hispanic men hopped out of the vehicle and went to the side door. It appeared that one of them knocked on the door. It was 7:15 p.m. It was also clear from the drone images that the camera on the outside of the north end of the building had turned so that you could only see the side of the camera pointing more up and to the right. Joe and Jack would review the other surveillance drones as well to see if they could confirm that the camera had moved.

As they continued to look at the streaming video, the door opened outward and both Rico and Jevon came out the door, fully armed. They shook hands with the two men from the van. They all went inside and then came back out with Jevon and Rico carrying one of the bales of cocaine from the warehouse. The van doors opened in the back of the truck, and what looked like an identical bale was pulled out and dropped on the ground behind the van. Colton Gilley and Grant Akers came through the door of the warehouse and began to remove all the identification from the real bale that they just brought out the door and placed it on the fake bale exactly where it should be. It looked like they had a gluing process down pat. The two guards carried the fake bale, with the original bale's identification stickers, and took it into the warehouse. Gilley and Akers picked up the real bale, minus the stickers, and carried it to the truck. The driver had already gone back and started the truck. The guy from the passenger side jumped up into the back of the van and took the real bale into the truck. Gilley closed the doors and turned the handle. He knocked on the back window and they left with their lights off.

"Son of a bitch. That's the best switch I've ever seen," Joe said. He had seen a few before but usually on board a boat.

"I've never seen a switch until now," Jack said. "That was amazing. So, now the fake bale with a real identification sticker is sitting in the warehouse and no one the wiser. The real bale worth $825,000.00 left in a truck. I wonder what's in the fake bale in the warehouse? I'll bet it weighs the same and probably looks the same. I'll bet it's filled with baby powder or something similar."

"I guess you'll know tomorrow after you test each and every bale, including the remnants of the destroyed bales."

Joe stood up and stretched. "I'm meeting Paul and his team at the Port Canaveral facility at midnight. It doesn't give me much time to get there. Can you take it from here? Can you get the video coming from the armed drone and see where it takes us? I'll bet it goes to a warehouse somewhere here in Miami. We can look at it together tomorrow. I'll tell Paul what we found tonight. I'll be back by noon tomorrow after watching the interrogation of Elana and Andy. Are you okay with that?"

"Of course. Let me get this straight. The rear admiral will call the first shift chief warrant officer and have him meet him somewhere, but not at his office. At the same time, I'll head in with Mark's men and Michelle to take a full inventory at 9:00 a.m. I have to be out of there by at least 2:00 p.m. You'll come back with Frank Cortez and his three officers, and Michelle and her four men will stay here in Miami tonight. We'll arrest the second shift as soon as they come in at 4:00 p.m. Is that correct?"

"Yes, that's correct. We've already tied all the phone calls to the burner phone held on to by Andy Marino. Calls to Elana and from the second shift to that phone have already been determined. If the inventory proves that there are between thirty and thirty-five bales that aren't cocaine, then we're good to go. Remember, some of the fake bales could have already been destroyed, and that's why you need to test those remnants as well. I'm sure that the paperwork says that there's no problem with the inventory. I'm sure they can account for all the bales than came and went since these original 130 bales were placed in the warehouse several months ago. That's some operation. If we find all of this to be true, they cleared almost thirty million dollars. I wonder how much they got. I wonder if it was worth spending the rest of their lives in jail. What did Elana Martinez get, maybe forty or fifty thousand dollars? Wow."

Joe gathered what he'd need and headed to his car. They had to keep this low key so that the Colombians, who were now being followed by the drone, wouldn't suspect anything. Joe didn't believe that they'd taken more than one delivery a week over the last three months. This should keep everything quiet for at least several days. The FBI and Homeland Security would have to follow up with the Colombians.

෴

The flying drone checked in with the technicians at 8:45 p.m. The van in the video was now identified as a Ford 2010 E250 panel van with license plates for Dade County. The plates belonged to ZAG Services, Inc. in west Miami near the airport. The address for ZAG Services proved to be an empty lot. The full jpeg video went to Jack immediately at 8:45 p.m. and he pulled up the GPS coordinates for the facility where the truck pulled in.

The drone could hover for the next twenty hours if needed. He went to Google Earth and downloaded the GPS coordinates and address for those coordinates. A warehouse, in a non-descript industrial park, came into view. In small letters on the building near the dock doors was a sign that read *ZIG Services, Inc. no solicitation.*

That's clever. The truck's registration is for ZAG Services with a fake address and this warehouse has ZIG Services by the door, The address was 2700 NW Seventy-Second Avenue in West Miami, near the Miami International Airport. The emergency phone number listed under the sign near the door was (305) 576-2341.

Jack was sure that was linked to several phones with no end in sight. The building was 10,000 square feet and considered to be in the Airport West Industrial Area of Miami.

The Colombians could land in Miami and practically walk to this hidden-in-plain-sight warehouse. It was a very nice set up. In the parking lot, there were only a few cars. The drone picked up the make, model, and license plates of those vehicles, and they'd soon have the owner's information—if they weren't stolen.

§

Joe arrived at Port Canaveral a little before midnight. Frank Cortez and his team members greeted him. Paul and two FBI agents had just arrived. On the way up to Port Canaveral, Joe had a lengthy talk with the rear admiral. Jake was going to bring the first shift leader in right before Jack arrived at the warehouse with his audit team. The first shift leader was fully cleared of any wrongdoing, and Joe needed him to be on their side as all this went down. Michelle's team had spent all week following the four second shift team members and nothing popped out that was alarming but they did pick up three branch banks where they'd made deposits that week. They also found out that two of the men had safe deposit boxes at the same banks. Joe got warrants to open the boxes after they were detained later tomorrow.

"Hi guys. Did you just get here?" he asked.

"What're you running on, Joe, adrenalin?" asked Paul "Yes, we just got here a little while ago. Shall we meet with Ms. Martinez first?"

"Sure, why not?"

Joe, Paul, and the FBI agents went into one of the interrogation rooms to meet with Elana. Frank's team had already started on Andy Marino who'd be court martialed, eventually. They didn't get anywhere, but they didn't need to at this point. He was nervous but unprepared to give up anything to the detectives. He was probably more afraid of what the Colombians would do to him and his family than he was of the Coast Guard.

Elana Martinez was escorted into the interrogation room in handcuffs and placed in a seat opposite Joe and the FBI team.

Paul took the lead. "Ms. Martinez, you're under arrest for attempted murder in the first degree, felony drug smuggling, and felony bugging of a federal official. You're also being charged with conspiracy to distribute drugs with known foreign felons. I'll read you your Miranda rights," he said. "You have the right to remain silent. Anything you say can and will be used against you in a court of law. You have the right to an attorney. If you can't afford an attorney, one will be provided for you. Do you understand the rights I've just read to you? With these rights in mind, do you wish to speak to me?"

"I've no idea why I'm here," she said.

"Ms. Martinez, we've got enough evidence on you to put you away for life. Perhaps you don't understand the charges. It wasn't just a Coast Guard lieutenant who was shot by someone warned by you, but he was also a representative of the FBI and Homeland Security. In addition, Lieutenant Traynor, sitting right here, with the same credentials, was also almost murdered on I-95 N on the same day. The email with the attachments sent to Andy Marino that same day by you, included bios, pictures, and contact information for both Lieutenant Silva and Lieutenant Traynor, which were used in an attempt to kill them. Do you understand?"

"Look, I don't know any of that. Yes, I sent pictures to Andy Marino. That's all I did."

"Ms. Martinez, you did much more than that. You received almost $50,000.00 in cash over the last several months from Mr. Marino. That same day, you deposited several thousand dollars into your account. We know this. It's a fact. If you don't cooperate, you'll receive the same sentence as the actual perpetrators of these crimes. Do you understand?"

"If I cooperate, what'll happen to me?"

"If you cooperate, we will inform the judge of your cooperation and ask for a more lenient sentence. Why don't you tell us about your involvement so we can decide how integral you are to all of this. Maybe you might just get a suspended sentence. Try us."

"Okay. Andy Marino and I've been dating for about six months. He knew I had financial problems. Not just for me but I needed money for my sister. She has breast cancer and no medical insurance. She's unemployed and my mother has very little in the bank. My father left us years ago. My sister means the world to me. When Andy told me he could help me out, I wasn't thinking. I jumped at the chance. He got me all that money in the last three months. I gave it to my sister for her medical bills. I swear to God that's all I did. He only asked me for a handful of files and I emailed the information to him whenever he requested it. I swear to God, I didn't know what he was doing with the information." She started to cry heavily and Joe gave her his handkerchief from his pocket. "Thanks." After she dried her eyes, she said, while looking at Joe, "I'm so sorry for what happened to you and the other officer. I'm ashamed that I got involved. I didn't know what else to do. I trusted Andy. What a fool I've been."

"Ms. Martinez, we're sorry for your problems and very sorry to hear about your sister," Paul said. "Will you write out exactly what you just told us and sign it. Will you also be a witness for the prosecution for any civil or military trials? If you do, we can make recommendations in your favor. Joe, what do you think?"

Paul asked Joe that question because he knew exactly what had happened to Joe's mother. Her life was taken by breast cancer in the prime of her life. Joe wasn't around when she died because he was involved in the same kind of situation that he found himself in right now. He was daydreaming and didn't hear the question. Elana brought him right back to his mother's death.

"Joe what do you think?" Paul asked again when Joe didn't answer.

"I'm sorry, Paul. I was nodding off. Elana, I never had the opportunity to be at my mother's side when she died of breast cancer. You have that opportunity to be with your sister and be there for her recovery. It's a shame you didn't tell anyone in the Coast Guard. We'd have helped you. I've been there and it's a lonely place. You still have some retribution due for having my best friend shot and having me almost killed on I-95. However, if you fully cooperate and help us put these people away forever, I'm a very forgiving man."

"Thank you, sir. I really mean it. I want to make this up to you. I never thought for a minute that this would have happened. I'll put everything in writing and put my fate in your hands. No matter what happens to me, I deserve it, but if you could help my sister, I'd be forever grateful. Again, thank you."

"One last question, Elana. Were you aware that the rear admiral's office was bugged by Andy Marino?"

"I swear to God, I didn't know. Why did he do that?"

"I believe he bugged the entire office, the landline phone, and cell phones to see if anyone knew what they were doing at the warehouse. When I was in the rear admiral's office that day, we didn't know about it being bugged. We talked about the FBI telling the rear admiral that they believed the Colombians got thirty to thirty-five bales of cocaine from the Coast Guard but didn't know how. By the time I got to the FBI office right after that meeting, I believe that Andy put in a rush order to you and asked for Mark's and my information and pictures.

"My cell was compromised by then and, after I got out of my FBI meeting, they were already on my trail and set up in Dania Beach to shoot Mark," Joe continued. "That's what your information to Marino caused."

"I had no idea and again I can't apologize enough for what I did. I would never have done anything like that if I knew what happened."

"Elana, I believe you. Go with the officer and we will

see what we can do for you. I'd certainly pray a lot, if I were you."

Elana was taken out of the room, placed back in a holding cell, and guarded by a female officer. She'd be here a while and, hopefully, her life might improve. She'd lose her job but might not have to pay the full price for her recklessness. Joe stepped out and said to Paul, "I used to be very trustworthy of everyone. Those days are long gone. Can you have your agents interview Elana's sister and mother and see if what she said was the absolute truth? If it was, then I'll error on the side of giving her a break. As far as that bastard, Andy Marino, that asshole is going down, big time. He should be prosecuted just for dragging that poor girl into this. How can anyone use people like this?"

"Money, Joe. It's all about the money. Life or death. All about the big score. Screw people. Just get the money. Sound familiar?"

"Unfortunately yes," Joe said.

They walked into the interrogation room holding Andy Marino. "I've been already quizzed by your cops," he said rather defiantly.

"Good. Stand strong. I hope that works for you. I just wanted to tell you that you won't be seeing any life outside of a military cell for a very long time. Perhaps, you'll enjoy the rest of your life in prison. We don't need your confession. We never expected one. The evidence we have is so overwhelming that they'll believe that you were nothing but a dumb greedy moron, controlled by the Colombians. In fact, when you get to federal prison after your full court martial, you'd better hope that there aren't any Colombians in the prison population. By the time we get through with you, cannon fodder would be a step up. By the way, your hidden accounts and safe deposit boxes will be found as soon as the ink is dry on the warrant. Good luck, Andy, you'll need it."

Since this was a military matter, Frank and his men took him to another cell in a different wing. They'd already contacted the military courts for a date and for an attorney to aid Mr. Marino.

This was a slam-dunk, compared to civil courts.

It was now around 3:30 a.m. Joe went to the back of the station and slept on a cot until 6:00 a.m. He had to be back in Miami by noon but he wanted to get back and see the rear admiral at the coffee shop around the corner from their offices. This was about wrapped up as far as the bugging and missing cocaine went.

As soon as he woke up, he called Jack and Jack gave him the full lowdown on everything that happened in Miami after he'd left for Port Canaveral. He'd meet Frank and his crew at the warehouse at 3:00 p.m. and, as they came on for the second shift, the team would pick the members off one by one as they walked in the door. Jack, Michelle, and her team would already be there and probably done with the audit by then. By that time, they'd know what bales were real and which were fake. The first shift chief warrant officer and his team would stay until the second shift arrived. Someone had to continue to guard the warehouse for the second shift as those men would be in jail by then. They'd still have to keep the lid on this case until the FBI and Homeland Security hopped on board to takedown the Colombians at the warehouse in northwest Miami.

CHAPTER 24

Joe made it to Miami by 11:30 a.m. He was moving fast. He pulled up and parked in the lot that he'd parked in yesterday when they went to the security office. He didn't want a bunch of strange vehicles in the lot in front of the warehouse, especially with government license plates. If it was crowded, anyone could have picked up that something was going on. He'd told Jack and the others to make sure they did the same thing when they arrived in the morning for the audit.

Joe walked to the side door and was greeted by two armed guards. He flashed his credentials and told the men that he was with the audit team. One of the guards stayed with Joe while the other went to get Jack. Jack came out immediately.

"Can I see your credentials, sir?" he asked, smiling.

Joe sighed and shook his head. "Cut the crap, Jack. I'm a little too tired for that."

"Please come with me, sir." Jack turned to the guards. "He's with us," he said and walked away without saying anything else. "Did you get any sleep, Joe?"

"Some, not much."

"How did the interrogations go?"

"As you'd expect. Elana broke down and gave up Andy Marino. She really had limited involvement. She needed the money because her sister has advanced breast cancer. Everything she got from him went to pay her sister's medical bills. Even though she almost got us killed, I can forgive her for that. She'll have some things to answer for, though," he added. "But she never knew what happened once she gave the information to Marino."

"I guess we kind of figured as much. What did she get, forty or fifty thousand dollars for her sister out of twenty-eight million? Got it stuck up her rear, didn't she?"

"We will check her story to make sure it's the truth before we give her any slack. If it's true, I can live with her getting a suspended sentence and being fired. She can't work here again, you know?"

"I agree."

"Well, what're you waiting for? Are you going to tell me what you found, or what?"

"Do you want the long version or the short version?"

"Short, then long before I pass out."

"We tested every bale in the warehouse and every remnant from the destroyed bales. In the warehouse, there are twenty-five bales that have no cocaine. We rechecked them and each of the twenty-five is mostly filled with baby powder and a few other materials to add to the weight. Each bale weighed exactly fifty-five pounds, just like the others that have one hundred percent cocaine. We also checked the shredded remnants of the bale covers and ten of the fifty destroyed had no cocaine. They showed residue of the same fake materials. So, we have thirty-five fake bales of cocaine at around $825,000.00 each, worth a total of over twenty-eight million dollars, at wholesale value. The street value is over a hundred millions dollars. Not a bad payday. Not a bad scheme, until they got caught."

"They won't be caught until the rest of them walk in for the second shift at 4:00 p.m. All the guys parked their vehicles in the other lot, right?"

"Yes and yes," Jack said. "Let me explain what we did, so you'll know when you talk to the FBI and the rear admiral again. Since the 130 bales showed up, there has been movement in and out with fifty bales destroyed, of which ten were fakes. There were an additional fifty bales that moved through the warehouse, in addition to the other 130 from the big bust. Fifty were destroyed, leaving 130 remaining. Of the 130 left, twenty-five are fakes. Add the ten and the twenty-five together and you get the thirty-five supposedly missing bales. The bales weren't missing at all. They were switched by our own men and sold to the Colombians. The FBI was right on target."

Joe patted him on the back. "Good job. As far as the testing, tell me how it was done."

"We used a cocaine purity test that enabled us to quickly get an idea about the purity of the cocaine in each of the bales. We put a small glass tube down the middle of the bale and extracted about twenty milligrams to be tested and we had the results within seconds. This test can't tell anything about the identity of the substance that may have been used to fill the bales. So we then used another test for cocaine cuts. This is the same test used for purity but it will tell you what the sample really is, since it's not cocaine. In ninety-nine percent of the fakes, we found fifty-five pounds of baby powder. The rest are the same cutting agents used to bulk up the end retail product. Not bad, huh?"

"How about the inventory identification tags used on each bale?"

"Each bale had the correct identification tag, but each of the fake bales had a special adhesive, not glue per say, that kept the tags on the fakes. We analyzed a few of the real bales filled with cocaine, and the adhesive for the tags on those bales doesn't match the fake adhesive used to reattach the real tags to the fake bales."

"Can you say that again? Maybe, I'm just too tired."

"We got them by the balls, Joe."

"Thanks for that deep analysis. Wake me up in an hour. We can plan how we'll snatch the second shift guys as they move into the warehouse."

With that, Joe crawled up into a corner at the end of the

warehouse and used his jacket as a pillow. He was out like a light.

∽∾∽

Everyone was in place by 3:30 p.m. Joe got up and had a soda and a candy bar. He felt a lot better. Michelle and her men were placed inside and outside the building. Frank Cortez and his crew stayed inside and would do the arrests. Each would be under court martial procedures since the second shift crew were all Coast Guard member. Jack and Joe would stay by the door as the others moved in. The first shift crew would also be around, in case of problems. The outside guards included a first shift crewmember who knew the men and could identify them as they got out of their cars. He'd notify Joe with a ringtone and a text. They also knew that each of the four to be arrested left their weapons locked in their lockers and only took them out for the shift. They'd be very careful, though, to make sure that, if the men had another weapon on them, they were taken down immediately, to avoid an armed confrontation.

At 3:45 p.m., Joe's phone chirped and the text said that the chief warrant officer was heading in. They knew, from the cameras, approximately which men came in first and about what time. Colton Gilley walked through the door and was immediately taken down by the first shift crew. He was placed in handcuffs, had his mouth taped, and was taken to the back locker room area. Nothing was said by anyone. Then Grant Akers pulled up, stepped out of his car and turned around to greet both Rico Fejos and Jevon Carter, who had just pulled up at the same time. Joe's phone started chirping like crazy. He thought that meant that more than one man was coming through the door. One by one, they came in and were greeted by guns pointed at them. Fejos was the last one. He jumped back and started to take off around the other side of the building. Pulling a gun out of his waistband in the back, he started to shoot at the door. Michelle's two guards and two members of the first shift were startled and had just started to pull out their weapons.

Joe ran to the back door and opened it slightly. As he did, a bullet came flying by his head and struck the cement near the top of the door. Joe kicked the door open again. He immediately dropped down and rolled right out the door. Fejos was only thirty feet away and had his gun aimed at the door. He was surprised to see Joe and was dead by the time he hit the ground. Joe hit him twice in the chest. He walked over and checked his pulse. Fejos was dead. Joe walked back into the warehouse and to the front of the building.

Michelle grabbed his arm, almost breathless from shock. "Joe, are you all right? What happened?"

Everyone stared at Joe, including Gilley, Akers, and Carter, now all in handcuffs and ready for transport. They looked as if they were in shock. One of them was now gone.

Joe holstered his weapon. "Fejos is dead. I believe it's Fejos. I didn't have time to see his face. All I saw was his gun aimed at me by the back door. He'd already missed me once. I'm glad he never saw any action or it could have been a different story. Muscle memory. That's all it is, muscle memory."

All the blood had drained from Jack's face. "Christ, are you all right? Why did you head out the back?"

"Our guards were way back behind the parked cars. I didn't hear any shooting, other than Fejos. I didn't want him taking off. One block over and he'd have been gone. He could have gone in any direction, you know? What would have happened if he'd gotten away? The Colombians would have been told about this in minutes. I couldn't chance it. As it is now, someone could know that bullets were flying. We need to keep this quiet, or as quiet as we can. We need to get these three over to Homeland Security lockup, now. Get a van and haul them away."

Jack gaped at Joe. He'd never seen Joe in combat mode before. The only one who was ever at his side when shooting started was Mark. None of the teams, inside or outside, had anywhere close to the experience that Mark and Joe had. The only ones who did were Mark's men who helped Joe and Mark take down the Russians.

Unfortunately, none of them had their guns out when the shooting started. Joe had taken off out the back like the Lone Ranger without Tonto. He really didn't have time to think about it but needed to stay on top of this.

Jack sighed in relief. It was almost over for the Coast Guard. They could hand it over to the FBI who would be in charge of taking down the Colombians, hopefully.

Chapter 25

After all the excitement was over and the three suspects were taken away, Joe pulled out his burner and called Jake. "Rear Admiral? It's Joe."

"You sound out of breath, Joe? What happened?"

"We've Elana Martinez, Andy Marino, and the entire second shift now in custody, minus one."

"Minus one?"

"Unfortunately, one of the guards, Rico Fejos, decided to shoot it out and lost."

"How did that happen?" Jake asked.

"I shot him when he tried to escape. He ran around the building and no one seemed to be ready to stop him. I ran out the back door and almost got killed. His bullet hit the top of the back door. I reopened it, rolled, and came up firing, unfortunately for Mr. Fejos. He got hit twice in the chest. If he'd made it another half block, he'd have been gone and the Colombians would have known about it almost immediately. As it is, we're trying to keep it quiet. The other three went to Homeland Security lockup and Elana and Andy are locked up in Port Canaveral. One will be a civilian case and the other a court martial."

"Are you all right, Joe? You always seem to be in the forefront of the action. Please take care of yourself. We still need you to tidy up after all this."

"I'm fine," Joe said. "By the way, we found thirty-five

bales that were complete fakes. Twenty-five of the bales are in the warehouse and ten that had already been recorded as destroyed. The wholesale value is around twenty-eight million dollars. Depending on how they cut it for resale, it could climb to well over a hundred million dollars. We pinpointed where the last bale went. It doesn't mean that the rest of them are still there in northwest Miami in that warehouse. We'll need to raid the premises as soon as possible to get back whatever's still sitting there, if anything. At least it stopped the bugging of your office and the flow out of our warehouse."

Joe sighed. "It still doesn't look good, sir. It was our men working with the Colombians. Without our men being involved, it might not have ever happened."

"So, can I now invite the FBI and Homeland Security in to take over?"

"As you know, I already met with Paul and Terry and they knew what our plans were to clean this up. I guess a call from you to them would make it official. If you still want me involved, I'll be glad to help. As a matter of fact, they probably need me for my Spanish linguistic skills alone. I also thought about it, sir. If our bales get cut into retail street product, it would, more than likely, be distributed in the greater Miami area by the Russian Mafia. As you know, I'm now fluent in Russian as well."

"I almost forgot, Joe. Of course, you'll represent the Coast Guard as this finally moves forward to include the takedown of the Colombians."

"We need to move faster, rather than slower, sir. This will hit the grapevine pretty quickly and we need all our teams in place by tomorrow evening, or it may be too late."

"I'll call Paul and Terry and my contact at Homeland Security and tell them you'll be meeting with them shortly."

"Since it involves the Colombians, and maybe the Russian Mafia, I should call my contacts at the CIA, just to see if they have any knowledge of what just took place. Remember, just outside our territorials waters, south of us, is where all this began. That's the CIA's territory. Mike Hanley and I are very good friends and have helped each other out over the years. You may not know him, but he's in charge of all drug trafficking outside the United States for the Caribbean basis, west to Mexico. He knows more about this topic than anyone in the FBI or Homeland Security. Do you want me to involve him? I believe we should, sir."

Jake hesitated. "You don't think there will be any territorial issues do you?"

"Of course, there will be issues, but it'll be over by midnight tomorrow. It's easier to ask for forgiveness than permission. Mike is a hell of a lot more flexible than going up the chain of command at the FBI and Homeland Security. I know. I carry their credentials."

"I trust you implicitly, Joe. Go ahead and make your plans. I'll inform my boss in Washington as soon as we get off the phone. Please be careful. I hope you don't have a death wish, Joe."

"What's with that, sir? You're the second person who's told me that today. Jack mentioned it just after the shooting. Evidently, he'd never been in a takedown before. His eyes looked like saucers. He's used to all the backdoor intrigue. I don't believe he's ever faced shooting before. He thought I was a little unraveled. But he looked like hell."

"Thank him for me. After all this goes down, you need time off. I also need to restructure the seventh district before someone else does it for me. You said you had a list of idiots that you'd like removed. Would you care to share that list with me? Any suggestions for replacements, Joe?"

"I've got several on the list, sir. As soon as this is over, it would be better to move more quickly than not. It would open our Coast Guard personnel's eyes that it's not business as usual, sir."

"I got you, Joe. Thanks. I'll see you in a few days."

享

The rear admiral made his calls and put Joe in charge of the planning for the takedown of the Colombian's warehouse out in northwest Miami, late the next night.

Joe needed to head out and meet with Paul and Terry, their staff and special agents, and the team from Homeland Security. He also needed to call Mike Hanley and let him know what was going on and that he should be ready if there was to be any offshore activity as a result of this operation.

"Mike, it's Joe Traynor."

"Hi, Joe. What high intrigue are you up to now?"

Joe told him and asked him for assistance outside the United States territorial waters, if needed by the FBI and Homeland Security. "I'm the liaison for them since the Coast Guard is affiliated."

"No problem," Mike said. "I have an unknown affiliated crew manning the CIA ship just past our territorial waters."

Joe guessed that they were Navy Seals but never wanted to ask or know. From time to time, a number of federal agencies would utilize a go-fast boat for its clandestine operations and meet Mike's ship immediately outside the territorial waters.

"Don't worry, the ship will be ready if needed," Mike promised.

The last time Joe met the ship was to drop off the Russians, who were then renditioned out of the country. Jeff Talbot piloted the go-fast boat at that time. "This time," Joe said, "I'll get a go-fast boat from Michelle Bower from Dania Beach and have it docked at the Port of Miami. I won't lead the charge of transitioning any of the Colombians, but I'll certainly aid in the effort and have the boat available for their use."

Mike grunted in agreement. "Okay, I'll get it set up for midnight tomorrow."

Joe called Michelle and explained the same thing. She was on board as well as her four men from her station. So far, she and they had been an enormous help, other than not getting their weapons out on time at the warehouse. *Oh well*, he thought.

Joe made it to FBI headquarters and walked into Paul's office. He and Terry were already preparing for the next day's events.

"Hi, Joe," Terry said, smiling. "Shoot anybody lately?"

"You too, huh? If everyone else had been ready, I wouldn't have had to shoot anybody."

Paul chuckled. "We know, Joe. Just kidding. Ha, ha. Tell us your plans."

"My plans? My plan is to go home and have a lovely dinner and spend the evening with my fiancée."

Terry shook her head. "Well, we know that isn't going to happen, so what's next?"

Joe shrugged. "I guess next is to take down a large warehouse in northwest Miami out by the airport. That would be my guess."

They spent the next three hours making calls and setting plans into motion. Joe called the drone team and told them to move the four surveillance drones over to the warehouse at 2700 NW Second Avenue in West Miami, near the Miami International Airport. The armed drone would stay put, 1,000 feet above the building and would constantly circle it while taking pictures of cars, people, and any other activity in and out of the building. A 10,000-square-foot building, if fully utilized, could hold literally a ton of cocaine and all the equipment needed to move it to the street.

Jack had gone back to the hotel and was receiving pictures taken by the larger drone since it stopped at the northwest Miami warehouse. He had already analyzed the vehicles parked outside the building. There were only four pickup trucks and two newer model Mercedes in the lot. Two of the pickup trucks' license plates didn't match the vehicle so Jack guessed that they were using stolen plates. The other two were listed as being owned by two Hispanic men. Jack went to the DMV's website and got driver's licenses for the registered owners. Those two individuals had lengthy records of convictions for drug use and sales. The two Mercedes, both 2013s, were registered to ZAG Services, Inc. with the same address as the building. They were the same registration as the panel truck that picked up the bale of cocaine at the Coast Guard warehouse earlier. Great, Jack thought, ZAG vehicles and a ZIG warehouse.

He had checked the number near the dock door and it was listed as the owner of the building. Evidently, ZAG services only rented the building from the corporate owner. So, Jack would have to continue watching the drone surveillance feeds to see how many people came in and out of the building. Unless there was an apartment in the warehouse, they'd have to come out sometime. In any case, the FBI and Homeland Security takedown teams should have more than enough men for the job.

Joe walked into the Hampton Inn, went to the room, and knocked on the door. He didn't want to just open the door and scare the crap out of Jack. He thought Jack had had enough scares for one day.

Jack answered the door, with the chain still on it, saw Joe, and let him in. Joe had a twelve-pack of Sam Adams *Oktoberfest* in one hand and a pizza in the other. Jack took the beer first and immediately opened two bottles. Joe put the pizza on the table and they both dove in. The twelve-cut sausage, pepperoni, and pepper pizza lasted about ten minutes. After twenty minutes, Joe and Jack had downed three beers each.

Jack burped. "Thanks, Joe. That was great."

"You're most deserving and most welcome. Tell me what happened back at the warehouse after I left. Oh, and tell me what the drone saw."

"First things first. I made arrangements for all 130 bales to be destroyed by the end of the week. There's no reason to keep that much cocaine for a trial. That's just really dumb. They've scheduled both shredder boats for tomorrow under the jurisdiction of Frank Cortez and his staff. Every bale was tested and all of it will be dumped into the ocean by the end of the week. There will be very limited need for the warehouse in the future. Just sitting there, it's a temptation and a disaster waiting to happen."

"That's great. So we will have a twenty-four-hour crew available until it's all gone?"

Jack nodded. "Yes. That's the plan. Both Elana Martinez and Andy Marino are still up in Port Canaveral and will be transferred down to the Homeland Security facility tomorrow morning. By the way, Andy saw the light. He's now singing like a bird but it's a little late, don't you think?"

"Yes, for Andy is it. How's Elana?"

"Born again. I think she's very grateful to you to be let off with a simple job firing and a suspended sentence. You know we can't get the money back and restitution will take her twenty years. I do believe she should pay back at least $150.00 a month for the next several years while on probation, and then, if there are no further incidents, we can let her off the hook. What do you think?"

"I think it sounds remarkably fair for someone who almost caused two deaths including *moi*."

"We all get it, Joe. She does, too. She'll be grateful. Trust me."

"What about the drone surveillance cameras? What did you pick up, if anything?"

Jack told him what he'd found over the last several hours. "I need to stay on top of it through most of the day tomorrow before the midnight takedown just to be on the safe side."

"Yeah, that's what we did up in Nashville, right up to the time we raided that building."

After their conversation, both Jack and Joe were exhausted. Joe called Julie and Joan to let them know he was all right and told them that he wouldn't be calling until the day after next because of the midnight raid tomorrow night.

Afterward, they both fell asleep within minutes of their heads hitting their pillows. Jack snored so Joe was grateful that they had separate rooms in the suite.

CHAPTER 26

The takedown was all set for midnight. The FBI and Homeland Security took charge of the operation and contacted the Miami police. The local police would serve in a secondary role. They'd place several of their patrol cars near the building's adjacent streets, right before the takedown took place, and block off the area within one square block of all the surrounding side streets, so if anyone escaped the net, they wouldn't be able to drive their way out. If they left on foot, they'd be immediately apprehended by a backup team placed outside the building near the parking lot perimeter. All the participating teams would meet in a CVS parking lot two blocks away at 11:00 p.m.

From there, the teams would go on foot and completely surround the building. At exactly midnight, the armed drone would take out the main door by the docks. The back door, on the other side of the building would have a team of ten FBI special agents, already in place, to take out anyone trying to escape.

Terry suggested that, during the day, they get permission from several of the building owners surrounding the warehouse to perform thermal imaging from their rooftops and, if not, from windows near the docks. By the time they went in, they'd have a pattern of people going in and out of the facility.

Jack told Joe that the drones had picked up two older

Toyota's, both driven by Hispanics, who got out of the vehicles and entered the building around 6:00 p.m. They
hadn't come out yet.

Joe believed that the two vehicles might have been the
same one that tried to take him out on I-95 N on his way to
Fort Lauderdale the day that Mark got shot.

By 11:30 p.m., the Miami police, guarding the perimeter
and the streets near the warehouse, would stop anyone leaving the facility after they'd traveled a few blocks beyond the
building, so as not to alert anyone inside. Anyone turning
into the building would be allowed to do so. If they were
still in the vehicles by midnight, they'd be among the first
people to be taken out. Dart guns were to be used on anyone
guarding the outside of the building. This was to keep noise
to a minimum, and they all thought it would be a good idea,
as long as the people using the dart guns knew exactly what
they were doing. But this wasn't a problem because the FBI
team used the darts regularly. With the thermal images pro-
duced, the takedown team had already determined that the
first team assaults would take place through the front door,
near the loading docks.

The first FBI teams would use stun grenades, also known
as a flash grenades. Joe knew that the stun grenades worked
well, since the grenades were used up in Nashville to take
out the meth warehouse. Joe and most everyone there had
used the grenades before but he wanted to make sure that
everyone, not on the immediate FBI teams going in, were
familiar with the capabilities and wouldn't be surprised by
the explosions caused by the grenades. The stun grenades
were designed to produce a blinding flash of light and loud
noise, without causing permanent injury. The flash pro-
duced momentarily activated all photoreceptor cells in the
eye, making vision impossible for approximately five seconds, until the eye restored itself to its normal state. The
loud blast was meant to cause temporary loss of hearing,
and to also disturb the fluid in the ear, causing loss of balance. They had to be careful because the concussive blast of

the detonation could still injure, and the heat created could ignite flammable materials in the warehouse.

The initial drone attack would prove to be quite effective, but the grenades would probably carry the day and incapacitate anyone inside the building. The second wave of officers would be in charge of securing the facility, and they'd go in immediately to prevent any destruction of computers or records. They'd need the records to see if they could connect the activities at the warehouse to the Russian Mafia.

"Our main priority is to get those in charge off the streets," Joe reminded the teams. "There are two Mercedes in the lot, obviously driven by people in charge. I want them, badly. The secondary priority is to secure all the bales of cocaine that might be left and any retail product ready to hit the street. Any money found will be secured by the FBI and Homeland Security teams, brought to Homeland Security headquarters, and locked securely in their vault. Unlike keeping 130 bales under guard, the Coast Guard has learned its lesson and these seized drugs will be immediately destroyed at sea tomorrow. Keeping the product as evidence is no longer a priority. A sample will to be sufficient, as long as we had valid videos and photos of the men and goods seized."

Everyone got to the CVS parking lot at 11:00 p.m. There were ten FBI special agents, ten Homeland Security officers, and several drivers for the Miami police cars that would monitor traffic after midnight and block the roads until the operation was completed. Already at the site, for most of the early evening, were several individuals manning the thermal imaging cameras. As soon as those assembled were ready for the assault, the thermal imaging staff would be pulled back to the CVS parking lot for assignments later. They'd go back into the building, after the takedown, and do thermal imaging on all the walls and potential hiding spots that could house drugs ready for distribution, guns, and cash, as well as anyone trying to hide. It was clear that bales of cocaine would stick out like a sore thumb somewhere in the warehouse—if they hadn't been broken down yet.

The strike teams went in separate directions, coming in from three different sides so they wouldn't be seen. The FBI team had three special agents, armed with dart guns, head up the line. They got into position first. Just like clockwork, they'd take out any guards walking the perimeter, with limited noise.

There were no guards. Whoever was working in the building had stayed in the building.

There was also one guy in his truck, just coming into the parking lot. He was immediately taken down, cuffed, and dragged down the street by the dart team. The rest of the first team had their stun grenades ready. Each team member had one grenade and a gun in their shooting hand. They waited for the drone to blow out the front door.

Exactly at midnight, a ball of fire came from the sky and a loud explosion blew the door from its hinges. The first team waiting to strike looked at the door but it was gone. There was a ten-foot-by-ten-foot opening where it used to be. Smoke billowed up from a small fire that had started in the pile of rubble that was left. The members of the team had synchronized their watches and, as soon as the drone hit the door, they ran through the opening. Within seconds, the stun grenades went off in the middle of the warehouse. The people standing around began to scream. They covered their ears with their hands, completely disoriented. There were ten individuals in the warehouse proper. All looked to be Hispanic. The second team came in and went immediately to the offices, grabbing two men holding their heads after the stun grenades went off. These two had to be the men in charge. They were well dressed but were now rolling on the floor in pain.

Joe went right in the front door after the first team hit and the second team secured the office. There were clouds of dust and smoke but Joe saw the two in the office, crying on the floor. He had two special agents separate the two in the office. The agents secured their hands and feet with zip ties.

"Take them straight to the Homeland Security facility, where they'll be questioned later," Joe told them. "Don't worry about their rights unless they can prove that they're United States citizens, which I don't believe they are."

He'd find out later. He was the only one on the FBI team who spoke fluent Spanish. Two of the Miami cops guarding the roads were Hispanic but they wouldn't be in on the interrogation activities that were soon to follow.

The warehouse was chaotic at best. Joe shouted at the top of his lungs for everyone to meet in the center of the warehouse with prisoners in tow. There were ten individuals rounded up, outside of the two in the office and the one guy who had just arrived.

None of those captured spoke English, so it seemed. Joe spoke to them in Spanish and they understood every word. He asked them who the two individuals in the office were. "The first one who comes forward with any information will receive a suspended sentence and possible placement in the Witness Protection Program." *What else do I have to offer?* At least he'd try to place them. He wasn't going to worry a lot about it.

Immediately, two individuals spoke up and wanted to talk. The other eight glared at the two but they seemed to understand the situation they were in. The others must have been lifers in the cartel. These two were very young and were scared to death. They were immediately separated from the other eight and placed in the office, tied up like the other two. The eight were placed in a Homeland Security van. None of them spoke English and were probably not citizens, either. They'd wind up with Immigration. However, Joe wanted those who shot Mark and went after him on the highway. He'd get that information from the two volunteers.

Joe went into the office and, in Spanish, asked, "What're your names and where are you from?"

They were brothers. One was twenty-one and the other was eighteen. Both came from Columbia. "We have no family and were brought to Miami to work in the warehouse," the older one said in Spanish. "The others have families at home and they'll be killed if the men say anything. But we have nothing to lose."

Joe knew that orphans made good workers but would turn on a dime, since, as the two men said, they had nothing to lose. "Who're the two men in the office?"

"The taller one is Esteban Montoya," the youngest brother said. He's twenty-eight and comes from Medellin, Columbia. His family is in charge of all the cocaine operations in Central West Columbia. It's one of the richest regions in the country. His family will be very upset about this. I'd watch my back if I were you."

"The other man is Rafael Valencia," the older one said. "He's thirty-four. He's from Cali, Columbia. It's on the western part of Columbia on the Pacific Ocean and is the kidnap capital of the world. Rafael comes from a very important family, as well. Both families got together and put this operation in place. That's all we know."

"Thanks for your help," Joe said. "You go with these men and I'll see what we can do for you. By the way, do you know who drove either one of those two Toyotas outside?"

The older brother told him which of the eight men were the drivers of the two cars. In fact, four of the eight were charged with taking down Joe. "Montoya was the shooter in Dania Beach. Valencia never gets his hands dirty. He never left this building, other than to party."

"Thanks."

The FBI agents placed the two brothers in another car and headed to Homeland Security to another, safer lockup area where they wouldn't be bothered.

Joe walked back into the warehouse proper, where the rest of the FBI teams were taking inventory. There were ten bales still sitting there. Joe looked at where the tags were cut out and he could tell that they all came from his Coast Guard Warehouse. It was clear that probably twenty-five bales had been already cut and made ready for street-level sale. He was really pissed about it, but he was glad they stopped it and got what they got. You couldn't worry about what happened. It was done. Surprisingly, though, one of the managing agents, in charge of the audit, told him that they found literally a ton of cocaine in retail bags ready for sale. There were thousands of the envelopes, probably worth millions.

Joe smiled. *That's good.*

The thermal imaging team came back into the building after everything had been secured. They went wall by wall, up and down, to the top of the twenty-foot ceilings. They went through the office space, the bathrooms, and the lunchroom. They'd found several spots where the walls were more tightly packed. Some of the FBI team members ripped the walls out where the imaging devices picked up the hot spots. In two spots, bags of money came tumbling out. In another spot, thousands of retail bags of cocaine were in plastic wrapped bags of several pounds each of ready-to-sell product. There were four small metal suitcases of money, all stuffed with hundred dollar bills. Joe didn't have to guess how much was there. He already had a good idea. A Halliburton aluminum waterproof briefcase held at least a million dollars in cash, in hundred dollar bills. There was at least four million in the walls.

He turned to Terry Owens and Paul Philips who'd just walked in. "Looks like your two salaries will be paid for the next twenty years, including benefits."

Terry gaped at the haul. "This is amazing. This isn't your first rodeo, either, is it?"

"No. I'm afraid not. But I don't want to get used to it either." He then told them about the two brothers and how he told him about Witness Protection. "I did it on the spur of the moment but if they go to jail or get sent back to Columbia, they're both dead men, you know? They gave up Montoya and Valencia. We need to go see both of them now and see if we can turn them and find out whom they were distributing through. I'll bet a million dollars it's the Russians. Maybe four million?" Joe said with a smile.

Paul nodded. "Let's wrap up here. Christ, it's almost 4:00 a.m. You tired, Joe? I am."

Joe went with them in their car. He'd go back and pick his up later or have someone drop it off at the hotel.

While in the car, Joe called Mike Hanley to make sure the CIA boat was ready. It was.

"I'll let you know what time the FBI go-fast boat will get there. It should be around daybreak.

"We'll be ready," Mike said.

Joe called Jake next. "Sir, it's a done deal. We took down the warehouse, secured the premises, and took all the men into custody, including the two in charge, who're both members of some pretty scary cartel families in Columbia. We also got the guys who shot Mark and tried to take me out. By the way, we only found ten bales left, but enough retail street-ready packs to keep Miami in cocaine for six months," he said. "Do you want to meet us at Homeland Security headquarters? We will be interrogating them for a short time and then renditioning them to Mike's boat, outside the territorial waters."

"I'll be there in a half an hour," Jake said.

Disconnecting, Joe closed his phone and got a few minutes of shuteye. He was starved and wanted a cup of coffee. Maybe they'd have some at the center. At least he could rest a little easier, now that they found the bales, the perpetrators, and closed down the operation. Joe didn't think it would be the end of it, with the two sons of the cartel now in custody. No one would ever know where they'd been taken, other than Mike Hanley, his CIA crew, and their bosses.

The cartels could search all they wanted, but they'd have to deal with the CIA now. Joe hoped that their end was coming soon.

CHAPTER 27

Joe and the rear admiral met outside the Homeland Security facility. Jack was already there, speaking to Paul and Terry. Joe deliberately asked his own investigation team, led by Frank Cortez, to stay back at the Coast Guard warehouse and make sure it was fully guarded and staffed until all the remaining bales were destroyed.

That would be a good use for his investigators. They were used to hours of routine to get to their end results. He knew that they'd be successful under Frank's leadership. Joe was thinking of asking Frank if he could recommend him to take over all security for the seventh district under Rear Admiral Barnes. It wouldn't hurt if he worked his way into that position. All he could do was move up the ladder, since everyone in security and even in the clandestine unit had already failed miserably. Joe had asked Michelle Bower and her crew to move back to the Dania Beach Station and work with the drone team to write up all the necessary reports that would document all the crimes committed by those now arrested. Elana Martinez and Andy Marino were moved down to the Miami location, in a separate area, from the rest of those who'd now be indicted. Michelle was way better at the required paperwork than Joe had ever been. She said she'd handle it and Joe knew she would.

"Sir, are you going to participate in our interrogations?" he asked Jake.

"I'll be an observer only. I understand the interrogation rooms have two-way mirrors so I can watch the action. Is that right? Can Jack join me? He's not participating in this, is he?"

"No. He never has and I don't know what value he'd add to the conversation. Most of the talking will be in Spanish, anyway. We'd better get moving fast. I'm needed for my Spanish fluency. First, we'll interrogate the men who did nothing more than cut the cocaine and get it ready for retail sale. However, in that little group are the two brothers who came forward and gave me the names of both those who were driving and those who were riding as passengers in the cars that tried to take me out. Those individuals will join the management team on the go-fast boat headed to the CIA ship. Mike Hanley is waiting for us. I just spoke to him. We need to get them shipped to the boat before dawn. The less public display, the better. The others will be handed over to Immigration who can deal with them. They're not our concern."

"I understand all of that, Joe. By the way, I forgot to ask you. How much did the total seize add up to?"

Joe shrugged. "It's hard to say. The reason is, not so much for the bales that were left intact. Those bales are worth $825,000.00 each, just as is. The retail value once broken down into powder and crack is a whole different story."

"How much different?"

"From my takedown experience, here in Miami, in Nashville, in Orlando, and at my own non-profit up in Albany when I was working there, prices varied, but not by much. As an example, the price of cocaine in New York varies, depending on a number of factors, including the buyer's familiarity with the seller, the location of the sale, and the quantity sold. Powdered and crack cocaine prices, particularly for smaller quantities, are generally higher in Upstate New York than in New York City, which serves as the state's distribution center. Here in Miami, it's just like

New York City. Nashville and Orlando are less populated and prices tend to be a little higher. According to DEA, in New York City powdered cocaine sells for $20,000.00 to $30,000.00 per kilogram, $900 to $950 per ounce, $120 to $150 per one-eighth ounce—eight ball—and $20.00 to $30.00 per gram this year. In rural New York, not unlike Nashville, powdered cocaine sells for $20,000.00 to $32,000.00 per kilogram, $800.00 to $1,600.00 per ounce, $160.00 to $175.00 per eight ball, and $50.00 to $125.00 per gram. In New York City and Miami, crack sells for $28,000.00 to $30,000.00 per kilogram, $1,000.00 to $1,500.00 per ounce, $27.00 to $45.00 per gram, and $7.00 to $10.00 per rock. In Upstate New York crack sells for $800.00 to $1,600.00 per ounce, $175.00 per eight ball, $50.00 to $125.00 per gram, and $10.00 to $40.00 per rock. Kilogram prices generally aren't available in Upstate New York or in any rural area."

"How the hell do you know that, Joe?"

"I just do. I guess," Joe said. "By the way, cocaine coming in to Miami doesn't just stay here. It winds up all over the eastern seaboard from here to Maine, not just New York City. It goes to the highest bidder and the best price gets most of the product. Their distribution systems rival Amazon and Target, just like the meth distribution system starting in Nashville."

"What did you say we got on the retail side?"

"There were thousands of individual eight-ball and one gram baggies. We couldn't count them all tonight. They'll be doing that for days but we need to stop and estimate and then destroy everything at sea. If we don't, the same problems will come up again. Do you remember the kid's game, Whack-a-Mole? All we can do is hit it in the head when it pops up. We don't have the manpower to catch everything coming in and going out. If we get twenty-five percent, it's a lot."

"I wish that wasn't true, Joe. But I know you're right. We can only do the best we can with what we have. We need more Joe's, Jack's, and Mark's but maybe that wouldn't even make a difference. Let's get the interrogations over."

They headed down to the room and Joe spoke briefly, in Spanish, with the worker bees. He told them they'd be imprisoned and then deported. If they came back and were caught, they'd wind up in a federal prison for life. They were very quiet and nodded their heads. No one spoke. They were removed from the room and sent to their cells, waiting for Immigration to show up. The rear admiral and Jack watched Joe as he spoke to the men. Jake was fascinated with the process.

They went to the interrogation room holding Joe's shooters who drove the older Toyotas. Joe told them where they were headed. "I don't need your cooperation. Attempted murder in the commission of another crime can mean the death penalty. I don't know that for a fact, but where you're headed on the go-fast boat with Montoya and Valencia means you won't be back."

They were shackled and brought out to a Homeland Security van, ready for the trip of their lives.

Finally, Joe went in to the room with Montoya and Valencia. Two Homeland Security interrogation officers, along with Paul and Terry joined him in the room. The rear admiral and Jack stayed behind the one-way glass.

"Gentleman," Joe said in English. "Do you speak English?"

Neither of the two men spoke. Esteban Montoya, the younger at twenty-eight, sneered at Joe and spat at him. Rafael Valencia, older at thirty-four, looked as if he could have cared less. This was nothing more than an inconvenience.

Joe went through their background. After the two brothers had given Joe the information, he'd forwarded it to Jack, who ran an international search on both Montoya and Valencia. Their Colombian roots in Medellin and Cali were confirmed. The fact that these two individuals were the sons of cartel heads came through with flying colors. They'd nabbed two bad guys but, even better, they'd taken out a future generation of cartel family owned businesses.

"Gentlemen, I really don't need your cooperation. By the end of the day, your Mercedes will be long gone. All the drugs seized at your warehouse will be immediately destroyed. Your facility will be completely gutted and every trace of you and your men will be gone. In fact, we will be knocking down your building by tomorrow afternoon. Everything will be carted away as if you never existed."

"What about us?" said Valencia.

"What about you? You don't exist. You were never in the United States, and you won't be going back to Columbia, ever."

"You can't do that," Montoya said. "We have rights. We're not U.S. citizens but we have rights."

"Not according to the United States Patriots Act, you don't. Not that it matters much, but since 9/11, Homeland Security has redefined terrorism to include gang activity and financial terrorism as violations under the Act. Under the Patriot Act, You can and will be renditioned to wherever the CIA sends you, just like those terrorists from the Middle East. They don't need the RICO Act. They only need to prove intent under the Patriot Act and it's a done deal. And, gentlemen, it looks like this is a done deal."

"What if we give up something to get something?" Montoya said.

Valencia looked at him with eyes that told him to shut up or he'd be a dead man.

It seemed to Joe that Valencia didn't get the gist of what was about to fall on his head.

"What if we give you our list of who we sell to?" Montoya asked. "Would that help?"

Joe looked at Paul and Terry and they nodded their heads.

The rear admiral was fully involved in the conversation from the outside looking in.

Jack felt like he was in a daze. He'd never witnessed Joe

like this before. If they could have rapped on the window, they would have.

Joe gave Montoya a yellow legal pad and a pen and told him to write down everything he knew including names, addresses, amounts, and locations where the drugs went. They took Valencia, under armed guard, to the waiting van. The van would run until they got what they needed from Montoya and then he'd join them. *He's getting what he deserves. After all, he shot Mark and almost took my life and career.* Joe wouldn't allow himself to feel sorry for him.

After Montoya handed the paper to the Homeland Security officers, Joe left the building. He stepped outside, called Mike on his SAT phone, and told him that the van was leaving the building in five minutes. It would take fifteen minutes to get to the Port of Miami where the go-fast boat was already running and ready to go. It would take less than a half hour after that to meet the Mike's CIA boat in international waters. Where Mike would take them, Joe didn't want to know. At least for now, his job was done.

The rear admiral joined Joe and Jack in the front of the building. "Joe, that was truly remarkable. How many names did Montoya put on the list?"

"There were at least ten names and addresses from here to New York City. I was right about that. More bang for the buck. Montoya and Valencia are remarkable businessmen. Unfortunately, they're also crooks and murderers."

"What's left to do, now?" Jack asked.

"We need to knock down the building or at least make sure it's done. We need to guard the bales and retail baggies, the thousands of packs, and make sure it winds up back with Frank at our warehouse to be destroyed tomorrow and no later. We still have to decide what to do with Elana Martinez. Andy Marino will be court martialed. The other three left from the second shift at the warehouse will be court martialed and the fourth's body shipped home. There should be a massive readjustment in the management of the seventh district, including your number three staff member,

George Pagan, sir. He has no clue about the personnel of the seventh district, sir."

Jake sighed. "I need to write this up properly, go to Washington to visit my boss, and explain what the hell happened and what we're going to do to prevent it from happening again. I may not be back, Joe. I may be asked to retire but at least I can go out, knowing that my men, my loyal men, had my back."

"Your loyal men and women, sir."

"Yes, of course. I'm truly sorry. Michelle Bower did a remarkable job and I know how much you respect Joan Talbot. Can we talk about all this in a week? I'll leave in the morning for Washington and be back by next Tuesday. Does that give you enough time back at Islamorada?"

"Yes, sir. Jack, can you stay another week? We really need your administrative skills and I need you to help me set up a computerized inventory and management plan and review all the personnel issues we encountered."

"Sure, Joe. I need to call my crew in Virginia. I'm sure they've forgotten about me."

"Not if I call them on my way to Washington and confirm your value to me."

"That would be nice, sir. Let the troops figure out what we're doing. Damned if I know," Jack said and laughed.

Jack and Joe hopped in their cars, waved to the rear admiral, and headed back to the Hampton Inn. Joe needed to make some calls, especially to Julie. With everything that had happened, he'd been a little neglectful in that area and wanted to make it up to her. Maybe a trip for a few days to Key West, just Julie and him, might help. Maybe she could take a few personal days. He planned on it being very personal.

CHAPTER 28

After breakfast, and after a short meeting with Jack, Joe headed back to Islamorada. He caught Julie on her cell phone as she headed out of the elementary school to go to the high school for meetings.

"Julie, hi."

"Hi, Joe. Where are you?"

"I'm headed home. We just wrapped up the case and I don't have to report in to the rear admiral until next Tuesday when he gets back to Miami from Washington. He has a lot of explaining to do, but I think he'll come out of this just fine. At least I hope so."

"Is everyone okay?" she asked.

"We came out of it without anyone injured. One of the men on the second shift tried to escape when we were ready to arrest him and the rest of his crew. He got shot and, unfortunately, he didn't make it." Joe left it at that. He didn't want to tell her that it was he who did the shooting. It would only upset her and he didn't want that. "What would you think about heading to Key West for a long weekend, starting Friday coming back Monday afternoon?" he asked her. "I don't have to meet Jake until Tuesday morning. We can leave right after school ends, so you'd only miss Monday. What do you say?"

"Actually, that's a great idea. I've missed you so much. There's no practice or cross-country meets this weekend.

It's an off week. I'm owed a few days, as it is. I can ask for Monday off as a personal day. I'll ask and I'm sure I'll get it. What time do you want to leave and from where?"

"Pack for the weekend the night before and I'll meet you at my station at 3:00 p.m. Friday afternoon. Don't worry about a thing. I'll make hotel reservations and book a few restaurants for dinner. We need this, Julie. I miss you and love you. Maybe we can look for an official engagement ring while we're there. I know the rear admiral has connections in Miami, but let's look around and see what you like first."

"I love you too, Joe. Sounds like a plan. Do we need to dress up?"

"I don't plan on it. Maybe something nice, but casual, for dinner and just our bang around clothes when we hit every bar on Duval Street."

"Every bar?"

"Yes, every bar, or at least *almost* every bar," he said, laughing. "See you then."

⁓⊱⊰⁓

As soon as Joe got to Key Largo, he stopped at Tillie's apartment to say hello. It had been a while since he saw her. He wanted her to know that everything seemed to be all right at this point. No promises were ever made, especially after everything she, Julie, and he'd gone through over the last year.

After a short visit, he headed to Islamorada and made it in less than a half hour. He was in no rush. He pulled in and walked into the offices. He dropped his gear on his desk, looked at his messages, and walked down the hall to see Joan. It seemed like a lifetime ago that he'd been back here. In reality, it had only been a few weeks but, then again, he and Julie were up in Walt Disney World during this investigation. He almost forgot about that. He needed to see how

Julie was holding up after turning down a very lucrative deal for the movie rights to her first book. God, he had a lot on his mind.

When he'd left a while ago, he and Jacob Cramer weren't on very good terms. Handing him the phone to speak to the rear admiral right before he left didn't do anything to improve the situation.

On the way down to Islamorada, Joe thought about changes that should and could be made to improve the seventh district. He was mulling around about asking the rear admiral to make some key decisions and he had it backed up with facts and good reasons. First, he wanted to have Frank Cortez, and his investigative team of three, moved down to Miami to head up all security for the seventh district. Dwayne Bullard, the command security officer, should be removed because everything that happened was under his watch. He only had a short time left before his retirement and he could be moved around, out of security, until that date. Frank and his team had earned it and they knew what they were doing. During the last investigation, Frank got a commendation from the rear admiral but, this time, Joe felt he should be promoted to lieutenant just like the promotion that he and Mark had received.

He also wanted Mark back in charge of Dania Beach but wanted him to work directly with him in Miami on a more official basis. He thought that Michelle Bower, after her recent performance, should be placed in Petty Officer George Pagan's spot as third in command of all personnel in the seventh district. She was the best there was in policies and procedures for personnel and was respected and well liked, especially by Joe and Mark. Finally, Joe thought about Joan. She wasn't involved in this investigation but she deserved to be in charge of the Islamorada Station and had less than two years to go before Lucy graduated. Then Joan could retire and work in Jeff's business, right next door. She deserved the promotion to warrant officer.

Jacob Cramer, who was a lifer through and through,

could be placed in charge of the Port Canaveral facility and report to the staff up in Jacksonville. Jacob would probably accept this role and not complain, not that Joe cared. He didn't want this to happen because he could get what he wanted from Joan. He wanted Joan in charge because she deserved it and Jacob had only gotten it through longevity and because he was a man. Joe remembered pointing out that the rear admiral was saved by both the men and women under his command. Joe doubted that, at this point, he'd forget. This would be the perfect time to offer the suggestions.

"Joan, how are you?" Joe walked into her office and gave her a big hug. "How's Jacob doing? Is he here today? I'd better stop in and see him too," he said when she nodded.

"He's fine," she said. "Same as always."

"Julie and I are heading to Key West for a long weekend. She's meeting me here Friday afternoon at 3:00 p.m. I've a lot to catch up with before then. Do you have time to go over the cases I left behind? I'm sure Jacob will remind me. By the way, before I make any suggestions, I need to speak to you alone tonight to see if you're in agreement. My suggestions will affect you, Joan. Hopefully, it will be for the good."

"Sounds intriguing, Joe. Want to go into town for dinner around 6:00 p.m.? It's been a long time since we did that. What do you say?"

"Great. See you then."

❧❧❧

Joe called his favorite Key West hotel to see if they'd any rooms at the last minute.

"Southernmost Hotel, may I help you?" said the receptionist.

The hotel was on the very end of Duval Street, right next

to the southernmost point buoy at the corner of South and Whitehead Streets. They were on the main street that housed most of the activity in Key West.

"Yes, I'd like to make reservations at your hotel, for two people for Friday, leaving Monday morning. We've stayed there before and I'd like your second floor deluxe guest room, king size bed and balcony overlooking the ocean. Your rooms still have refrigerators, flat screen TV, and Wi-Fi, correct?"

"Yes, sir. All our deluxe rooms have those amenities. We've four rooms available for the weekend, Friday through Sunday, leaving Monday morning for $402.33 per night, plus tax."

"That would be fine. I want the room closest to the ocean and the one that offers the most privacy. It's a special week-end. We're coming down to pick out an engagement ring and wedding rings. We will be married in May of next year."

"That's wonderful, sir. Your room will be ready and waiting for you at 3:00 p.m. We will add a few extra amenities for you fiancée's pleasure."

"Thank you very much." He gave her the credit card number and got his confirmation.

Next, he called two of their favorite restaurants. The first was La Trattoria, located at the center of Duval Street. It had been honored numerous times with the People's Choice Award as one of Key West's favorite Italian restaurants and as the best romantic dinner where the locals ate. The next restaurant he called for Saturday night reservations was the Conch Republic Seafood Company on Green Street. Joe thought that the view and atmosphere combined made it the perfect location for one of the best seafood restaurants in Key West. It overlooked the historic seaport with terrific views. On Sunday, they'd head to the Margaritaville Café for what the locals called the "real Key West experience."

Joe liked to plan but this weekend all he wanted to do was relax and go with the flow. Maybe, just maybe, Julie would finally pick out an engagement ring. He didn't have to buy it now, but it would be nice to see something that she really wanted. He hoped for the best. The best part of Key West was going to the bars like Sloppy Joe's, his personal namesake, he thought. They'd hit the Hog's Breath Saloon, Bourbon Street Pub, Green Parrot and a few others that the locals went to when out on a weekend.

Joe got to Key West quite a bit when he was on a cutter chasing down drug boats that were then hauled into the Key West Coast Guard Station, right down the road. Julie loved the saying, "See you at Sunset!"

Beginning two hours before sunset, Mallory Square came alive. The sunset celebration culminated in the glowing pink and red sun sinking into the Gulf of Mexico. The nightly festival allowed visitors from all over the world to take part in this memorable event. The sun going down at Mallory Square was one of the most beautiful sites anyone could ever see.

Joe finished all his calls and went to his officer's quarters. He started a load of laundry. He couldn't remember the last time he'd done so. He opened a few beers still in his refrigerator, ate some cheese and crackers that were left over, showered, dressed, and met Joan at the front of the station to go to dinner. They headed over to a nearby café. Joe wanted wings and shrimp. Joan had an appetizer and a large salad.

"So, what's up, Joe? You seemed so preoccupied when you got here. Have you come down yet from the clouds?" she said, smiling.

"It seems like I've been working seven days a week since I arrived last fall when Tillie got hit by the truck. I haven't stopped and, actually, I'm getting kind of tired of the whole thing. I've exactly one year left under my contract and I'm not sure if I want to stay in the Coast Guard. I'm getting sick of chasing dirt bags, including our own. I don't know what else to do. I could go back and work in Troy with the Troy Education Consulting Group. I don't think Julie would ever want to live up north. She had her fill of that for five years at Brown University. I could go into administration at the Miami Police Department or in the sheriff's department down here. I don't know. Maybe I'm just tired. However, I do want to bounce something off of you."

"Sure, Joe, anything. What's up?"

"How would you like to be promoted to warrant officer and run the Islamorada Coast Guard Station, in addition to your other duties, for the next two years before you retire?"

"How would that happen, Joe? I'm not sure I could handle it."

"Don't kid yourself. You've handled it for the last twenty years without the title. Don't you want to get paid for it and add it to your final salary that's gets boosted up for your retirement?"

"Well, of course," she said.

"Jake asked me for suggestions on re-staffing the seventh district. I want to recommend you to take over Islamorada and move Jacob to Port Canaveral."

"I'd like to be considered," she said, after Joe explained why he wanted certain moves made. "When will Jacob be told?" she asked.

"Jake will be back in Miami by next Tuesday. I'll be back late Monday with Julie and then I'll head up to Miami for an early Tuesday meeting. If accepted, I'd like the changes to be made no later than four weeks from the approval date. That will give everyone time to make moves. Since Jacob lives at the station here, he doesn't have to worry about selling property. By the way, Julie and I'll be looking for a house before the wedding, if we decide to stay in the Keys. That will probably be the case, no matter how I feel about it. I'll make it my home for Julie's sake."

"You'll adapt, Joe. You always have. Go away this weekend and forget about everything except your plans with Julie. Come back refreshed and start over. That's my motherly advice and you'd better take it," she said, laughing.

"Yes, Mom. I'll try."

They finished eating. Joe paid the bill and they went back to the station. He needed to finish his laundry, pack, and call Mark and see when he and the extended family would be back to Dania Beach. He gave Joan a big hug and a kiss on the cheek and headed for his quarters. He needed rest more than anything.

☙❧☙

Julie got to Islamorada and parked next to Joe in the Coast Guard officer's lot. She had an extra set of keys to Joe's car and hit his car's opener to pop the trunk. She loaded her bags into his car and locked her car up for the weekend.

Joe came out of his quarters, stopped, and gave Julie a big kiss and a hug. He opened his trunk and threw his bag in. He put the small cooler with a few beers and snacks in the back seat. " Are you ready to go?"

"Yes, sir. I'm on board, sir!"

"I like that 'sir' stuff. Makes me feel important, you know?" he said, laughing.

"Sure, Joe. Hit the road."

The trip was a little over an hour, maybe an hour and a half at most, going at a snail's pace on a Friday afternoon. Joe thought of his trips to Cape Cod, going over the Sagamore Bridge. It was hit or miss, bumper-to-bumper traffic or clear sailing, depending on the weather and season. They arrived a little before 4:30 p.m. and Joe pulled into the hotel parking lot.

The smells, the sounds, just being there felt so different. Living in the Keys was an all-year-round vacation but this was different. This was a vacation designation spot and everything was waiting for them.

Everything would have to wait because Joe had a few ideas of his own. They checked in. He got the key, unloaded the car, and headed up for the second floor. He opened the door to a suite and was shocked. It was beautiful. He guessed that telling the young lady at the reservation desk about the rings had made a difference.

There was a bottle of champagne sitting in a bucket of ice that couldn't have been delivered more than a half hour before. There was a tray of cheese and crackers, fresh strawberries, and Godiva chocolates waiting for them.

Julie's eyes went wide with pleasure. She moved the tray onto the table by the couch and signaled to Joe to get over there now. He obliged immediately.

Within minutes their lovemaking began. It went quickly at first and then slowly and deliberately, minutes later after their first orgasms.

Joe looked into Julie's eyes. "You've no idea how much I love you and how much I missed you."

"I think I got a pretty good idea, Joe. You know?"

She grinned, walked across the room naked, and brought over the tray.

Joe opened the champagne and filled the two fluted long stem glasses. "To you, Julie. Only to you."

They tapped their glasses and emptied both quickly. Joe grabbed a few strawberries. Julie ate a few chocolates and then she grabbed his hand and took him back to the bed.

"You didn't make up a checklist this time, did you?" He remembered the memorable weekend in New York City when he asked her to marry him on the steps of Saint Patrick's Cathedral.

"No. I have that list memorized. Do you want to test my memory?"

"I believe you. I really do."

It was getting close to 6:00 p.m. Joe made reservations at La Trattoria for 7:30 p.m. They both got dressed and sat outside on their private balcony, overlooking the ocean.

"Joe, this is beautiful. Thank you for this. It's great. I love you."

"It *is* beautiful. Let's walk on down Duval toward the

restaurant. I want to stop at a few jewelry stores on the way, just to see what they have for engagement and wedding rings. We're just going to look. Don't panic. Here's the list that I downloaded for jewelry stores on Duval Street alone."

Joe handed her the list of stores on the way. Included on the list were Emeralds International LLC, Tanzanite International, Italian Jewelry, Pacific Jewelry, Diamonds International, Island Silver/Shell Necklace, 220-B Key West Charms, Neptune Designs, Capricorn Jewelry, and Aria Key West. All the stores were on Duval.

"Can we visit Diamonds International first, Joe? That's seems to be the in place for diamonds. You don't think I didn't look up a list of jewelry stores as well? You know what you've turned me into, don't you? I'm now a serial list maker, all thanks to you," she said with that "Julie look" that meant more than mere words.

She found several designs that she liked, mostly low-key but elegant. She was looking for something that she could wear alongside her grandmother's ring. She decided not to combine the two but to wear them separately on her ring finger, to honor her grandmother. When Tillie passed, Julie would then switch Tillie's ring to her other hand and wear only Joe's rings on her ring finger. Julie always made decisions and stuck to them. That was one thing that Joe truly admired about her. She knew what she wanted and stuck with her choices.

The weekend went very well. Julie found a ring and got all the information about it. Joe would ask the rear admiral if he knew anyone who could match the diamond and the setting. If not, the rings she chose at Diamonds International were beautiful, affordable, and exactly what Julie wanted. He offered to buy all three on the spot but Julie declined. She wanted to wait and not make a lifetime decision hastily. They could always go back to Key West, any weekend, even for the day.

They went to all of Joe's favorite bars. They saw the beautiful Key West sunset at Mallory Square and had wonderful dinners. They headed out, relaxed and back in love, around 3:00 p.m. on Monday. It was three glorious full days that neither wanted to ever forget. She stayed at Joe's Monday night and they both headed out early Tuesday morning.

Julie switched gears and went to the high school first, instead of to the Key Largo School. This was her pattern whenever she stayed over at Joe's place. Some of her friends at school laughed and commented on her change in venue on those days. She laughed it off and told them they should be so lucky.

Joe's next few days would be filled with politics and anxiety over the changes that needed to be made. He hoped that Jake would take his recommendations to heart. Joe only wanted what was best for the seventh district. Jake was concerned about forced retirement.

At thirty-four years old, Joe was concerned about the rest of his life. He really had to think long and hard about staying in the Coast Guard. The pay was fine, not great. The retirement was fine, not great. Getting shot at all the time and being followed by crooks and murders wasn't a positive job motivator. He'd talk it through with the rear admiral when the time was right. He'd learned at Rensselaer Polytechnic Institute in his MBA course work that the author of substantial change couldn't stay and be the everyday manager. Those were two separate skills. Joe knew that and was struggling with exactly what to do about it.

If you stayed after you made all the changes, you wound up being resented by everyone from the top to the bottom. It was just the way it was. He could always go back and work with Mark, doing the same investigations over and over again. But he just didn't want to do that anymore.

CHAPTER 29

Joe had a lot on his mind as he headed back to the Coast Guard headquarters in Miami. The ride there gave him time to think about everything that he knew was coming. He and Julie had a wonderful time in Key West. He wished that it had never ended. *Wishful thinking.*

They discussed their wedding plans for next May for both New York City and for Key Largo. The wedding at Saint Patrick's and the party afterward for around thirty to thirty-five people would cost almost as much as the full-blown affair in Key Largo for 125 guests. Joe hadn't spent a dime since he'd been back in the Keys. This would make up for it.

Whenever he was on an investigation, he either got reimbursed immediately or only had to use the Coast Guard government Visa card for everything. Joe had saved almost $40,000.00 at this point. He'd also gotten a bonus of $15,000.00 from the rear admiral for a job well done up in Nashville and Orlando.

Julie's ring was around $12,000.00. She said it was foolish to spend more than that because she wanted a house of her own more than a ring. Joe agreed with her. Neither came from money, and a house in the Keys seemed like a much better investment for the future. The wedding reception in New York City was almost $300.00 a person, over $10,000.00 in total. The reception in Key Largo after their second ceremony at Saint Justin Martyr Church was less than $5,000.00. Those two ceremonies and the ring would take a big bite out of Joe's life savings, almost $25,000.00 in total.

Julie got two checks from her publisher for $30,000.00 each, and that $60,000.00, after taxes, would cover the down payment and the closing costs for a house, leaving not much to move in, decorate, and buy furniture. Neither cared about that. The house was everything to Julie. If Julie's grandmother, Tillie, ever got sick and couldn't keep up her apartment, Julie wanted her to come live with them.

In her spare time, Julie had already looked at a few houses in Key Largo, Islamorada, and Tavernier, near Coral Shores High School. All the houses were in the $300,000.00 range with two bathrooms and a minimum of three bedrooms. Storage was an issue because there were no basements in the Keys. They were at flood level already.

Houses in that range tended to be smaller, in the 1,200-square-feet range, but that was fine. Julie wanted a house near the water and wouldn't mind paying a little more for a bigger lot so they could add on to the house if they needed to. She wanted a house all on one floor, in case Tillie ever did come to live with them. Climbing stairs would be out, especially after Tillie had been on her feet as a waitress for close to fifty years. Taxes weren't bad in the Keys because the rich, in their mansions, tended to pay a larger portion and never had kids in the school district. Their kids mostly attended the private schools that popped up, or even attended the various Christian schools that were attached to local churches.

Joe knew and fully understood Julie's concern. She could never talk to Tillie about it because her grandmother was stubborn and wouldn't listen to anyone, including Julie, or even Joe. He would do anything for Tillie. She had always been there for him, and he'd be there for her. His only issue was where the hell would they wind up? Would they stay in the Keys? Would they move to Miami? Would Julie accept the movie deal and commute to Burbank, California, to meet her contractual obligations with Disney? There was too much to think about, but Joe always made lists and crossed the items off as he accomplished his goals on a daily basis. He couldn't help himself. The act of writing out his thoughts helped him to clarify what was important to him, and to Julie.

He walked into headquarters, passed through the machine, smiled at the guards, and headed to his office. He'd stopped around the corner for his Duncan Donut fix— regular coffee and two donuts. He couldn't function most mornings without it.

Unfortunately, in the Keys, Duncans were few and far between. He unlocked the door to his office and barely had a chance to drop his stuff on his desk when Al Cummings came running him to tell him that the rear admiral wanted to see him right away.

"Al, can you ask him if I have time for a piss? Thanks."

"He wants you right now, Lieutenant."

"Just as soon as I take a piss, Al. All right?"

"I'll tell him that, sir. Exactly."

"You do that, Al. I'll be in to see him in a few minutes." *Watch your Irish temper, Joe. Not the time or place, even if he is an obnoxious ass.*

Joe headed to the men's room, shaking his head. *How could anyone be as anal as Al Cummings?* he wondered. Joe did his duty, washed his hands, combed his hair, and threw some water on his face to help him stay alert. He wanted to be there this morning as much as he wanted to dive in the Hudson River at high tide. At least that was his father's expression. Joe smiled and knew he owed his father and brother a call, one of these days. He'd been neglectful. His father was getting along quite nicely now that his heart operation was a complete success. He was on the way to full retirement, kicking and screaming at Joe's brother, Pete. Pete had come a long way. He just didn't listen to John Traynor as much anymore or simply told him to stop. Pete was becoming his own man, thanks to Tanya Fields, of course.

Joe knocked on Jake's open door. "Good morning, Rear Admiral."

"Good morning, Joe. I'll be right with you. Did my attack dog bother you this morning?"

"No more than usual, sir. Is there a test, when you enter the Coast Guard, to see if you can be as anal retentive as humanly possible and then the brass have the person groomed to work for a rear admiral twenty years later, sir?"

"I don't think that's possible, Joe but you never know," Jake said and laughed. He told Joe exactly what happened when he went to Washington to meet with his boss and a committee formed to review exactly what had happened and what was needed to correct it moving forward. "I received a warning in my jacket but at my level and years of service, it doesn't matter any. This is as far as I'm going. I've got one year left before retirement and I was offered the opportunity to clean up this mess before I retired so I can leave on a good note. Is that something you can help me with, Joe?"

"Yes, sir. I can, but we need to talk. I've about one year left under my agreement, as well. I believe my contract expires during the same month that you agreed to retire."

"What're you saying, Joe. Are you leaving us at the end of the year?"

"It depends, sir. Right now, I believe that when my contract expires, I'll be leaving the Coast Guard. I'd love to help you clean up Dodge City, though. I'd feel really good about that, sir. I don't know what the future will bring but, at that point, I'll be married, we will have bought a house in the Keys, and Julie will have finished her contractual obligation for her *Girl's Life* trilogy. Hollywood may be beckoning her and I'd gladly tag along with her. She means everything to me, sir, absolutely everything."

"I know the feeling well, Joe. This will be our thirtieth wedding anniversary this year. I owe my wife, Becky, everything, as well. She's put up with more from me than I ever would have. Perhaps, you're right. When you need to move, you should move and not think about what you could have done but didn't. The regrets will kill you, Joe. Take it from me. I know all about regrets. The biggest regret, though, I finally get to fix with your help. Care to join me?"

"Yes, sir. I will, gladly." Joe then went through all the changes that he believed the rear admiral needed to make. The drugs would be sunk at sea later in the day. They also got half a million dollars, from the final count of the seized cash. The money would be used for the court martials and the cost of closing up the warehouse and sinking the drugs.

Jake balked about George Pagan but Joe gave him a detailed reason why he should go. "You can't fire the bottom of the order. Someone at the top was fully responsible, or even derelict in their duties, and has to go. That person is George Pagan. You also have to let the head of security, Dwayne Bullard, go as well. He could retire and be immediately replaced with a competent officer, Frank Cortez."

Joe made his recommendations about Michelle and Joan and those recommendations were approved. "So, you finally were able to get rid of Jacob Cramer, huh, Joe?" Jake said, laughing.

"Get rid of? No, sir. Strategically moved to where he can't possibly make a bad decision." Joe hesitated briefly. "Well, maybe, sir."

Jake chuckled. "Wow, are you now politically astute, Joe?"

"Hardly, sir, and you know it. If politically astute means promoting the women in the Coast Guard to positions that they should have held years ago, I guess I'm politically astute, Jake. You know I'm right."

"Yes, you're right. I've been an asshole for not recognizing it a long time ago. I guess that's why dinosaurs like me need to be replaced, and soon."

"Sir, no kissing up, but next to Tom Jones, you're the best officer that I've ever known. You're a man of your word and you don't back down, sir. You also accept the blame without blaming others. You, sir, have all my respect. By the way, can we use some of the cash we got to pay the rest of Elana Martinez's sister's hospital bills? I know it's rather unusual, but I want to let people know that we take care of our own in good and bad times, sir."

"Good segue, Joe. Yes, you can have up to $150,000.00 of the money for that purpose. We won't advertise it because we don't want people lining up at the door. But if we get some good publicity out of it, at least it might negate some of the crap that we're now standing in. And by the way, thank you, Joe. That means a lot to me."

After the meeting, Joe headed to his office. He needed to find out when Mark was coming back. Mark was cleared for duty a few days earlier and he'd waited until Joe thought everyone was out of danger. It wasn't so much that Mark was afraid for himself. He'd wanted to make sure that Louise, MJ, Jennifer, and Louise's parents were safe when they got back to Fort Lauderdale. Mark was ready to go. He just wished that he were part of the final takedown of the Colombians. He was smart enough to know that he shouldn't jeopardize his career for one investigation. His arm was healing and his range of motion allowed him to function at eighty percent, for now. He'd continue to build up from there.

Joe called Jack and told him that everything was in place. The rear admiral wanted to see Jack, before he left to go back to Virginia, and personally tell him how grateful he was that Jack had jumped right in and did an incredible job. Jake knew that offering Jack a job down in Miami would probably be turned down, since Jack only had a few years left and that Joe was thinking about leaving as well. Jake had nothing to offer him at this point. Jack was brilliant and should continue coming up with new, innovative investigative techniques to catch the bad guys. At least the Coast Guard had a go-to-guy whenever they needed one.

Chapter 30

Joe was in his office when the phone rang. It was around 11:00 a.m. He was going to let it go. He was thinking about Julie and her books and the movie rights. He wondered if she did the right thing in turning Disney down until her trilogy was completed. But it was important for Julie to make her own decisions about her life. As he'd told her, when they were in the luncheonette around the corner from the Islamorada Station and first expressed their true feelings for each other, he never wanted to be a hindrance to her career.

He'd been floored when she'd told him that day that she'd always loved him and she wanted to know if he loved her in the same way. He did and he'd told her so. But he still wanted her to decide for herself what was best for her—not because he didn't love her and didn't want to spend the rest of his life with her, but because he was older than she was, and she hadn't experienced the same things that he had, at this point in their lives. And he didn't want to stand in her way. He knew that when he got back to the Keys, they should really sit down and discuss their future plans—not so much about their love for each other or about their impending wedding day, but about where they'd be in two years. This last investigation, with Mark getting shot, weighed heavily on Joe, and he wasn't sure if he'd continue in the Coast Guard when his current contract was done.

The phone kept ringing. Joe sighed and, at the last second, picked it up. "Joe Traynor speaking."

"Joe, it's Cal Roberts calling. Remember me?"

"Of course, Cal. How are you?"

"We've got a problem, Joe. I've put you on speakerphone. I'm sitting here with Trinity Hightower. You remember Trinity, don't you?"

"Of course, Cal, I remember all of you. We're grateful for everything you did for Julie and me when we were up there at the Disney meeting at Hollywood Studios. I don't think Trinity slept a wink for the entire weekend with making sure we were both okay. How are you, Trinity? What can I do for both of you? Name it. How's Archie doing?"

"Archie is fine. Joe, I need to put Trinity on the phone with you. It's a private matter and I hope you can help her. It's serious or I wouldn't have called you."

"I understand. Go ahead, Trinity."

She picked up the phone and pressed the private button removing it from speakerphone. "I've got a family problem and I hope you can help. Do you have time to talk right now?"

"Sure, go ahead."

She sighed. "I'm at my wits' end. My little niece, Kiki, who's fifteen years old, is a sophomore at Colonial High School in Orlando, the same school that I and my sisters attended. She took off from my sister's house yesterday with her best friend, Glenda Davis, for parts unknown. We believe she's headed to Miami to find her father who hasn't been in her life since she was a baby. She cleaned out her savings of about $300.00 in cash. Kiki had a big fight with my sister, Hope, and took off. Evidently, she had been doing some research online about her father, Quentin Lonell. He's a jazz pianist and has toured all over the country. We think he is appearing in Miami, but there's no address for him. Trust me, Joe, I know how to do online investigations and research. The only thing we found was that he was in a jazz group that appeared in a club on South Beach for the last week. After that, we've got no idea. I called every hotel in the area of the club. He could be staying with someone or shacking up somewhere. We just don't know where."

"Trinity and Hope, huh? Any other sisters?"

"Faith. And I don't want to hear about it." She started to laugh and it broke the tension. "My father, Marvin Hightower, is the pastor of our local Baptist Church, and, yes, Joe, my mother Mavis, leads the choir. Can we be any more obvious?" she said.

"Well, I'm one hundred percent Irish. We're all drunks and all we eat is corned beef and cabbage and potatoes. I'll tell you my mashed potato story someday when I see you."

"What can I do about this, Joe?"

"First, pack a bag for a week. It's Tuesday. I'm sure we will find her, Trinity. It's about four to four-and-a-half hours from Orlando to Miami, about 350 miles, door to door. Use your police car and put the flashing lights on all the way. You can make it in under four hours. I know. I did it," he said. "You can stay at our Coast Guard condo. I'm staying here this week. I'll give you the address and GPS coordinates. It's about a block from my headquarters downtown on Brickell. If you leave in an hour, you can be here by 4:00 p.m. I'll call Julie and see if she can come up and help as well. We'll do everything we can to find your niece, Trinity. In the meantime, I need to get a hold of Jack before he heads back to Virginia. He's our technology genius. If she's on the streets of Miami, he'll find her. By the way, as you know, Mark got shot on our last investigation, which just ended. I'll try to bring you up to speed on that when you get here. He was in San Diego recuperating and now he and his family are on their way back to Fort Lauderdale. This is perfect timing. He's champing at the bit to do something. This is it."

"Thank you. Cal was right. You're a good guy, Joe, and so is Julie. Thank you. Thank you. Thank you. I'll go home, pack, and head out. What do I tell my sister and my family?"

"I won't kid you, Trinity. She and her friend could be in a world of hurt if she's been here since yesterday. You know and I know that teenage girl trafficking is an epidemic in major cities like Miami. If she didn't get a ride in a car, then she probably took a bus to Miami. Trains are too expensive and don't run all the time. She doesn't drive, does she?"

"She has her learner's permit. You can at fifteen in Florida, but she has no access to a car other than her mother's run down old Honda and that's parked in front of the house. Her friend won't be fifteen for another month, so she can't drive. I already checked the bus station here and buses leave for Miami every couple of hours, Joe. I've no idea which one she took, if she headed there."

"Okay, we'll check from this end immediately. If she got off a bus here from Orlando, we'll find her. We'll pull every camera angle in the bus terminal to see if she arrived and at what time. Get your rear end here as soon as you can, Trinity. Please drive carefully. I know you're upset. Anyone can tell, but just get here safely. Let me talk to Cal for a minute." When Cal came on the line, Joe said. "Cal, Trinity is heading down here as soon as she can leave. Please tell her not to worry her sister and to make sure her sister doesn't come with her. We don't have time for hand holding, especially if it ends badly. You know what I mean. We'll pull out all the stops and try to find her as soon as humanely possible. As I told you, we've the state-of -the-art technology to help out."

"Thanks, Joe. You're a good guy. I knew I could count on you. Trinity is beside herself but she's professional enough when the chips are down. She'll be a help and not a hindrance. Thanks again."

"Tell her to call as soon as she hits the Miami area." Joe hung up and called Jack. He caught him right as he walking out of headquarters after speaking to the rear admiral. "Get back here, now, Jack. We've an emergency and I mean life and death. I'll explain it to you as you walk back into the building."

After he hung up from Jack, Joe called Mark, who'd just arrived at the airport in Fort Lauderdale. He told him what was happening and to get down to Miami. Mark was back on the job. Joe called the drone team that had been hanging around the Fort Lauderdale area, waiting to be dismissed. Joe wasn't sure if they were needed but he wanted them around if he needed some surveillance done.

He thought, if things got rough, he might even need the armed drone. The armed drone had a few extra features that included laser technology and the ability to seek out heat sources in a building from its lofty position high in the sky. He also wanted to keep the smaller drones available if he needed a fixed camera or two, in positions where no one could normally reach, like on the top corners of buildings, just like at the Coast Guard warehouse.

Joe walked into the rear admiral's suite and was once again greeted by Al Cummings. "Yes, Joe. Can I help you?"

"No, but the rear admiral can."

"He's in a meeting, Joe. It will be a while."

"Thanks, Al." Joe turned back to his office and dialed the burner phone he'd given the rear admiral.

"Joe, what's up? I'm in a meeting. Can you make it fast?"

"Sir, can you give me five minutes? It's really important."

The rear admiral walked out of the meeting, past Al Cummings, and headed to Joe's office. "What's up, Joe? You look worried."

"I am, sir." He proceeded to tell Jake about Trinity's niece and what may very well have already happened. All Joe wanted was permission to drop everything and find Kiki. He told Jake what Cal Roberts had done for the Coast Guard during the Orlando and Nashville investigation and how he and Trinity personally had their backs at the Disney meeting for Julie.

"You've got whatever you need, Joe. If you need any money, let me know."

"I may have to grease a few palms down here at the level I deal with, Jake. Can you throw me a few thousand dollars?"

"No problem," Jake said. He walked back to his office, closed the door, with everyone waiting for him in the conference room to continue his meeting, and opened his office safe. He took out $10,000.00 in hundreds, wrapped the bills in his Miami Herald, and walked back to Joe's office. "Here, if that's not enough, let me know."

Joe smiled. "Thanks, Jake. You're one of the good guys."

"Ditto." The rear admiral went back to the conference room.

Joe wondered what everyone thought about what just happened. He smiled to himself, with a shit eating grin, thinking about mister anal retentive, Al. If it were up to Al, Joe would be filling out paperwork until the end of the month. *What a good guy Jake is.*

❧❧❧

Joe met up with Jack a few minutes after he called. They put their heads together and Jack got his marching orders. The first thing he'd do is go to the bus station and check with the ticket clerks to see if they could identify either girl. Then Jack would check every camera and every angle for buses that arrived in Orlando within the last three days, in case Trinity was wrong. Not Trinity so much but the girl's mother might not have noticed when Kiki really left. If she was unsure of the time, Hope might have told a white lie about the time she "knew" Kiki and Glenda took off. It happened all the time with teenagers.

Joe knew the truth of the matter. Hell, he snuck out of the house so many times growing up, he could tell exactly when his father got up to take a leak every night. He'd be back in bed by then with no one the wiser. Joe thought that kids today were even brighter and had access to technology that made everything easy. He prayed to God that she and her friend were okay. Trinity would be beside herself. Joe could hear in her voice how much Kiki meant to her. He also heard in her voice that she and her sister might have different opinions on how to raise a teenage daughter.

CHAPTER 31

Jack went back to the condo and unpacked his bag. He turned on his laptop and started up all his high-security encrypted programs. Once up, after five minutes, Jack went to the bus website, hacked in, and checked the cameras for the last few days. Trinity had emailed Kiki's most recent picture. The picture was of her and her girlfriend at Walt Disney World on a class field trip. Her girlfriend, Glenda, was also in the picture. Trinity's sister, Hope, said they took off Monday night, so he'd look for her on camera footage for yesterday to see if they hopped on a bus.

No such luck. Jack went back to Sunday and, finally, the two girls popped up, taking a 3:00 p.m. bus that was clearly marked for Miami, Florida. Jack checked the schedule and found they'd have arrived in Miami by 11:00 p.m. Sunday night with multiple stops along the way. *Well, Hope was wrong. How could Kiki not be missed late Sunday night?*

He called Joe immediately and let him know. "Joe, she left Sunday night, not on Monday. Both her and her girlfriend popped up on the screen getting on the 3:00 p.m. Miami bus. Hope had the wrong day. You better ask Trinity when she gets here. It could prove to be more difficult after twenty-four hours of being missing, even if we know where they were headed."

"I hear you, Jack. Keep working. Make sure they arrived. I'll be at the condo in a little while. I've got a bunch of errands to do. We need groceries. Julie's coming here tonight. She's using some comp time and then personal. She jumped right on board as soon as I mentioned Trinity's situation. Do you want a pizza? Pepperoni?"

"Sausage and peppers would be good too," Jack said. "See you in a little while."

He went back online and watched the Orlando 3:00 p.m. Sunday night bus pull in at 11:08 p.m. that night. Hopping off the bus were the two girls with two small carry-on bags and their pocketbooks. *Well at least we know they got here. Two days is a long time to catch up in Miami. God knows where the hell they went. They probably tried to get a hotel room for the night and then look for Kiki's father the next day, which would be yesterday and a Monday. I need to find her father and keep looking around the bus station area, inside and outside, to see what direction they went. I need to talk to Joe. I need their email addresses, passwords, cell phone numbers, and the kind of phones they use. I need an electronic trace to see whom they've been talking to since Sunday, if anyone.*

⌘

Trinity called Joe when she got near Fort Lauderdale, heading south on I-95. Joe gave her the exact directions on how to get to the condo and the code to the parking garage. He said he'd meet her at the garage as soon as she arrived. She was to call him and he'd walk down. Joe, at Jack's request, had called Trinity earlier to get the email, phone, passwords, and other information that Jack needed to go online for his trace.

Trinity called her sister from the car and asked for that information. Hope called her back and Trinity pulled off to the side of the road to take down the information. Hope said they had Time Warner for internet service and Verizon for phone service. Kiki had an older model iPhone and paid for

it out of her babysitting money. She got Glenda's information as well. Joe had told Trinity that they discovered
Kiki and Glenda getting on the Orlando bus on Sunday afternoon at 3:00 p.m. Trinity asked her sister about that and
she said she didn't know Kiki was missing because she said
she was staying with Glenda over the weekend as she had in
the past. When Hope spoke to Glenda's mother, she said
Glenda told her that she was staying at Kiki's house for the
weekend. She told Joe that neither mother was paying attention to their daughter and now they were feeling guilty.
Trinity told her sister she believed that they'd be fine and
they'd catch up with them. She didn't need to hammer on
her. Hope felt bad enough. Trinity prayed that was all that
would happen. Her sister would never be able to live with
herself if something happened to Kiki and Glenda. *Parent-
ing is a fine art.*

While waiting for Trinity to arrive, Jack told Joe that he
found them coming off the bus at the Greyhound Bus Station, located at 16000 Northwest Seventh Avenue in downtown Miami. Jack did a MapQuest on the location since he
wasn't all that familiar with downtown Miami. The bus
terminal was less than a mile from the condo at Brickell
Plaza.

Joe had just arrived with pizzas in hand. He had a
twelve-pack of Oktoberfest in the other. They ate one pizza
in less than ten minutes. Joe told Jack to wait for Trinity
before diving into the second. He was glad he bought two
orders of Buffalo wings as well.

When Jack came up for air, he told Joe about the video
of their arrival in Miami. He'd also looked at all the cameras surrounding the buildings in all directions. He checked
from 11:00 p.m. Sunday night through the next hour after
arrival. "The two girls were standing outside the terminal
around 12:30 p.m. when a young, light-skinned black man
came over to them. Kiki gave the young man what appeared
to be a hug. It looked like she was introducing him to Glenda and they were all smiles. Kiki grabbed the young man's

hand and they started down NW Seventh Avenue.”

"Well I'll be damned,” Joe said.

“The young guy appeared to be in his late teens. He was tall, thin, and all smiles.”

“Jack, can you blow up their picture. I want to see the guy's face. It sure sounds like she knows this kid if she was smiling ear to ear. I wonder how she knows him. We need to get online and get her and Glenda's emails and tweets and anything else we can think of. Trinity will go ape shit when she sees this. I really hope Kiki knows him and it's not someone she met online. That's how they get these young girls to head to Miami. Get a good-looking kid to talk to her online and have her fall in love with him and follow him anywhere. I really hope that's not the case but I'm not optimistic at this point.”

“I hear you, Joe. I'll get right on the emails and tweets and find out who this kid is if we can. I'll blow up his picture and match it to every record I can find including car registrations, driver's licenses, school ID cards, anything. I'll run my facial-recognition program from here and see what I get. I hope he's not in the juvenile detention system. You know they close those records to the public. I can still get the reports, but I really have to cover my ass on the way out of each system. Yes, Joe. I've done it before,” Jack said, smiling, when Joe opened his mouth to protest. “I've also been trying to trace her father as well. But I don't think that's the main reason she's down here, do you?”

“Not after hearing what you saw on the video. Jack, we'd better break it to Trinity in small doses before she comes unglued. I'm really glad that Julie's coming up here to be with her. Trinity needs a woman who knows what she's going through. God knows that Julie's been through enough crap and Trinity knows that. They'll be good for each other until we get Kiki and Glenda back safe and sound.”

෴

Before Trinity arrived, Joe wanted to make sure that she was qualified to help out when she got to Miami. It was great of Cal Roberts to promote her and Joe thought highly of her after meeting her in Orlando. She did an admirable job in shadowing Julie and him for the weekend. They became friends, but being friends didn't make her qualified. So one of Jack's first duties, when he arrived at the condo, had been to do a thorough search on Trinity Hightower that included her professional and personal activities. He knew that she was twenty-eight years old and single. She wasn't seeing anyone at the moment. It was evident from their meeting and conversations up in Orlando that education, her job, and her family was everything to her. That mirrored Joe's responses, as well as Julie's.

Jack's quick investigation had come back, giving Joe even more respect for her and her abilities than he had before. He was pleased to have her on this team, as long as she kept her emotions intact. He believed she would. Having her team up with him, Mark, Jack, Julie, and Mark's team, including Michelle Bower, would prove interesting. He didn't realize, until Jack told him, that Trinity was as big a tech nerd as Jack was and he proved it by handing him the report.

Trinity Hightower came from a very religious family. Her father Marvin was the pastor at the local Baptist Church on the west side of Orlando. Her mother Mavis was the church choir leader for many years. Trinity, and her sisters Hope and Faith, were fully involved in the church until they grew up and moved away. Her sister, Hope, now thirty-five and the oldest, married very young and had Kiki with her husband, Quentin Lonell. He left her right after the baby was born. He just couldn't take the pressure. He was a jazz pianist and traveled the country with a quartet. It was believed that he wound up in Miami, near South Beach, playing at a few jazz clubs.

Faith was the second oldest at thirty-three, married to Antoine Lawrence, age thirty-four, and a very well-respected software engineer in Orlando at a new high tech company. They had two daughters ages six and four. They attended her father's church to this day. She'd take over her mother's music ministry one day. Faith was a fulltime mother at home.

Trinity was the youngest daughter and the first police officer in her family. Joe knew that she had a Master's Degree in Criminology from the University of Central Florida, located in Orlando. After graduation as salutatorian from Colonial High School in the western part of Orlando, she received her bachelor's degree in Criminology and, immediately afterward, went full time for her masters. Upon completion, she attended the Orlando Citizen's Police Academy and was immediately hired once she finished the program. She was ranked first in her class.

She was now in the doctoral program in Public Affairs, which was an interdisciplinary program drawing from the strengths of faculty in Criminal Justice, Health Management and Informatics, Public Administration, and Social Work. The Criminal Justice Track prepared her for academic positions in colleges and universities as well as research and leadership positions in public, nonprofit, and private agencies. Joe hadn't known that and was surprised. She chose police work over all the others.

Joe read the report on the doctoral program at Central Florida University. It stated that the program included a dynamic mix of an interdisciplinary faculty with students of varied backgrounds, which created a stimulating environment to examine contemporary organizational, institutional, and community problems and issues. Graduates possessed the theoretical, analytical, and ethical foundation to produce new knowledge that impacted policies and programs and enhanced institutional and community performance. *She wants to contribute to changing society's thinking about criminology. Wow. That's one hell of a challenge.*

He also discovered, from her writings that Jack had dug up, that Trinity would like to be the first woman to be chief of the Orlando Police Department. Chief Cal Roberts was the first African-American chief of the department. She'd like to be the first African-American female chief with a PhD. She was now a member of the adjunct faculty at the university, in the criminology department. She specialized in examining crime, criminals, and justice policy. She taught courses in Leadership, Crime Analysis, Juvenile Justice Leadership, and Police Leadership. Joe had known none of this and was enlightened.

Trinity was promoted as a detective in the Violent Crimes Section, taking the place of Jim Butler. Jim Butler was found guilty of participating in the murder of Joe's long-time friend and mentor, Tom Jones. Trinity was stationed at police headquarters on South Hughey Avenue, in downtown and sat at Butler's old desk. She was the youngest patrolman promoted to the detective ranks.

He also found out, anecdotally, that there was skepticism in the department because the detectives had their own favorites to be promoted from the ranks and because she was an African-American female. They simply dismissed her as being a token. Over the last six months, she closed more cases with Archie Higgins, her partner, than anyone else in the division. She used her education and high-tech skills to close in on murderers, drug pushers, and her specialty—sex abuse of young females. After a while, the squad members asked her for her assistance in their cases. This pleased Joe. She rose above her circumstances and proved everyone wrong. Joe believed that about himself, too.

Trinity was very close to Kiki but he didn't know that she was her Godmother. He found out from Cal that she'd been talking to Kiki about college choices and was extremely upset with her sister, Hope, who thought that carrying a big stick should be the mother's choice of discipline. Cal said that once he got to know Trinity and became a part-time mentor, he knew that Trinity had been upset at her own father for a time for being a strict disciplinarian, but he never hit his daughters. Trinity's beliefs, backed up by her own research, was that her sister, Hope, was a very bitter woman who was left behind by the man she loved and never got over it. Any talk about Quentin Lonell was forbidden in her house. Joe imagined that Trinity could see this event of Kiki's leaving long before it happened and that, as Kiki got older, she'd want to see her father, regardless of his lack of fatherly skills and her mother's apprehension. Joe also knew that Trinity wanted to find Kiki and Glenda and have them back in their families' arms. After that, they could discipline her. Trinity's only hope at this point was Joe and his team. He wouldn't let her down.

℘℘℘

When Trinity called from the parking garage, Joe went down and got her. He gave her a hug, grabbed her bag, and told her that they'd find Kiki. She had tears in her eyes and brushed her arm across her face to hide them.

"Don't worry, Trinity. We don't always play by the rules that you're forced to follow. Whoever is responsible for this will pay a huge price. We will get the girls back." Heading up the stairs, he told her exactly what they found up to the minute. He also told her, while looking her right in the eye, that she'd checked out as well.

"I'm not surprised, Joe. I'd have done the same thing, regardless of who's friends with whom. I don't blame you one bit."

"Not only did you check out to my satisfaction, Trinity, I'll spend any time you want in your foxhole. You've done a remarkable job to date. Just like Cal offered me and my team jobs in the Orlando Police Department, I'll get you in the Coast Guard as an officer, immediately, if you ever so choose."

"Thanks, Joe. However, you must have read that I'm going to be the first African-American female chief of the Orlando Police Department, even if it kills me."

"I did read about it, and you've got our support. I couldn't think of anyone better, with a little more seasoning."

"Seasoning it is, Joe, and then it better happen or I'll kick ass."

Joe laughed. "Trust me. I believe you." Then he laughed some more.

She did too. "I don't know where the hell that came from but I've got to use it again somewhere."

He opened the condo door and introduced Jack. Mark was there with his crew, including Michelle. Julie was due in a half hour. Joe ordered more pizzas and beer and made reservations for everyone at the Hampton Inn at Brickell Plaza, right around the corner. It was going to be a long night.

Julie arrived, threw her bag in the bedroom, and called dibs. She hugged Trinity and everybody else in order. Mark got a big hug and a kiss. He and Louise meant everything to her and Joe, and everyone in the room knew it. The bad guys were going to have a very bad day tomorrow.

CHAPTER 32

After a quick meeting, a few hellos, and pizza, wings, and beer, those heading to the Hampton Suites left and said they'd be back in the morning. Joe and Julie took the one bedroom and Trinity had the other. Jack said he'd sleep on the couch but wanted to work as long as he could, downloading the pictures from the cameras.

It didn't seem to matter where they were headed outside the building. It was clear that Kiki knew the young man in the video and she looked quite pleased when he arrived. They walked away hand in hand with Glenda following them like a little puppy dog.

Jack downloaded the facial recognition program to see what he could find out about the young man before morning. He isolated him from the two girls and then blew his picture up. He had pictures of both sides of the young man's face and a front view. He couldn't do better than that.

The pictures were a little grainy but his enhancement software cleaned them up. Jack's program ran the photo against all government websites, starting with the State of Florida and Miami areas. Within fifteen minutes, he had identified the young man as Geraldy Herard, born in 1994, making him twenty years old. Geraldy was tall, at six feet, two inches, but weighed a paltry 140 pounds. He was obviously a light-skinned black man. He had the bluest eyes Jack had ever seen, next to Joe. Geraldy had a Florida driver's license. That was how Jack identified him. He also had a 2008 Honda Civic registered to him. He lived at 1200 NE Fifty-Ninth Terrace. That was right down the block from the Little Haiti Cultural Center. He lived in the heart of the Little Haiti section of Miami.

Jack downloaded Google Earth and identified the house as a nondescript two-family duplex in okay shape, nothing to write home about. He went deeper into his research. Geraldy never graduated from school in the United States. Jack checked immigration records and the records showed that Geraldy arrived in the United States as a sixteen year old, immediately after the Haiti earthquake of 2010. He was sponsored by his uncle, Claude Philador, now age fifty. Claude and his wife, no children, resided in a penthouse apartment on NE Second Avenue, only two miles from Geraldy.

Claude Philador was a successful businessman, owning several apartment buildings and two restaurants in Little Haiti. Claude arrived in the United States from Port-au-Prince, Haiti, with his parents, at age ten, and became a citizen when he turned sixteen. Geraldy, also from Port-au-Prince, just became a citizen at age nineteen, last year in 2013. *Sounds like an American success story.* Claude's mother was the aunt of Geraldy's mother. She came to the United States last year when Geraldy became a citizen and lived at the same address.

Geraldy had a juvenile record that had been sealed. *How interesting.* Jack unsealed the records within minutes. It was nice to have government clearances and even better to know how to get information. Geraldy had been in trouble with the law since he arrived. He had four arrests by the time he was seventeen. All were for breaking and entering, coupled with assault. He never used a weapon, so he was smart. He appeared to have stopped his criminal ways for the last three years, or at least he'd learned how not to get caught. He had no high school diploma and evidently no formal education, which would be the case for most people who came to the

United States from Haiti under humanitarian conditions. It looked like the uncle bailed him out or was Geraldy working for the uncle? *Time will tell.*

Jack was still up at 6:00 a.m. when Joe got up and headed to the bathroom. He walked into the kitchen and, evidently, Jack had already gone out to Duncan Donuts and gotten the large economy size coffee and two-dozen donuts.

"Bless you my son," Joe said, smiling. "Did you sleep at all?"

"I'll sleep later when you go hunt down the bad guys. I don't do that crap. However, I may have a lead that could help find the girls quickly."

He went through what he found and Joe was thrilled. As Julie and Trinity got up, he told each one what Jack had found. "Find the kid and we find the girls," Joe said. "At least it's the start we needed."

Michelle and Mark and their team came through the door at 8:00 a.m. They all eyed the donuts and coffee and thanked Jack. They all figured he'd stayed up all night on a shift they weren't used to.

After breakfast, Joe took a shower first, followed by Trinity, and then Julie. Trinity would join the team in the hunt. Julie would stay behind and help Jack continue to look at videos and set up a surveillance plan for both Geraldy's and Claude's houses. The team of four from Dania Beach would split into pairs of two and follow whoever came out of each house. Joe called the drone team and had two surveillance cameras placed at Geraldy's house and two placed at Claude's. The smaller drones could be moved in minutes. The Broward County airport, where the drones had stayed during this entire time, was only fifteen miles from either of the houses.

When they launched the armed drone, if needed, from the time it was launched, it could be above either house within a few minutes, leveling off at 1,000 feet, where it would be unseen.

The plan was to pick up Geraldy as soon as he left the

house or was seen on the street. Time was of the essence. If the girls were at his house, they'd chalk it up to no hit, no foul. If they weren't there, it would probably mean that Geraldy dumped them into the sex trafficking black hole. It was now Wednesday and they'd left Orlando on the bus at 3:00 p.m. Sunday, arriving in Miami at the Greyhound terminal at a little after 11:00 p.m. that night. *This isn't good.* He wanted to say something to Trinity but was unsure of how to go about it, so he excused himself and asked Julie to join him in the bedroom. Jack's eyebrows went up a little and Trinity's eyes followed them as she headed to the shower.

Joe closed the bedroom door and turned to Julie. "I don't want to alarm anyone but this isn't good. They left Sunday and it's now Wednesday morning. I'm glad we found Geraldy but I think you know what I, Mark, and the team might have to do to find out what he did with the girls. I think Trinity is strong but she might not be up for what we have to do to get the girls back. This may follow the same pattern as hijacking the Russians out of the country and dropping them on the CIA boat. I don't even know if Trinity knows what we're capable of doing to protect this country and our loved ones—not in that order."

Julie nodded. "I'm not even sure how you did what you did. If you're worried about impending gray areas attached to finding the girls, I'd go with your gut and your heart. You need to do this for Trinity."

They walked out of the room. Trinity had finished her shower, was dressed, drinking coffee, and eating a Boston Crème donut.

As they walked into the kitchen, Trinity grinned "God, these are good, Joe. I can't remember the last time I had a donut. How about you?"

"Every day I can I get the Duncan number two meal, regular coffee and two donuts. Chasing down the bad guys keeps me in shape," he said, smiling. "Trinity, we need to talk. What I'm about to tell you may unsettle you and, depending where you fall with regard to certain gray areas, you may not want to hear this."

"I want my niece back, Joe. At this point, I don't care how we get her and Glenda back. I want them back. I'll worry about the consequences later." Joe told her his plan. She nodded. "Whatever it takes, Joe. You've no idea how much I appreciate what you and your guys are doing for my family and me. Things like this show how much friendship means."

"You can actually thank Jake, my rear admiral, when we get them back. He told me to do what I had to do after I told him what happened."

ღღღ

Joe called Mike Hanley and told him what happened. He told him all about Trinity Hightower and what she did for him and Julie and how desperate they were to find out where the girls were and bring them home. Joe didn't want Geraldy renditioned. He only wanted Mike and his team to scare the living crap out of him. He wanted Geraldy to believe that he'd never see the United States or his mother again. Screw his uncle. Joe believed that Claude didn't get that rich by playing by the rules. Geraldy didn't move up to middle class, after arriving in the United States four years ago, by playing by the rules. Geraldy's mother didn't arrive in Miami without pull. Joe wanted to even up the sides, that was all.

"No problem, Joe. You get him to the ship by 8:00 p.m. tonight, and he'll be peeing his pants in ten minutes. You'll have your information within an hour after he sees the lock-up room with the chains attached to walls."

"I don't have access to a go-fast boat tonight since everything happened so fast and I'm winging it," Joe told him.

"A CIA go-fast boat will be docked at the Miami port by the time you arrive. The keys will be in the ignition but we can't help you until you arrive outside the territorial waters of the United States."

Joe knew where and what that meant. It was getting to be old hat by now. "As soon as we get him, sometime after 4:00 p.m., hopefully, I'll call you on this phone. We might be there even earlier. Thanks again, Mike. You rock."

☙❧

Mark's men found Geraldy in a Little Haiti coffee shop around the corner from his house around 3:15 p.m. They didn't move but waited for instructions.

"I want you to follow him and keep in touch. Trinity and I will be heading up to Little Haiti right now." He hung up the phone and turned to Trinity. "We're on. Let's find your niece."

It was a good forty minutes, with traffic, heading up to North Miami. Joe pulled in near where Mark was parked in the black Chevy SUV. The windows were blacked out and it looked exactly like a government vehicle in any FBI movie ever made. Trinity and Joe hopped into Mark's truck.

Mark simply smiled at Trinity. Michelle was sitting there in the passenger seat. "Hi, Trinity," she said. "First time in an FBI movie?"

"God, is that what this is? It feels a lot weirder than arresting people up in Orlando. I can't believe the access you have to everything and, I may add, some of the smartest people I ever met."

"Gosh, thanks a lot, Trinity," Joe said as if he was Gomer Pile.

"Really. Julie told me how you were in these situations. I guess I have to be here to see it for myself," she said.

"You've no idea," Mark said. "Jack told me, when he called me in San Diego to see how I was doing, that Joe scared the living shit out of him when he shot the guy outside the drug warehouse. There are two Joe Traynors. The first is the mild-mannered, really nice guy who loves puppies and small children and, of course, Julie, but who wouldn't? And, then there's the change-in-the-phone-booth, ass-kicking, take-no-prisoners Joe Traynor, who'll stop at nothing to solve his cases. Welcome to Joe number two, Trinity."

"Nice to meet you, Joe number two. I'll take Joe number two any day if I can bring my niece and her friend home safe and sound."

Everyone in the SUV could tell that Joe had his game face on. Jack had rarely seen it, but Mark was used to it. Mark thought it scared Michelle and maybe even Trinity but Trinity said she was glad Joe was ready to do whatever it took and she hoped he never got mad at her and looked like he looked right now.

Joe checked his weapons. " Let's go get 'em, guys," he said, and meant it.

Just then, Geraldy walked out of the coffee shop and sauntered down the street as if he didn't have a care in the world. Mark pulled up behind him and followed as slowly as possible. Two of the crew walked behind Geraldy, looked around for witnesses, saw no one, and grabbed him quickly. They covered his head with a black cloth, taped the hood around his neck, and threw him in the back of the SUV. Mark hit the gas, turned the corner, and headed toward the ramp to I-95 S to the Port of Miami.

⌘

"Who are you? What're you doing? I'm a citizen of the United States. I demand my rights," Geraldy said.

The only one who spoke was Joe. He finally understood, after having the men watch Geraldy all day, that the guy was no more in love with Kiki than the man in the moon. If he were, they'd be arm in arm right now, staring at each other in the coffee shop. Glenda would be right there with them. Kiki would never leave her best friend, according to Trinity. They'd been inseparable since they were toddlers.

Geraldy would pay a big price if he didn't cooperate.

"You came into this country under false pretenses. You came to commit crimes against young women. You're in the sex-trafficking business. You stole two girls from Orlando on Sunday night. We want them back, and any other girls you put into the same position. If you don't tell us where they are, you'll pay the ultimate price, young man."

"I don't know what you're talking about. I didn't do nothing. You can't do this to me. I have rights."

"You said that already. Where you're going, nobody will ever find you. I hope you kissed your mother goodbye this morning. How about your uncle? Did you kiss him good-bye, too?"

Everyone could see it in Joe's eyes. He'd hurt him if he had to.

"I ain't saying nothing," Geraldy yelled. He was scream-ing at the top of his lungs. The two guys, who grabbed him before, unrolled a foot of duct tape, placed it across his mouth, tore off some more, tied his hands behind him, and taped his legs together. They arrived at the Port of Miami in under a half hour. Heading back toward Miami was a lot easier than heading north with the commuters.

Joe got out of the SUV, looked around, and spotted the go-fast boat. It was a non-descript boat with two huge en-gines. He and Mark and two guards grabbed Geraldy, lifted him out of the truck, and threw him in the back of the boat. Trinity and Michelle stayed with the SUV.

Joe told them to be back in two hours. He was pretty sure he could get what he needed from Geraldy.

He turned to Michelle. "Stay in touch with Jack and Julie back at the condo. You guys will continue watching the surveillance cameras outsides both houses just, in case there's any major activity in and out. You'll also be in charge of telling the drone techs when and where the armed drone will be needed."

Trinity hugged Joe. "You guys be careful."

They made the CIA ship in less than forty minutes. The seas were a little rough. One of Mark's men was an experienced ship's captain and owned a similar go-fast boat. By the time they got to the ship, Geraldy was almost in shock. They dropped him off with Mike's men, hauling him over the side of the ship.

Mike brought Geraldy to the lockup. The guy was scared shitless. They left him in there for fifteen minutes, which seemed to be a lifetime as far as this twenty-year-old kid was concerned.

Joe went into the holding area. "You've got one chance to make this right or you're going to be renditioned out of the country, never to be seen again."

Geraldy had finally stopped complaining about his rights. He gave Joe everything he required, including giving up his uncle, the bank safe deposit boxes, where the girls were located, and how many had been taken just like Kiki and Glenda in the last year. "When the economy didn't come back, my uncle started to supplement his income by selling young girls to foreign nationals now located in Miami. Many are sex-slaves and all are forced labor, as well serving as domestics and prostitutes whenever the call is needed."

"What did you get out of this, Geraldy?"

"I got $10,000.00 a girl if they were under sixteen. I got twenty grand in cash early Monday morning when I handed them over to my uncle's men. Kiki thought I was her new boyfriend and the love of her life. I was trolling online in a teen chat room a few months ago and met her. I knew she was pissed at her mother so I invited her down here. I told her we could look for her father, as well as hook up. She didn't have a clue. As for Glenda, what a piece of work. She did everything Kiki told her to do. What a waste. What're you going to do with me now? You promised if I gave my uncle up, you'd protect me."

"You'll be staying on this boat until we get the girls

back. If we don't get them back, you'll be shark bait. Do
you hear me?"

"Yes, sir."

That was the first "yes, sir" Joe had gotten from him. It
was time to go back. Joe wasn't really sure what would
happen to Geraldy. He knew he'd never be able to trick
some poor teenage girl ever again. Joe would have Mike
hand him over to Homeland Security and have them deal
with him. They could revoke his citizenship. That was what
they should do and send his ass back to Haiti. He'd probably just pick up girls down there instead. Human waste, that
was all he was.

℘℘℘

They got back right on time. Michelle and Trinity were
standing outside the SUV waiting for them. Joe had called
them from sea and told them to call Jack and Julie to have
two surveillance drones go to Claude's penthouse, as well
as the armed drone.

The other two drones were to go to where the girls were
being held captive. Joe would head to Claude's and press
the doorbell with Trinity standing right next to him, backed
up by two of the crew.

Mark, the other two crewmembers, and Michelle would
head to where Geraldy said they were holding the girls. Joe
wanted Claude to call his men and release the girls without
a shootout.

It would be hard for Joe and the crew to explain why
they didn't call the local police to get involved if things
turned out bad.

Joe had dealt with the Miami Police Department and he
couldn't wait the month or so they needed to process the
paperwork to go knock on a door that he'd be knocking on
in less than an hour.

They headed north, kept to the speed limit, and were

anxiously awaiting the confrontation that Joe knew would eventually come to fruition. Dirt bags never knew when to give up. The team would make them.

<h1 style="text-align:center">Chapter 33</h1>

The girls were being held with five others two blocks from Geraldy's house in Little Haiti. From there, they'd be shipped all over Miami and points south. There was big money in trafficking young girls. Selling young girls at $50,000.00 a pop was a quick $350,000.00 for about a month's work. It really didn't take a lot to convince the girls that Geraldy, with his beautiful blue eyes and Café au Lait coloring, was the love of their lives. He wasn't the only one either. The uncle recruited the best-looking young guys in town, all Haitian, all with beautiful blue eyes and charm.

If Kiki had wound up in someone else's arms, they probably would never have found her. Actually, Geraldy's running around Little Haiti like the cock of the walk did him in. He thought he was untouchable, just like his Uncle Claude. Claude would be in for a big surprise when the doorbell rang, and it wouldn't be trick or treat.

The plan was in place. Mark, Michelle, and two others from their team had gone to check out the address where the girls were being held captive. They'd wait to see what happened after Joe and Trinity's confrontation at the penthouse with the uncle. Mark's other team members went with them as backup. Joe didn't want any violence where the girls were held. Mark and his team not only had their weapons but had dart guns as well, and they'd prefer to use those rather than have a shootout. They didn't believe there were a lot of men guarding the girls. Usually, they didn't need a lot of men because they controlled the girls through fear of being killed, or raped, or both. If the girls came out of the building, which was the plan, hopefully, the crew would hit their captors with darts first and then with guns, if required. They hoped not.

They had two surveillance drones already in place. The drones moved down the street from Geraldy's house to the new address that supposedly held the girls captive. The drone team, in constant contact with Julie and Jack, would let the team know, if and when, there was any movement before they had to reveal their positions.

Joe and Trinity would simply go to the penthouse lobby and speak to the two armed night security guards sitting at a desk with a bank of cameras, monitors, and a phone system. They'd politely ask to speak to Mr. Philador. Joe would take it from there. The two locations were less than two miles apart in distance but millions of dollars apart in lifestyle.

The armed drone hovered overhead about 1,000 feet in the sky. The penthouse was on the top floor of the building, the tenth floor. At least whatever Joe needed to do would be confined to the top floor and the roof. The drone had been sending pictures back over the last half hour. There were no curtains to spoil the view of the penthouse. It took up the entire tenth floor and was over 4,500 square feet. Jack had already downloaded the building plan and went right to the uncle's penthouse layout. The surveillance drones took pictures in every window. There were four bedrooms, a large office-den area, a living room, a dining room, and a professional kitchen. There were maid's quarters that looked like a mini-suite of a large bedroom and sitting area. The office or den had an open view and a large LED TV hung from the back wall. In the room were also a large leather couch and chair and a beautiful mahogany desk. Joe decided that this was the room that he'd take out first if there wasn't any cooperation.

Trinity and Joe walked up the steps to the front door of the building. They'd parked their vehicle down the street and out of the way, in case there was any fallout from what Joe had planned to do if there was a lack of cooperation. Both of the other two crewmembers went to the back of the building to make sure there was no escape, if it got that far. Joe and Trinity had to keep the front of the building covered. Neither believed that the security guards would risk their lives for this gig. As Joe and Trinity scanned the area, they saw no other security people walking around the building. Evidently, being the bad guy in the community kept everyone else on their toes.

As soon as Trinity and Joe walked in, both with their weapons fully secured and ready for anything, they headed straight to the security guards at the desk and told them that they'd like to speak to Mr. Claude Philador.

"Whom may we say is asking for him?" the first guard asked.

"Please tell Mr. Philador that Geraldy is safe for now but we'd like to meet with him in the lobby in the next five minutes."

The guard called up to Mr. Philador, who said he didn't have time for such nonsense. The guard relayed the message to Joe and Trinity. Joe picked up his phone and dialed Jack. Quietly he said, "Jack, send the first one through, immediately followed by the second. Take out the TV and the desk, couch, and chairs."

Totally pissed off, Joe knew it showed in his tight smile and narrowed eyes, so he yanked down hard on his temper. He looked at Trinity. He didn't want to frighten her. She obviously knew something was about to happen. Her eyes went wide as she slowly brought her gun out and behind her back while the guards were distracted.

"If I were you two," Joe said to the guards, "I'd quietly leave the building for a few minutes. They don't pay you enough to participate any further. Do you understand?"

The two rent-a-cops got up slowly from their chairs and

raised their arms with their palms opened forward in a sign that they'd be leaving.

As soon as the door closed behind them, a loud BOOM could be heard, immediately followed by another loud BOOM. The drone used its laser capabilities, drilled a hole right through the thick plate glass, and blew the TV and office into a million pieces. The armed drone went back to its position. The other two surveillance drones went to the scene of the hit and took pictures from different angles. Everything was smoldering. It looked like the sprinkler system had gone off and took out the flames from the burning wreckage.

The phone began to ring down at the front desk. Joe picked up. It was Claude. "Who the hell are you? You just blew up my office. The TV is gone and the couch and chairs are on fire. My wife is screaming at me. Thank God we don't have kids. You could have killed us. What do you want? Where's Geraldy? Everything is ruined. The sprinklers are on."

"You don't ask the questions, we do," Joe said. "You've got five minutes to call your men at the house where you're holding the seven girls. Those girls are to walk out the front door, unguarded and unharmed. If not, your penthouse has a world-class drone aimed to blow you right to hell. Sorry about your wife, but for better or worse as they say, you know? Does she know what a dirt bag you really are, Claude?"

"I'll call them right now. What guarantee do I have that you won't kill us, anyway? Where's Geraldy? What about my stuff?"

"You're lucky to be alive. If you so much as move a foot, other than to make the call, I'll let the drone hit you one final time. You've got no guarantees, except the guarantee that if you don't do as your told, you'll be disintegrated within the next two minutes. Your choice."

"I'll make the call right now. Where are you? Are you downstairs? Let me talk to the security guard."

"You've got no security guards. Make the call now, Claude."

∽∾∽

Joe's phone rang. It was Mark. The girls were walking out the front door, all seven. They were in various stages of undress, mostly in their night gear, ready for bed. They looked like they'd been drugged, and none of them could walk a straight line. Two men looked out the window and, as they did, Mark and the team hit them with the darts right through the window. The two crewmembers, walked past the girls into the house. There were two others standing there with their hands up, speaking Creole. Not even Joe understood Creole, a version of French spoken in Haiti and in Little Haiti.

The team hit them with darts as well. After they fell, the four of them were gathered up and had plastic zip ties binding their arms and feet. They were all tied together in a neat little package, back to back. Mark called Homeland Security to pick them up. The FBI and Homeland Security could deal with them and then pick up Claude at what was left of his penthouse.

As the girls came out, one by one, Mark and Michelle immediately knew who Kiki and her girlfriend were. They were the only two African-American girls. There were two Latino girls and three white girls, along with Kiki and Glenda. All looked like they were sixteen and under. One of the Latino girls looked about twelve. Her fate would have been worse than death if she hadn't been rescued. For that matter, none of them would want to live after being sold down the road. These were the lucky ones.

Trinity and Joe showed up at the house where the girls were in less than ten minutes. Trinity took both Glenda and Kiki into her arms, hugged them, kissed them, and shoved them into the back of the SUV. They were going home with

Joe and Trinity. The other five would be placed in the hands of the FBI, where they'd be identified and sent home. None of the girls were physically harmed. Their mental state was another matter, for another day.

Mark, Michelle, and the team would wait for Homeland Security to pass off the guards captured in the house. Geraldy was already on his way to Homeland Security, either to jail or to be deported. He deserved both. Joe and Mark were sure that Geraldy and the other men would give up Claude. Joe had a few safe deposit box numbers in his possession. A warrant to open the boxes could produce not only cash, but perhaps records of where others girls had previously been sent. Unfortunately, this wasn't their battle. Everyone thought that sex trafficking of young girls only happened in third world countries. The truth was that it happened right here in the United States and, unless these men were dealt with, many more young girls would suffer.

૯ᠵᠥᡘᠥ

Trinity, Joe, and the two girls were on their way back to the condo. Trinity would take them home tomorrow. Mark would clean up, hand off everything, and head back to Dania Beach with his crew. He was glad to be back and over any apprehension that he had about being shot again. Adrenaline kept him going and safe. The only reason he was shot in Dania Beach was because he was targeted. He vowed that it would never happen again. He still couldn't believe that Joe used an armed drone to take out a penthouse in Miami. Joe had more balls than anyone he ever met—ever.

Trinity called her sister, Hope, who was staying with their parents. "Hope, we have her and Glenda back. She's groggy and drugged but unharmed. We're so fortunate to have men and women like Joe, Mark, Michelle, and the crew to drop everything and save two little girls from a fate worse than death. I have to go. They're exhausted and we're going to the Coast Guard condo. Julie and Jack are waiting for us."

"What happened?"

"What happened? You wouldn't believe what we did if I told you. I can't talk about it, ever. Just say it's done and over and pray to God that the next little girl gets the same chance as your little girl.

"Tell Joe I love him."

Trinity laughed. "Yes, I'll tell Joe you love him. He'll be glad to hear that."

Joe called Jake. "Rear Admiral Barnes? It's Joe, sir. It's done and over. We rescued five other girls, in addition to Trinity's niece and her girlfriend.

"How much damage?"

"Damage? Just a minimum, sir. The only ones who paid, and will pay even more, are the uncle, the kid, and the four guards who took the girls hostage and were ready to sell them. Just thinking about it makes me really pissed, sir. They're rounded up and will be taken by Homeland Security and the FBI to be processed.

"Any idea what will happen to them?"

"No, sir. I don't, but I think they'll be out of business. Unfortunately, someone else in Miami will simply replace them and start all over again. You can only do so much. I'm glad we got Trinity's niece back. That's what I'm glad about, sir."

"Great, Joe. I'll see you tomorrow."

Yes, sir, see you tomorrow. Thanks." Joe hung up and smiled at Trinity.

"I've no idea how to repay you for this, Joe. I've never been part of anything that was solved this quickly, with this intensity, and with these results. This is truly remarkable. I know I can't say anything to anybody about this, ever. You people deserve a medal, all of you. How do you do this every day? I couldn't do it, I'll tell you. Julie must be worried every day, knowing what you do for the country and for people in trouble. I've never had anyone go to the lengths to help me like you guys did, and I'll be forever grateful. You've no idea how happy I'm right now. You took out a penthouse with an armed drone. How did you do that?" she asked. "How did you even think about doing that? How the hell does your mind work? I'm not complaining. Trust me. I'm just in awe."

"Well, Trinity. We're a full service provider and our customer service is second to none. If you've got a problem, we're here to resolve it, or you get your money back, guaranteed," Joe said with a smirk.

"You don't like praise, do you, Joe?"

"No," he said.

She smiled. The girls were sound asleep in the back. Half an hour later, Joe carried Glenda and Trinity carried Kiki to the elevator and then through the condo door.

Julie hugged Trinity and Joe. "Welcome back, John-boy."

Joe stared at her. "Where are we, at the Walton's?"

She just smiled.

Jack hugged Trinity and told Joe there would be no kissing involved. They put the girls in Trinity's room and shut the door.

"Can we keep them in there safe and sound, until they're twenty-one?" Jack asked.

"It certainly would be nice. Wouldn't it? What do you have to eat? Better yet, I need one or two or six beers. Got any?"

"I knew you'd be asking so there's a case of Oktoberfest in the refrigerator and six subs. Take anything you want. Trinity, how about you?"

"I've never been a beer drinker until right now. I'd love one."

Everyone laughed.

"Yeah. We're officially done rescuing people for the night," Joe said.

Maybe for the rest of my life. I don't know if I can take

*much more of this. I know it's needed, but I'm not sure I'm
the one to do it anymore. I guess I'm just worn out.*

CHAPTER 34

Everyone was still all keyed up from last night. Trinity was already up with Kiki and Glenda eating breakfast. It was only 7:00 a.m. Jack was up as well. He always got up early. Sleeping on the pullout couch probably didn't do his back much good, but he sat there sipping his coffee with the girls.

Joe came out first in his sweats, followed by Julie with her hair going every which way. "Don't look at me. Coffee, please," she said.

Joe looked at Jack eating a bowl of cereal with the girls. "What're you eating?" he asked.

"Trix. There not just for kids, you know?" Jack said with a smile.

The girls laughed. Trinity looked amused as well. She actually looked relieved. Joe didn't blame her. He knew how he felt losing his mother to cancer at such a young age. But that was no comparison to Julie's losses. Everyone was still amazed how resilient she really was growing up. That had a lot to do with Tillie of course. She'd treated Julie like an adult since she was ten years old. They were in it against the world and Tillie had treated her like a partner unless Julie needed to revert back to being a child once in a while.

Joe remembered when he first met Julie. Tillie gave Julie a wide berth and Julie hovered between little girl, teenager, and then an adult. Even though Tillie was old school, she knew better than to dictate to a little girl on how she should act after losing her parents. Both came out of it for the better.

Someone once said the best thing to do about ninety-five percent of everything was absolutely nothing. What would happen would happen. Worrying about it, never resolved anything. That was Joe's philosophy, and it had rubbed off on both Tillie and Julie, a long time ago.

Trinity touched Joe on the arm. "Can I speak to you alone for a minute, please."

"Sure, let's go to your room."

"You've done so much for us, Joe," she said when they'd shut the door behind them. You saved their lives and I hate to ask you for one more favor, but since we won't be back here for a while, I need to mention something to you. Kiki told me last night that she did come down here to see Geraldy, which was the biggest mistake of her young life, and she admits that now, but she also wanted to see her father. She said ever since she was a child that she's heard nothing but bad things about him from my sister. She said she wanted to see for herself. We went online on my iPad and Quentin is appearing in a jazz club less than a mile from here. Is it possible, and I'm only asking, can we go see him tonight and head back tomorrow? I'll tell my sister we're finishing up the paperwork, and she'll have to believe me. What else can she do? Then, we will head out in the morning, early. In a way, this is partially my sister Hope's fault, as well. It's ninety percent Kiki's fault and she knows it, especially dragging in the very gullible Glenda."

"I don't see a problem. I'll ask Julie to stay one more night and Jack can take Glenda to dinner and a movie, if that's all right. I don't want to place him in a position that he's uncomfortable in. These days, everyone is watching everyone, it seems, except for the poor girls who are kidnapped and sold into slavery. It seems everyone missed that."

"Instead of that, as I don't want him to be uncomfortable

either, we can order a big dinner brought in for them and you've got Netflix in the condo. I checked. We should be home by 10:00 p.m., or so. Then we can stay up with them, watch another movie, make popcorn, and then hit the sack around midnight. Sound like a plan?"

"Even better," Joe said.

When he announced the plan to the rest of them, everyone was in agreement. Julie had never been to a jazz club so there were a lot of firsts for everyone.

"The will be my first babysitting experience," Jack whispered in Joe's ear.

Joe laughed. He had to meet the rear admiral by 10:00 a.m. right around the corner. Jack would go with him. Julie would hang with Trinity and the girls and go to lunch in the Brickell Plaza. They'd all meet up around 5:00 p.m. Trinity had seen a barbeque place down the street when she first got into Miami. They'd stop there and let Glenda pick out what she wanted for dinner. Jack preferred ribs.

The Quentin Lonell Trio was appearing every night for the next few weeks at The High Note Jazz Club, at 1465 SW Eighth Street in Miami. There were two shows a night. The first, the one they'd be attending, went from 7:00 p.m. to 9:00 p.m. with an hour break and then the second show was from 10:00 p.m. until midnight, and that show always went a little later.

Trinity hoped that Kiki could see her father at the 7:00 p.m. show and speak to him after 9:00 p.m. when the Trio went on break for an hour. Quentin Lonell had been on the road ever since he left Kiki's mother when Kiki was a baby.

Tickets were hard to come by since he was so well known and respected in the jazz circles. His real home was now in Chicago, spent equally between there and Greenwich Village in New York City. He spent several weeks in Los Angeles, Miami, and Dallas when not in either Chicago or New York City. That was another reason Kiki wanted to come to see her father, because he wouldn't be back for another year. If she had conveyed the message to Trinity, her own Godmother, then Trinity probably could have convinced her mother that now was the time. Kiki was old enough to know what a good parent should be. Her mother, Hope, held her too tightly and almost lost her because of it.

❧❧❧

Joe and Jack walked across Brickell Plaza and up the front steps to Coast Guard headquarters. They went through security and up the stairs to the rear admiral's office. First, Joe stopped at the men's room. Jack waited outside. Then they dropped their things off at Joe's office right down the hall and walked into the rear admiral's suite. Al Cummings, as always, was there to greet them. Joe introduced Jack to Al. Both were polite but Joe didn't think they'd be drinking buddies anytime soon. They walked into the conference room and were greeted by the rear admiral's complete direct and indirect staff. As they walked in, the rear admiral stood erect and started to clap in honor of Joe and Jack. The rest of the team did the same.

"Everyone, those who don't know Joe and Jack, I'd like to personally introduce them and tell you exactly what they've just done." Joe and Jack sat at the opposite end of the table and waited, embarrassed, for the rear admiral to continue. "If it weren't for these two gentlemen, their other team members, including our team from Port Canaveral and Dania Beach, I wouldn't be here today," he said. "I owe them my career and probably my life, if this continued on the destructive path that it was headed down."

He then told the assembled group exactly what had happened, how it happened, and the recommendations that were made to resolve all the issues they faced in the aftermath. The rear admiral asked Jack to speak briefly on his involvement and then the meeting was turned over to Lieutenant Joseph Traynor to offer his assessment of the entire situation, his and his team's recommendations, changes in personnel, and installation of new technology systems, software, protocols, and policies—so none of this would ever happen again. By the time Joe had finished, everyone was paying rapt attention. There was some nervous coughing and minor noises but, otherwise, you could hear a pin drop.

Joe finished up his presentation by saying, "I hope no one here thinks that everything that I've done, said, or recommended was self-serving. Those recommendations were made with a clear conscience and belief that these changes offered would move the seventh district into the twenty-first century. Right now we're not there. We will be when everything is implemented. By the way, my contract expires, one year from the end of this month. I don't plan on continuing in the Coast Guard. I rejoined last year, after a five-year hiatus, for several important reasons, none of which had a long-term career as the ultimate goal. I'll be most pleased to assist the rear admiral over the next year and, hopefully, all the changes will be completed by then."

The rear admiral thanked Joe for his service, loyalty, and expertise. "By the way, I'll be following Joe out of the service at the same time. I'll be retiring at the end of next year as well. My bosses in Washington gave me the opportunity to correct all those problems that occurred on my watch. Not too many people get to fix their mistakes. Fortunately, with Joe's help and your help, we can end on a high note and ensure the continued success of the seventh district."

Everyone at the table stood, clapped their hands, and turned to each other, shook hands, and smiled. They were now all on the same page.

Joe nodded to the rear admiral, said he'd call him later on their burner phones, and then walked out of the meeting, followed by Jack.

Once outside the room, Jack turned to Joe. "You never told me that you were leaving the Coast Guard. Why? You just made a name for yourself. Did you see their faces? They were awestruck, Joe. Why?"

"Do you know how many people I've had to kill in the line of duty in the last year? How about in the first ten years I was taking down drug runners with Mark? It wears thin, Jack. I don't want to do it anymore. I've got a life with Julie and I don't want to blow it. How many marriages have been ruined by the ambition of those trying to move up the ladder of success in the military? How many policemen have lost their families and wives because all they dealt with was the slimy side of life? I don't see a future for me in this arena. That's all."

"Wow. I didn't know you felt this way about it. I knew you've been under the gun forever, but I never suspected what a toll it took on you. All I could see was the praise and glory for a job well done. You're right, though. None of that's worth losing Julie. Has she ever said anything about it?"

"Never. But that's doesn't mean I don't know how worried she's been about me. Every time I came back from a job, you could see the anguish in her eyes. She's been worried about me and I don't want her to live her life like that. She has a wonderful life ahead of her as a nationally known writer, a mother, or anything else she wants to be. I need to be there for her, just like she's been there for me."

"Everyone knows that you've been there for Julie and Tillie since you met Julie in fifth grade at ten years old. You've never wavered in all that time. That's why when you call, we come running, Joe. You're that important to us."

"Thank you, Jack. Now, I don't want to hear any more about it, okay?"

"Yes, Joe. I know."

ᏋᎧᏋᎧ

Joe and Jack met the ladies back at the condo around 5:00 p.m. just like they planned. Julie had called the rear admiral earlier in the day and asked him if he could get four tickets to the jazz club for 7:00 p.m. show. She explained why and, of course, Jake said he'd get right on it. He called Julie back at 3:00 p.m. and told her that he'd secured a reservation for a table for four, a few tables back on the right side of the raised stage. The tickets and dinner were paid for, compliments of Jake. She thanked him profusely.

They could watch the performance without Kiki's father even noticing them. Jake loved Julie and it was obvious. They'd met previously and he and his wife were invited to their wedding in New York City's Saint Patrick's Cathedral and in Key Largo's Saint Justin Martyr Church, Julie and Tillie's parish church of longstanding.

Julie told Joe to call the rear admiral on his burner phone.

"Rear Admiral, Julie told me to call you."

"Yes, Joe. I just wanted to thank you again, one more time, for what you and your team did. On top of that, you managed to save two little girls from harm. I commend you. By the way, I've already called Mark, Michelle, Joan, and Frank Cortez. I told them what you'd recommended for changes for the seventh district. I told them that I wholeheartedly concur. I asked each one of them to personally join me in cleaning up the mess that I'd created. Each one said they'd be honored. Joe, I'm honored that they'd do so. I also told them that there would be a big promotion ceremony in a few weeks and my assistant would personally call each one and invite them to this promotion ceremony with their families in attendance. I'd also like you to attend as well, since it was your recommendations in the first place."

"Sir, I'd be honored. I'm going to take a week off after I get through my stuff at Islamorada. I'm woefully behind in the criminal investigations down here. Most of those are in need of Russian and Spanish translations. Can we meet the week after I come back? We really need to implement those changes even before the ceremony, sir."

"I agree, Joe. Let's plan on it then. Two weeks from to-day, we can meet here."

"Thank you, sir. It's an honor serving you."

❧❧❧

Trinity spent a lot of time with Kiki. She, Julie, Glenda, and Kiki went shopping in the Plaza and both girls got new dresses and shoes, even though Glenda wouldn't be going. That was fine with Glenda. She loved her new outfit and was going to wear it in the condo for movie night, she'd said.

Everyone smiled. Things were getting back to normal—whatever normal was going to be from now on. Glenda and Kiki would be grounded for life, or a month, whichever came first. Crisis had a way of solving those issues.

Joe drove his government car. The streets were packed around the club so he simply placed his FBI and Homeland Security parking sticker in the window and left the car near the building. They walked down a few doors to the club, went up to the roped off door, and told the bouncer who they were. He unchained the rope.

The look on Kiki's face was remarkable. It was Christmas and Easter all rolled up into one. They were guided to their table. Joe pulled out Kiki's chair and everyone sat down. The waitress took their orders. They had club sand-wiches and drinks. Kiki had a non-alcoholic margarita and was grinning from ear to ear. Joe got a beer. Trinity and Ju-lie asked for white wine.

The Quentin Lonell Trio came on at precisely 7:00 p.m. and started their set with a Thelonious Monk standard jazz repertoire, including "Round Midnight," "Blue Monk," "Ruby, My Dear," "In Walked Bud," and "Well, You Needn't." Monk was the second-most-recorded jazz com-poser after Duke Ellington, which was particularly remark-able, as Ellington composed more than 1,000 pieces, whereas Monk wrote about seventy. The Trio consisted of Quentin on piano, a percussionist, and a bass player. They were fantastic and had been together for years. They were considered one of the best jazz trios in the country.

The place was packed. There was a cornucopia of people of all colors. Jazz transcended race, religion, color, and economic status. It was clear this trio was a hot ticket. Kiki seemed very impressed with her father. Trinity hoped that the initial meeting with him, after the set, would go as well. They hadn't seen each other for most of Kiki's fifteen years. Kiki didn't even have a picture of him. Trinity always thought he was the most handsome man she'd ever seen. He looked very similar to Eric Bonet, the jazz singer who used to be married to Halle Berry. He was that good-looking and not even forty years old yet.

Kiki was enthralled. Trinity was staring straight ahead. She'd only heard Quentin play piano a few times at her parent's house when he and Hope were just married. Why he took off, she never knew. He was a bum. He was no good. Yet, there were always two sides to every story. Before tonight, she'd doubted that she'd ever hear his side.

Nine p.m. drew quickly near and, as they finished their first set, Quentin thanked everyone for coming, while introducing the other members of the Trio. As he looked around at the audience, he spotted Trinity. At first, he wasn't sure who she was, but then it hit him and he smiled from ear to ear. He didn't notice his daughter or the others at the table.

He raised his finger at Trinity, as if to say, "I'll be there in a minute," and turned to his crew. "I'll be back in a few minutes."

They had an hour to kill and there was food for the Trio back in their dressing room. Quentin stood up, pushed his stool in, and walked over to the table.

"Trinity, I can't believe it's you. Thank you for coming to my show. It's wonderful to see you. Who're these people you're with?"

"This is Julie Chapman and Joe Traynor. They're friends

and colleagues. I'll explain it to you sometime. Quentin, I'd like you to meet your daughter, Kiki. Kiki, this is Quentin Lonell, your father."

"Kiki? Is that really you? Wow. You're so grown up and so beautiful. How are you? I've got so much to say to you but, as you know, I'm on a tight schedule here with the next set happening soon. Where are you staying? Can I see you tomorrow?"

"Unfortunately, we're leaving in the morning to head back to Orlando. I'm sure that Kiki has a lot to say to you and to ask you where you've been, but I need to speak to you quickly outside for ten minutes to catch you up on what has just happened to your daughter. Do you have a few minutes?"

"Sure. Let's go out back. Kiki, I never stopped loving you. I want you to know that. Can I see you sometime soon if not tomorrow? I really do love you."

Kiki had a tear in her eye. She nodded. Trinity excused herself from the table, nodded at Joe and Julie, and walked to the back door to tell Quentin what just happened to his beautiful daughter, who up until that moment didn't have a father.

They went outside the backdoor and Trinity told Quentin what had happened to Kiki, in detail, and how she was almost sold into the sex trade. He was in shock. They made plans to see him in the morning at 7:00 a.m., an ungodly hour for a nighttime jazz musician but he said he'd be there.

"Why did you leave Hope?" Trinity asked. "You just had a daughter and seemed very happy. You just got up and took off, never to be seen again. She's bitter, Quentin. You have no idea."

"In my defense, I just didn't leave her. We were married for two years and I caught her cheating with my best friend. I wasn't sure if Kiki was even mine. I forgave her and asked her to go to New York City with me. I was just starting the Trio and we'd be based there and in Chicago, where we're still playing to this day. She refused to go with me. She wouldn't leave your parents. I didn't know if Kiki was mine and I never had a test done. I was a loser, Trinity. I took off. I convinced myself that I was right and she was wrong. I've felt that way ever since. Looking at Kiki, I've got no doubt that she's mine. I don't need a test. Why I didn't call, I can't tell you. I was a coward and afraid. I'd like nothing better than a chance to make it right. I just think that Hope will never forgive me or give me the opportunity to make it right with Kiki. Hope did cheat on me, Trinity. Of that I have no doubts. I ran into my friend when he was in Chicago. He apologized to me, so I know it happened. It's not a good excuse, though, and you have no idea how sorry I am. Can you tell her that? Can you tell Kiki that for me?"

"You can tell her in the morning. I'll make sure we've got enough time for you to talk to her before we leave. I'll never tell her about her mother. She's not to ever know about that. Do you hear me, Quentin? Hope's still her mother. She did wrong. But she's raised her by herself forever. That has to count for something."

"Of course, it does and I'll never get between Kiki and her mother. I promise you that. I have to get back. I'll see you in the restaurant at 7:00 a.m. tomorrow."

They headed inside. Trinity nodded to Joe. They got up and Joe left a sizable tip for the waitress, even though the bill was taken care of by the rear admiral.

When they got outside, Kiki's head was spinning. Trinity told her his set was beginning and they had to get home. They promised Glenda they'd be there by 10:00 p.m. "She has her new dress and shoes on, just waiting for us. We can't disappoint her, Kiki."

"I know. Let's go. Can we see my father before we leave?"

"We're meeting him for breakfast with Glenda before we leave for Orlando."

They headed back to the condo. Julie smiled at Joe, as if to say that the world would be okay by tomorrow.

EPILOGUE

Trinity hugged Julie, Joe, and Jack before she, Glenda, and Kiki left to have breakfast with Kiki's father. Joe cleaned up the condo, took out the garbage, and helped Julie carry their bags down to their cars. They both said goodbye to Jack and set up a date for him to bring down his new girlfriend to meet Joe and Julie before their wedding in the spring.

Jack said he'd definitely come this time. He had promised before but never got around to coming down except for Mark's fortieth birthday party last year at the Hard Rock Hotel in Fort Lauderdale. Joe told him that this was the same thing and he had to come down, especially since he was going to be in the wedding.

Julie followed Joe all the way back to Key Largo. She'd stay at her grandmother's apartment for the night and Joe would head back to his Islamorada Coast Guard Station. He had a lot of catching up to do, especially since Joan Talbot was being promoted to commander of the station, along with a new title of warrant officer. Joe hadn't seen her since his recommendations to Rear Admiral Barnes were approved. Jake promised Joe that he'd call Joan directly and offer her the promotion. She'd accepted and there would be an official presentation in a few weeks after the dust settled. Jake also called Michelle Bower and offered her the position on his staff, taking the place of George Pagan.

She was flabbergasted to say the least. She immediately called Joe but he was unable to take her call. He called her later and told her to accept the position without question. She deserved it and proved to the rear admiral that she could handle anything presented to her. She was pleased, to say the least.

Traffic was light and they pulled into Tillie's apartment complex around 2:00 p.m. Joe stayed for a half hour and then headed out to Islamorada. He and Julie had already picked out the rings they wanted for the wedding. Jake's connections in Miami didn't have the ring settings that Joe and Julie had chosen. Joe had called back Diamonds International in Key West and told the owner that they were interested in purchasing the settings for the engagement ring and the wedding rings. The owner knew that Joe was in the Coast Guard and that Julie was a native Conch, so he took that into consideration when he gave Joe a final price. He discounted the two-carat diamond engagement ring by twenty percent, saving Joe $2,400 off the $12,000.00 price. The wedding rings, simple in design but elegant, were $500.00 each so Joe saved another $200.00 off the $1,000.00 price. In total, Joe spent $10,400.00, plus sales tax of 7.5% or $11,180.00. Joe still had the $15,000.00 bonus from the rear admiral, from the Nashville operation, to cover the bill. In addition, Joe hadn't spent a dime since he'd been on the job in Islamorada. He had $40,000.00 saved along with the $15,000.00 bonus. All his student loans for his MBA at RPI were now paid in full as well. He was debt free.

When they bought a house, Joe would have enough money to buy decent furniture for Julie. *She grew up with a thirteen-inch black and white TV with an aluminum foil antenna.* Joe laughed to himself. She deserved better. The rest would go toward the weddings in New York City and Key Largo. He wouldn't have much left from the $25,000.00 he'd committed.

Julie agreed to spend the following Saturday in Key

West to get the rings sized and then have all three sent up to them in Key Largo, fully insured.

While Joe was hunting down crooks in Miami, who turned out to be his own Coast Guard members along with some nasty Colombian drug runners, Julie had spent all her free time—beside finishing her second book, serving as a teacher aide, guidance counselor, and assistant cross-country coach—scouting out homes. She found the exact house she wanted in Tavernier. It was located at 107 High Street, less than four short blocks from Coral Shores High School on the Overseas Highway in Tavernier. It had three bedrooms, two baths and was 1,800 square feet in size. The house was a single story and sat on a lot one hundred feet long by seventy-eight feet wide, which was considered a good size for the Keys. The house was only fourteen miles from Tillie in Key Largo and Julie's elementary school, and only seven miles from Joe's Islamorada Coast Guard Station. The vacation and weekend trips were about eighty miles each way to Key West, which didn't seem to happen enough.

The total mortgage would be $1,433.00 a month, including taxes with only $30,000.00 down and $5,000.00 in closing costs. They could afford the house right now. It was built in 1988, so it would need updating over time, but it had a one-car garage, which was important to both of them. Also, flooding, especially in the Florida Keys, could happen in any home, but insurance companies and the federal government deemed certain areas at higher risk than others. They identified zones prone to flooding from natural disasters or geography for insurance purposes. The federal government designated areas with a minimal risk of flood as "Zone X." This house, fortunately, was an "X Zone" and the FEMA flood insurance, although expensive, was the cheapest of all flood insurance at less than $1,500.00 a year. Property taxes in the Florida Keys weren't prohibitive, due to a large commercial property tax base paying the bulk of county and school taxes.

Julie could easily pay the down payment and closing costs on the house. She got two checks from her publisher for $30,000.00 each and that $60,000.00 was in the bank, less taxes of $15,000.00 already paid. Buying a house was everything to Julie. If her grandmother ever got sick and couldn't keep up her apartment, Julie wanted her to come live with them. Julie wanted a house near the water and wouldn't mind paying a little more for a bigger lot if they needed to add on to the house. She wanted a house all on one floor in case Tillie ever did come to live with them. Climbing stairs would be out, especially after Tillie had been on her feet as a waitress for close to fifty years. With this house, she got everything.

It was a block from the ocean. She thought Joe would love the property as much as she did. When everything was settled down, she and Joe would go look at the house. She was prepared to offer $375,000.00. The asking price was $395,000.00, but one of her teacher friends at the high school knew the owners who'd retired and were moving into a more manageable condo down the road. They were looking for good people to buy the house and the teacher certainly thought that Julie would be an asset to the area. Julie thought they'd accept her preliminary offer and asked her friend to bounce it off the owners before anyone else looked at it. It had only been on the market for eleven days.

❦

Joe pulled up in front of his officer's quarters, opened the door, and dropped his bags on the floor. He looked into his refrigerator and smiled. Joan was really good about keeping his refrigerator stocked with Sam Adams Oktoberfest beer, extra sharp Vermont Cabot cheese, pepperoni and crackers. God he loved Joan. He grabbed a quick beer, took a shower, changed his clothes, and walked down to the main office.

Joan was in her office. She turned and smiled.

"Hi, Joe. How the hell are you?"

"Better than ever, Joan. How the hell are you?"

"You have to ask? Thank you for you know what."

"You're welcome and you deserve it. Has Mr. Cramer mentioned anything to you?"

"He mentioned that he got a big promotion up to Port Canaveral. Was it?"

"Of course, it was," he said, smiling. "When does he leave and when do you take over?"

"Next Monday morning, at 7:00 a.m. officially. I'm a warrant officer, or at least I'll be in a few weeks. Are you coming to the ceremony?"

"I wouldn't miss it for the world, Joan. You know that. Are Jeff and the kids invited?"

"Of course."

"I'll ask Julie to go as well. Can I?"

"Of course."

Joe walked into Jacob Cramer's office and offered him his congratulations. Jacob shook his hand and Joe headed for his office. He needed to talk to the rear admiral. Jake asked him to call him when he got settled back in Islamorada.

"Jake, can you talk now?" Joe asked as he sat back in his chair. He couldn't remember the last time he was here sitting in his office.

"Let me close the door. Do you think we still have bugs?"

"God, I hope not. I couldn't take that anymore, could you?"

"No. I couldn't," the rear admiral said. "I know you're thinking about leaving us when your tour expires, but I've made a lot of calls and I want you to listen to me before you make up your mind. I called my boss up in Washington DC. He wants to meet you next week. We spoke at length and he understands your value almost as much as I do. He has a few ideas of his own. He'd like you to move to Washington and work at the high command but I told him you'd have no interest in that. Is that correct?"

"Yes, that's correct."

"Next, he wanted you to meet with the head of Homeland Security and the FBI on openings in the Miami and Florida Keys area. He also knew that you were tight with the Miami CIA rep, Mike Hanley. He knows you could go in that direction but I told him you were tired of shooting people. Is that about right?"

"Yes, sir. I'm very tired of living every day on the edge. Julie has never said anything to me, but I know she doesn't want to live that way either."

"I've got a much different proposal, that you can think about over the next year, and the job will be waiting for you. You can continue as a lieutenant in the Coast Guard and keep your years for retirement and added officer's benefits and renew your contract for one year at a time, just like Tommy Lasorda and the Dodgers. Like that analogy?"

"I'd like it better if it were the Yankees. Then I'd take a ten year contract, sir."

"Smartass. I know you would. May I continue, Joe?"

"Yes, sir."

"You, Joe, can be in charge of the Military Education Office with a duel title of Lieutenant in the Coast Guard and Vice President for Institutional Research at the Florida Keys Community College in Key West, starting whenever you want. Let me read you their overview. 'Located in the National Marine Sanctuary in Key West, the Florida Keys Community College offers associate's degrees, advanced technical diplomas, certificates and vocational training. Degrees are offered in arts, computer programming, computer technology, marine engineering, diving technology, business, marine technology and nursing. Law enforcement and corrections are offered in five different vocational courses. Certificates at this college are offered in two different areas of business, marine propulsion and addiction studies. An advanced technical diploma is offered in emergency medical technician basics." Jake paused a moment, as if expecting Joe to interject. When Joe remained silent, Jake continued. "Barry University also operates out of the same site for four-year masters and Ph.D. degrees as well. You'll work with both entities. Joe, we send our military, all branches stationed in Florida, for further education and degrees. It's no different than how you got your degrees from Miami Dade College, the Coast Guard Academy, and then RPI for your MBA. If you took the job, liked it, and excelled, you could wind up as the Superintendent of the Coast Guard Academy. It wouldn't take as long as you might think. What do you think, Joe?"

"That's a very intriguing offer. It could combine my education, my experience from my three years at the Albany Coalition for Families, and of course, I could teach Spanish, Russian, and other topics associated with the intelligence division of the Coast Guard. Let me bounce it off of Julie. God knows, we've enough to think about right now. I can't just think about myself, Jake. Julie keeps getting calls from Marcia Manning, Vice President from Disney in Burbank, California. She's been keeping in touch with Julie, at least every month or so. She knows that Julie is finishing her second book within the next few weeks. She offered Julie another $300,000.00 on top of the original $300,000.00 they offered for her first book. They also sweetened the deal, giving her a say over the finished product, which she didn't have before. They'll also locate part of the movie sets at the Hollywood Studios in Orlando to cut down on her travel time. They're making it very hard for her to turn down the offer. We're also buying a house in Tavernier very shortly. Julie doesn't know it, but I got a call from the realtor asking me our intentions. Evidently, Julie has found a house and wanted to surprise me. So much for a surprise. I have to keep it quiet though. I don't want to blow it for her. Buying her own house, after all that's happened to her in her life, means everything to her. She wants to take care of Tillie now, just like Tillie did for her. Can I get back to you next week? Julie and I are purchasing rings this weekend in Key West and probably a house as well. And please keep that to yourself."

Jake chuckled. "Sounds a bit overwhelming. Whatever you want to do is fine by me. Call me early next week and we can get together. If I were you, I'd take a trip to Washington, DC and meet the big boss. It can't hurt. Perhaps Julie can go with you. I know her career means everything to you. I believe that your career means as much to her as her own. Stay safe. Please, for once, stay safe."

After Joe hung up, he locked his door and headed to see Julie and Tillie. They had a lot to talk about. He called Julie. "Do you need anything picked up?"

"No, but Trinity called. They arrived back in Orlando safely. Her sister and her family are extremely grateful to you, Joe, for saving Kiki and Glenda. Trinity said she'd call you next week to personally thank you. Cal Roberts called, as well, and said to say hello and thanks. I love you, Joe. Get here soon."

"I love you too, Julie. I'm on my way."

As he was driving, he wondered where life would lead them in the future. He and Julie had a lot of decisions to make very soon. He hoped they'd pick a path that would lead to a great life. *So far so good.*

The End

About the Author

Daniel J. Barrett was born in Rutland, Vermont, and has lived his entire life in Troy, New York, ten miles north of Albany. He is a graduate of both Siena College in Loudonville, N.Y. with a BS in Finance, and from Rensselaer Polytechnic Institute in Troy, NY, with an MBA in Management. He has had a varied career, first as a commercial banker, then as the chief accountant and manager of financial and strategic planning for a large division of a major international corporation. He has extensive international experience, traveling worldwide.

Barrett has also served as the first executive director for economic development for a county in New York State, and as the first lay director for a Catholic shrine in Massachusetts. For the last twenty years, he has served as a financial, strategic planning, and educational consultant to corporations, non-profit organizations, colleges and universities, and government agencies.

Currently, he serves as a grant writing and development and strategic planning consultant for many non-profit organizations in the Capital Region of New York State and Vermont. Barrett continues to live in Troy and has been married to his wife, Sandy, for forty-five years. They have three children, Sean, Eileen, and Ryan, and four grandchildren, Shannon, Caden, Megan, and Declan.

An avid reader, and inspired by numerous authors, Barrett has read over 1,300 books in the last five years in preparation to write his first novel, *Conch Town Girl* (Black Opal Books 2014). He continues to work, as a consultant, serving those most at risk in the Capital Region, and is now working on another novel.

www.ingramcontent.com/pod-product-compliance
Lightning Source LLC
Chambersburg PA
CBHW060950120726

47910CB00002B/576